"You win, Elias," Sarah said.

He bent his head, so close his beautiful lips were nearly brushing hers. She saw that there was too much heat in his eyes, and his breath was ragged when he spoke. "What do I win, Sarita? A kiss?"

There was mocking cruelty in the words. She saw everything in those fleeting seconds while his lips poised over hers. Saw his rage and his pain and his piercing desire. Without thinking, she touched his face. "Stop, Elias," she whispered. "We'll destroy each other."

He closed his eyes, as if her fingers hurt him. "Your father already destroyed me," he said, so low she could barely hear. "He destroyed us both." When he opened his eyes, there was such heat, such hatred and so much hunger that Sarah could not look away. "We are ghosts, Sarita. Ghosts cannot hurt each other."

Dear Reader,

The blissful days of summer may be drawing to a close, but love is just beginning to unfold for six special couples at Special Edition!

This month's THAT'S MY BABY! title is brought to you by reader-favorite Nikki Benjamin. *The Surprise Baby* is a heartfelt marriage of convenience story featuring an aloof CEO whose rigid rules about intimacy—and fatherhood—take a nosedive when an impulsive night of wedded bliss results in a surprise bundle of joy. You won't want to miss this tale about the wondrous power of love.

Fasten your seat belts! In these reunion romances, a trio of lovelorn ladies embark on the rocky road to true love. *The Wedding Ring Promise,* by bestselling author Susan Mallery, features a feisty heroine embarking on the adventure of a lifetime with the gorgeous rebel from her youth. Next, a willful spitfire succumbs to the charms of the tough-talkin' cowboy from her past in *A Family Kind of Guy* by Lisa Jackson—book one in her new FOREVER FAMILY miniseries. And in *Temporary Daddy,* by Jennifer Mikels, an orphaned baby draws an unlikely couple back together—for good!

Also don't miss *Warrior's Woman* by Laurie Paige—a seductive story about the healing force of a tender touch; and forbidden love was never more enticing than when a pair of star-crossed lovers fulfill their true destiny in *Meant To Be Married* by Ruth Wind.

I hope you enjoy each and every story to come!

Sincerely,

Karen Taylor Richman,
Senior Editor

Please address questions and book requests to:
Silhouette Reader Service
U.S.: 3010 Walden Ave., P.O. Box 1325, Buffalo, NY 14269
Canadian: P.O. Box 609, Fort Erie, Ont. L2A 5X3

RUTH WIND

MEANT TO BE MARRIED

Silhouette®

SPECIAL ▼ EDITION®

Published by Silhouette Books

America's Publisher of Contemporary Romance

For Tara Gavin,
who has given me room to find my voice...but also
pulls me back from the precipice when necessary.
Many thanks.

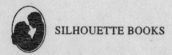 SILHOUETTE BOOKS

ISBN 0-373-24194-1

MEANT TO BE MARRIED

Copyright © 1998 by Barbara Samuel

Printed in U.S.A.

Books by Ruth Wind

Silhouette Special Edition

Strangers on a Train #555
Summer's Freedom #588
Light of Day #635
A Minute To Smile #742
Jezebel's Blues #785
Walk In Beauty #881
The Last Chance Ranch #977
Rainsinger #1031
*Marriage Material #1108
Meant To Be Married #1194

Silhouette Intimate Moments

Breaking the Rules #587
*Reckless #796
*Her Ideal Man #801

*The Last Roundup

RUTH WIND

is the award-winning author of both contemporary and historical romance novels. She lives in the mountains of the Southwest with her husband, two growing sons and many animals in a hundred-year-old house the town blacksmith built. The only hobby she has since she started writing is tending the ancient garden of irises, lilies and lavender beyond her office window, and she says she can think of no more satisfying way to spend a life than growing children, books and flowers.

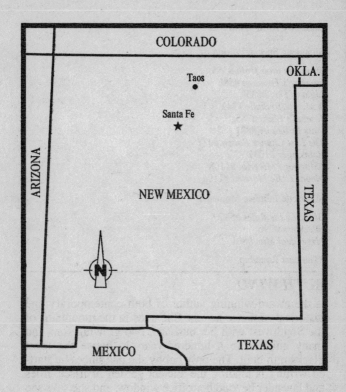

Prologue

They knew Sarah's father would be angry.

No, not simply angry. Angry was a thunderstorm crackling over the valley, pouring torrents of rain into the arroyos and over the fields of sage; fierce but quickly spent. Angry was a bee sting. Angry was a bull behind the confines of a barbed wire fence, being teased by children with a red bandanna.

Her father's fury would be worse.

They drove through the night in Eli's battered sedan, the stars overhead clear and bright as they left Santa Fe and headed into the northern mountains on the narrow road toward home. They held hands, silent, each trying not to imagine what would happen when they got there. Trying not to imagine the scenes they would face.

Sarah could not avoid it. The closer they got, the threadier her heartbeat grew, the more tightly she clutched Eli's long, slim hand, that hand she loved so much.

Her father's wrath would be wilder than a thunderstorm.

It would be like the torrents of hail that sometimes came in late spring, beating young plants to death. It would be a nest of rattlesnakes, striking virulently at a wary intruder. Her father would be like the bull set free, tearing the fence down with no thought for what the barbs would do to his hide, set only on vengeance.

Sick, she put her face to Eli's arm, and as if he knew what she thought, he lifted his hand to her face. "Will he hurt you?"

"No." Not physically. Never, in all her life, had he ever raised a hand to her.

But whatever they had expected, it was not the sudden flare of police sirens and lights that roared to life when they crossed the city line, the three cars that surged forward when the sedan passed, as if they had been waiting....

Eli swore in Spanish, words she only vaguely understood as profane. She knew he was scared. For what seemed an endless time, he only stared in the rearview mirror at the trail of police, flashing red against the black, black night. "They knew we were coming," he said softly. "Sarah, they knew."

Sarah could not even find the breath to whisper. There was a noise in her ears like a roar of rain. It was her fault the police were here, she realized. Sarah had called her mother. So she wouldn't worry any longer. So she wouldn't have to pace the floors again tonight, as Sarah knew she'd been doing since they ran away three days ago.

Eli pulled over and turned to her. His dark eyes were unreadable as he took her by the arms. "Sarah," he said, a broken word.

With a sob, she flung her arms around him, burying her face against his neck, feeling his hair grow moist with her breath. She clung to him, weeping because this was worse, so much worse than they had expected.

Fiercely he gripped her face in his hands and kissed her. Deeply. Then he let her go as a cop with a gun came to the window, and a voice over a megaphone said, "Elias Santiago, get out of the car with your hands up."

Sarah wanted to grab him, to pull him back into the car and take off—but he slipped from her grip, kicking open the door with his foot, his hands raised before he even left the car, so there would be no mistake.

Oh, God, please no mistakes.

Instantly he was approached by a group of dark-uniformed police, who swarmed him like ants.

Sarah scrambled out and cried, "Don't hurt him!" as they turned him and flung his body hard over the trunk of the car. Handcuffs flashed in the wildly surrealistic light, and Sarah covered her mouth with her hands, knowing the bull had had his revenge.

Then Eli was gone, whisked away, and she couldn't help crying out his name, one time. "Eli!"

He didn't look at her, only stared forward, his face blank as the police car roared away.

Chapter One

Twelve years later

To celebrate her thirtieth birthday, Sarah Greenwood resolutely shoved away her depression and treated herself to a shopping spree. She bought an elegant red wool suit and a pair of Italian shoes without even blinking at the price tags, then walked the drizzly, crowded streets of London until she saw an appropriately cozy bistro, and asked for a table by the window. She ordered a very good glass of merlot and the plowman's platter—taking pleasure in the green cheese and strawberries and crusty bread, buttering the latter heavily without sparing a moment's thought for the calories.

Afterward, she leaned back and expansively ordered a second glass of wine and watched the passersby, taking stock of her life thus far. Mentally she ticked off the pluses: an excellent job that had provided wealth, a modicum of renown and respect, and world travel. Here she was, a young and healthy woman in one of the most wonderful cities in the world, staying in a fine bed-and-breakfast near the Thames, and with money enough for whatever she wished in the way of material goods.

Who could ask for more?

A small voice, the same voice that had tsked over the butter on her bread and the second glass of wine, said nasally, *How about a friend? Or a husband, or anyone to share this day with?*

Sarah took another tiny sip of her wine. She had friends. Plenty of them.

Acquaintances, the voice countered.

Sarah ignored it. She was in a profession that required people to be driven to succeed. Everyone she knew was as driven—and successful—as Sarah herself. They worked friends and lovers in as time permitted.

What lovers? the voice sneered.

A sore point, actually. She didn't meet men she wanted to date, much less sleep with. There had been only two she'd permitted into her bed over the past decade, and both had shown a distressingly serious wish to be married shortly thereafter, so she'd sadly let each of them go.

What about—

To cut off the voice, Sarah flagged the waitress and ordered cheesecake. "It's my birthday," she said aloud, embarrassed at ordering so much rich food in public.

The waitress congratulated her and hurried off to get the cake. The voice happily drowned out, Sarah settled back once more, letting the conversation of the diners wash over her pleasantly. English accents always made everything sound so much more cultured, so calm. She heard the rolling sound of Arabic coming from one corner, and German from another—she was, after all, in the middle of London at the height of the tourist season.

And then, from a table not very far away, she heard the

sound of home. Could it be? She did not look over her shoulder, even though it was quite tempting. Instead, she narrowed in on the voices and listened, picking out the lilting rise and fall of syllables, inflected Spanish and hints of Indian cadence. English as it was spoken on the New Mexico plateau.

Home.

Her careful charade shattered, and her blues came back in a fierce rush. The truth was, she would rather have had dental surgery than spend this day all alone. She was sick and tired of traveling. She was homesick for the Taos valley, and people who were real, and a life that still had meaning when she wasn't at work. Even work, truthfully, had had little joy lately.

It was time to go home. Her father's health had been poor the past couple of months, and her mother had asked her several times to come for a visit. Standing in sudden decision, she put money on the table to cover everything, and hurried out.

Four days later Sarah gripped her bag tightly in her left hand and followed a plump woman down a pathway that hugged a long adobe wall. She was conscious of the August heat, white-hot sunlight pouring down from a turquoise sky to sear the back of her neck and the part in her hair, putting dampness on her back and between her breasts. She was aware of the weight of her bag—she had not really known what or how much to bring. She would not, she vowed, put on a pair of jeans again for a least a month. Taos was much hotter than she remembered. Even for August.

The path opened at last into a three-sided courtyard. "Here we are!" Mrs. Gray sang out. "Isn't it lovely?"

Glad for the opportunity to set the bag down for even a minute, Sarah let it go with a plop and straightened, stretching her back. She brushed a loose, limp tendril of hair from her face, and the view suddenly penetrated her weary brain. "Oh!" she said softly.

Nothing could be further from the London world from which she'd flown. The courtyard was filled with cosmos, a riot of pink and white and lacy green against sand-colored walls. On three sides was the house, fronted by a deep gallery furnished with wooden benches in the old Mexican style, and pots of purple and red petunias, thriving in the coolness of the shadowed recesses. The windowsills and door were painted turquoise.

On the fourth side of the square courtyard there was a low rounded wall and a gate, and beyond—a breathtaking view of the valley. Without thought, Sarah stepped forward, a strange pain deep in her chest. "I always forget," she said, her hand fluttering up to her throat, "how it looks."

The woman smiled in understanding.

From the gate, the hill fell steeply away, revealing wide green fields bounded by violet mountains, round and furry-looking in this light. A tangle of sweet peas against a fence gave a splash of bright pink, but the rest was all green and blue, all shades, every possible hue of both.

Faintly dizzy, Sarah looked at the woman. "It's perfect," she said.

"How long has it been since you were here?"

Sarah didn't have to think about it. "Not counting overnighters, almost twelve years." Even the overnighters had been scarce, maybe one or two a year. As few as she could get away with. "Is it especially hot, or am I remembering wrong?"

"It's hot this summer." The woman waved for Sarah to follow her as she unlocked the door to the old house. "And what brings you this time? You studying something?"

"No." Sarah ducked into the coolness of the living room. "My father is ill. I've come home to help my mother take care of him."

"Oh, I'm real sorry, honey." The woman patted her arm.

"You're a good daughter to do that. Not all children would nowadays."

It made Sarah feel guilty to accept the praise. It wasn't as if she had rushed home the moment she heard he was sick. Picking up a blue glass tumbler, she held it out toward the light streaming in through the small southern windows. "Maybe," she said, and smiled wryly. "But don't think too highly of me. I should have been here two months ago when he first got sick, but I couldn't get away."

"Who is your mother, sweetie? Maybe I know her."

In a town of four thousand, that was entirely likely. "Mabel Greenwood."

"*Greenwood!*" Her face lit. "Well, I've been going to church with your mother for eight years. Isn't that something! And you're the famous photographer. Oh, she brags about you, all right." The face split into a huge smile. "All those New York models, all that glamour."

"I enjoy it." A lie, but a white one. She *had* enjoyed it. Once upon a time.

"Have you ever met Cindy Crawford?"

Sarah nodded, and to preempt the next question, added, "She's as nice as you'd imagine." That was what people wanted to hear, that the celebrities they admired were good, kind people—just as they thought they would be themselves if they ever hit the big time.

"Oh, that's something." Mrs. Gray leaned forward conspiratorially. "We don't lack for celebrities around here, either. Last winter I saw Amy Irving having breakfast."

Sarah was loath to rush her, but she was desperately jet-lagged, and she wanted to be able to collect herself, come to terms with being home, before she had to confront the reality of being *home*. It had been one thing to decide, on a gloomy day in London, that she needed to heal the rift with her family. It was quite another to find herself actually standing on home ground and dealing with having to face her parents—and everything else.

Scaredy-cat, whispered her voice.

She made a soft sound, brushing her hair out of her face, and stuck her hand out. "Thank you, Mrs. Gray. This is going to be perfect."

The old woman took the hint. "Sure thing, honey. If you need anything, just holler. My number is posted on the wall. The house is yours as long as you need it."

"I thought it was only free for a month."

"Leave that up to me." With a casual wave, she let herself out, closing the heavy door.

In the blessed silence left behind, Sarah pulled the pins out of her hair, simultaneously kicking her shoes off. Thick adobe walls kept the heat outside where it belonged and she looked in the fridge for something cold to drink. Finding a bottle of water, she took it out and wandered the rooms of the vacation cottage she'd rented. The main room, a combination kitchen and living room, opened into a bedroom on one side of the courtyard. The third wing was across a small covered breezeway. Curious, she padded barefoot across the bricked path, and into the double doors on the other side.

On the threshold she paused, feeling again that strange thick pain in her chest. The room was a studio, probably originally built by one of the artists who'd flocked here in the twenties and thirties. The whole north wall was glass brick, allowing a cool, clear light in. The two windows to the south were tall and narrow, and showed the same view of the valley as the courtyard. At one end was an open door that led to the small darkroom Sarah had wanted.

Sarah closed her eyes, wondering why that simple, familiar view made her feel so emotional. Why that pain kept sticking itself between her ribs. Maybe, she thought with a sigh, she was more disturbed by her father's health than she'd admitted.

Or maybe it was harder to come home—or leave home—than she'd allowed herself to acknowledge. Firmly she closed the doors and headed back into the main house to take a shower and nap. She'd promised her mother she'd be there for supper.

Thunderheads rolled in over the valley in the late afternoon, coming simultaneously from the south and west to knot up over town. Eli Santiago, whistling tunelessly as he ambled back to his truck after a meeting with a graphic designer who would create new packages for Santiago Herb Teas, looked up at the dark sky gratefully. The clouds made the air cooler almost instantly, and a good rain would be excellent for the crops.

From the corner of his eye he caught a shimmer of golden hair, bright against the grayness. In the same spirit of genial admiration he'd given nature's view, he turned to get a better look at the woman striding up the hill across the street. A tourist, probably, heading back to one of the bed-and-breakfasts hidden among the narrow, twisting streets that led away from the plaza. It was hard to see her features, but the body was nice indeed, slim and long legged, with narrow shoulders and softly moving breasts under a gray T-shirt. Her calves showed that walking was nothing casual for her, and he imagined that thick blond hair swinging in a ponytail as she marched around a lake in Chicago or California.

Tugging his keys out of his front jeans pocket, he grinned to himself. One of the assets of living in a tourist town was the women.

Buoyed by the successful meeting and the sexy walk of the woman, he leapt into his three-quarter-ton GMC, his pride and joy, and started it up, taking pleasure in the rich rumbling sound of the engine. He punched a cassette into the stereo and turned it up loud, cheerfully singing along with U2.

Luck was with him, and he made it to the corner without fighting a stream of cars for the privilege. With a grin, he noticed the blonde was stuck at the light along with him, and he admired her legs at close range. Damned nice thighs—tanned and muscular. Delectable breasts, full but not overblown. Good hair, too, a thick honey and sunshine that lay against her shoulders in a smooth line that fell forward to hide her face as she examined something on her shoe.

All at once, Eli was struck with piercing recognition. He wasn't quite sure what brought it on—maybe the crook of her knee, or the trio of silver bracelets that slid down her tanned forearm, or the angle of her head—but suddenly he realized she was no ordinary tourist.

Sarah.

Her name tangled over his nerves, and a sensation of heat and fear and cold rejection washed through him, all in seconds.

As if she felt his gaze, she lifted her head suddenly, frowning, and spied him, his arm hanging out of the open window of the truck. Their eyes met for a long, long moment, hers that strange pale blue-gray that had always slain him. The expression was hard to read: surprise, of course, but some little flame of something else, too. He didn't like to think what showed in his.

For one fleeting second, staring into those once beloved eyes, Eli was again eighteen and painfully, wildly in love. Remembered emotion swelled through him, that fierce and passionate and faithful love that had fallen to such bitter ashes. The hatred that had burned in him since—for Sarah, but even more, for her father.

He pressed his hand to his ribs and felt an urge to cross himself, as if against the evil eye.

Behind him, someone honked, and it startled both of them. Sarah looked at the driver honking. Eli looked at the light and saw it was green, and the man honked behind him again. He didn't know what else to do, and gunned the truck around the corner, coals burning in his gut.

He didn't look back, didn't stop as he'd half considered doing. He simply drove on, trying to put the startled pale eyes out of his mind, trying to keep the memories far, far away.

Some things were better left undone.

As she watched the big black truck roar off, Sarah found her hands were shaking. So were her knees, knees that wobbled as she crossed the street under the darkening sky. It took great effort to hold her head at a natural angle, and as soon as she was off the main drag, she halted beneath a cottonwood and leaned on a smooth adobe wall, pressing her palms and forehead against the coolness.

Fragments of memory assailed her—Eli on his horse, looking like some romantic figure from history, straight and tall and handsome, his hair very long in those days, falling down his back in sleek, heavy blackness. Eli bending over her, the first time he kissed her, shyly, not entirely sure of his reception. Eli's hands, those elegant, long-fingered brown hands that were so strong, and so gentle and so clever.

Oh, God.

She pressed her forehead harder into the wall, as if the pressure would halt the memories. Her reaction was ridiculous—it had been a long, long time. Everyone had some tragic tale of first love, and grown-ups didn't allow such memories to poison their entire lives.

How could she have forgotten she would have to deal with Elias?

Before each of her scattered visits to Taos in the past, she had carefully prepared herself for the possibility. Each time, she'd been braced, had even rehearsed imaginary conversations in which they were both distantly friendly and very calm and perhaps secretly admiring. She had created scenarios in which she turned up an aisle at the grocery store, and ran into him and his wife, with maybe a couple of children in tow. She had imagined seeing him at a gas station with a child on his hip. She had imagined—

Oh, many, many situations. Dozens, over the years.

Oddly, this time, she had forgotten to mentally prepare herself. She'd been very tired the past few months, weary of city life, of the hustle and bustle of the modeling world, sick of the travel she'd once enjoyed. The only thing she'd thought about was quiet. Silence. The blue of the mountains against the blue of the sky. The peace of finally healing the rift with her parents, something she should have done long ago.

A ragged man with a filthy backpack walked along the edge of the road ahead of her, and Sarah straightened. Heading down the winding road that led to her parents' modest home, she forced herself to breathe normally. In. Out.

This was no casual overnight visit, and over the next few weeks Sarah could count on running into anyone she'd ever known. The town was too small to avoid it. But it was unnerving to see Elias just as she'd made up her mind to make peace with her dying father. Feathery red tails of anger brushed against her need to forgive, tails attached to deeply buried, very painful memories that she really had no interest in facing. They'd been nicely buried for more than a decade, and there they could stay.

She could face her father, and make peace with him. She would not dig up anything else. Period.

But that, as the old saying went, was easier said than done. As she walked, memories spilled out of their hidden place, flashing in kaleidoscopic tumbles, like the revolving red light on a police car.

Elias de Jesus Salimento Santiago. The syllables spilled unbidden through her mind, lyrical and lilting. *E-li*-ass d'*Hay*sus Sa-li-*men*-to San-*ti*-ah-go. The sound was still beautiful, like a song or poem. She'd written the words on a hundred pieces of paper, and along the margins of her spiral notebook in history class, and on a scratch pad while she baby-sat late at night and talked to him on the phone.

Elias.

Resolutely, Sarah lifted her chin. With the rigid self-control that had seen her rise to the top in one of the most difficult, competitive careers going, she shoved everything about that all-too-brief period away from her mind.

Several years ago, she'd discovered that walking banished her demons with a firmness that still surprised her. And it did not fail her now. Simply putting one foot in front of the other, walking around the curving road, past a field lush and green with recent rain, gave her a measure of sanity. Even as she remembered her unfinished business with Eli Santiago.

After a few blocks, her heart had stopped pounding and her breath came naturally, and she found herself realizing it had been ten years—twelve. He probably had a passle of children and an adoring wife by now. High school, some-one had quipped, was an event to be survived. It had no bearing on the rest of a person's life.

First love was always wild, always intense, always more full of color than other relationships. That did not mean it was particularly important later on.

Feeling better, Sarah lifted her head and rounded the cor-ner to her parents' house. Her mother was in the yard, trim-ming marigolds. Her formerly golden hair had faded, and there were new lines in her beautiful face. Still, Sarah felt something warm and rich move in her at the sight of Mabel gardening late in the day as she'd always done. "How are the roses this year?" Sarah said mischievously, opening the gate.

Mabel looked up and gave a little cry. "Sarah!"

Sarah wrapped her in a heartfelt hug, smelling the fa-miliar scent of lavender on her neck. "I'm so glad to see you, Mom."

"Thanks for coming, baby." Her mother squeezed her hand.

Sarah nodded. "How's Dad?"

A short hesitation. "He's all right. He was a little agitated earlier, so he had to take a sedative. He made me promise to bring you in to see him when you got here, but I doubt we'll be able to wake him up."

"All right."

"We can look in on him, then have supper out in the backyard, where we won't disturb him." She squeezed Sarah's hand and smiled. "Then we can have a nice visit."

A quick, odd pinch touched Sarah's heart. She let her mother lead her inside the house, with the evocative smells from childhood in the air, and the familiar red corduroy couch and her father's easy chair with its footstool.

In his room her father, Garth, lay sound asleep. His color was too red, and she could hear the labored sound of his breathing—a complication of the asthma he'd had all his life. A big black cat slept on his feet.

It was strangely unnerving to see her bluff, burly father so still and quiet. A stubborn man who had lived with one constraint all his life, he had refused to give up his ranching-family habits of red meat, eggs, butter and bread, and he'd been fifty or sixty pounds overweight for most of his life. Now his stoutness was reduced by half. "He isn't still smoking, is he?" she whispered.

Mabel snorted softly. "Only because he can't get to them."

Sarah smiled in understanding, feeling suddenly lighter. Her stubborn father was still himself.

"I'll be out back," her mother said. "Come out when you're ready."

Somehow, Sarah found herself tiptoeing into the room to sit on a straight-backed chair her mother had left near the bed. The room held a scent of Old Spice and something that made her think of Saturday-morning chores in child-hood.

Her father shifted, rubbing his nose in a familiar way, but did not wake, and Sarah found herself smiling gently. She was weary of everything in her life, but she was also weary of the long war she had waged with this hard-nosed policeman. They were too much alike in some ways, and too different in others, but she loved him. She had missed his acerbic humor, even his blustering.

It was time to end the war. Impulsively, she stood and kissed his brow, very, very lightly.

He stirred, and his hand—that big, strong, dark hand—came up and gripped hers. "Sarah."

"Oh, Dad, go back to sleep. I'm sorry to wake you."

"I'm sorry about the baby, sweetie. I was only doing what I thought was best."

A deep sense of dread twisted in her gut. "Go to sleep, Dad."

But he was already drifting off, his breathing labored. His grip on her hand eased. Sarah stepped back, and un-consciously wiped her hand against the leg of her shorts, staring at him, an involuntary rush of images rising against her inner eye, flashing red against a black night.

Swallowing, she stiffly moved into the backyard, where her mother was humming as she set out plates on a wooden table covered with a bright blue umbrella. Chamiso in full yellow bloom clustered against the fence, along with clumps of cosmos. Breathless, Sarah stared at the plants, trying to shove away the emotions her father's words had kindled.

"It's almost ready," her mother said. "Come sit down."

"Mom."

Something in her voice must have told Mabel something was wrong, and she looked up warily.

"Dad woke up, for just a minute. He said something about the baby." She forced herself to take a long breath, then blew it out. "Please tell him that is not a subject I want to discuss, okay? I can't."

An odd expression crossed the older woman's face, but then she put down the fork she was holding. "He wanders a little when he takes some of these pills. You'll get used to it."

For a moment more, Sarah paused, wondering if she was strong enough to bear even the small step of healing her war with her father. Because she saw suddenly that everything was interconnected—her father and the baby and Elias and all the tangled mess of betrayals.

Her mother reached out, and Sarah noticed that there were veins showing under the thin flesh, and a couple of knuckles were gnarled with the beginnings of arthritis.

"Please, Sarah," she said. "Please, let's just sit down and eat."

And for one blazing moment Sarah thought that this had always been her mother's way, to avoid whatever was most painful, never confront it.

But the sight of that aging hand would not let her be cruel. She folded the fingers gently into her own palm and managed a smile. "Good idea."

She would deal with her father and her mother, period. They would simply have to respect her limits. She would not discuss the past, or allow it to be brought to her attention. They would go forward from this moment, as if nothing had ever happened.

It was the only possible way to cope with it.

Seeing Sarah roused a restlessness in Eli that he found difficult to shake. He stopped for some supper before heading back to the ranch, and ordered a hamburger and home fries. Leaving the meal half-finished, he drove around aimlessly. Up and down the twisting, narrow lanes, where his ancestors had walked for nearly three hundred years, around the ribbon of road that circled the outskirts of town and back into Ranchos de Taos, the site of a church made famous in hundreds of paintings.

His blood felt hot in his veins, hot with hatred and anger and vestiges of sorrow that lingered no matter how he tried to banish them. He could not go to the ranch with this much emotion still boiling in him. Someone would see, and when they learned Sarah had returned, they would remember his agitation tonight. He couldn't bear the speculation, the accusations, the sly proverbs that would prick him.

So he drove and drove and drove, in the truck that he loved. He turned the radio off, and watched the storm roll in, dark and beautiful, over the endless fields of sage and chamiso, turning them a pale gray-green below the mountains circling the valley like a ring of soldiers in blue wool. Adobe walls captured the ghostly light of the incoming storm, and shone like the lost cities of gold that Coronado had once believed them to be.

The land calmed him. It always had. He was as intimate with these views, this light, these hills, these fields as he was with his own body. And it was not just his own memory and knowledge, but that of his father and grandfather and great-great-great-grandfather before him, all those men who had lived here and walked here for generations.

Even so, even with the calm, he found himself where he must have known he had to go, to wait for her. He parked beneath the thick arms of an ancient cottonwood tree not far from her parents' house. She would come by here on her way back down the hill, as she had when they were kids.

Sarah. He didn't kid himself about being in love with her after all these years, but he was honest enough to admit there was unfinished business between them. That business stuck in his throat, hot and thick, in a way he'd thought he'd outgrown.

Through the windshield he watched lightning twig over the horizon. Walking rain danced across the land to the west. Not long now till the storm broke over town. He welcomed it, welcomed the release of pressure he felt it would bring.

He kept an eye on the rearview mirror as he waited, and the gesture brought back a tangle of memories—both bitter and sweet. This had been their meeting place after Sarah's father had forbidden their relationship. In those days, they'd both grown adept at lying. Sarah lied by telling her parents she had to baby-sit. Elias lied by omission, never explaining exactly what he was doing. His mother assumed he was with friends.

Instead, they met secretly under this very cottonwood, and spent their evenings driving around, afraid to go any place where someone might know them. They often got out of the car and walked along the Rio Grande gorge, tossing rocks to the silver ribbon of water far, far below.

Often they had made love.

The memory burned a little and he moved his head, feeling stiffness in his neck.

They'd been so very young, he thought now. So young, and passionate, and full of the melodrama of their situation, the children of families engaged in a mutual hatred that had begun more than a century ago, when a Santiago man raped a Greenwood woman and was hanged for the crime. Elias had heard the story told many ways, and over the generations it had taken on the mythical power of a legend.

Eli glanced in the rearview mirror to the empty street. Sarah had known the story, too, of course. There was no one in town—no native anyway—who did not know it, or know that the families had been battling ever since in a feud of such virulent hatred that one was wise to leave any room if two members of the opposing families found themselves together.

He shook his head. The feud was 150 years old. After the hanging of Manuel Santiago, it had led to the stabbing death of a Greenwood boy in the 1860s and the beating death of a Santiago in the second decade of the twentieth century. In the 1930s a minor war broke out that lasted nearly seven years, and took with it a half-dozen assorted Santiagos and Greenwoods, including one woman.

In the years between there had been a host of lesser injuries, acts of vandalism, pranks and troubles.

Including prison for Eli.

He rubbed his bottom lip, wondering how things might have been different if the art teacher at the high school had called roll by last name instead of first name the day he and Sarah met.

Even so many years later, he remembered the day with a strange clarity. He noticed her immediately, a pretty girl in a blue shirt that made her eyes and hair glow with some inward fire. He thought she looked like the sky, blue and gold and full of light. And when she smiled shyly in response to his flirtatious teasing, he'd been euphoric.

It was only days before they'd found out their respective last names, and by then it was too late. The connection between them had gone quick and deep almost immediately, and neither was inclined to give any weight to the silly old story of the backward generations that had come before them.

They had underestimated the hate. In spite of the soul-satisfying melodrama of the old story, neither of them had taken the old feud between their families seriously until it was way, way too late.

The first fat raindrops began to splat down on the hood of his truck, loud in the quiet, and Elias looked up to see a flash of gold in the rearview mirror, just as the skies opened up and rain roared down in a thundering deluge.

He turned around in the seat, and saw Sarah standing on the other side of the tree as if frozen, oblivious to the rain soaking her to the skin. With a quick gesture, he moved over and flung open the passenger door. "Get in!" he yelled over the torrent of sound.

For a moment he thought she was going to refuse, but a bright flash of lightning blazed over the landscape, quickly followed by a clap of thunder that was all too close, and she bolted for cover.

Dripping wet and out of breath, she ran to the door, and halted. "I'll ruin your seats!"

"Get in, Sarah."

With a shrug she jumped up onto the seat and slammed the door behind her, then wiped water off her face. "Thanks. It's wild out there," she said.

Eli narrowed his eyes. She sounded so polite, so unruffled. "It is."

Cocooned in the cab, with rain pounding all around them, they looked at each other face-to-face for the first time in over twelve years. Eli had heard bits of news about her over the years; he'd seen some of her photographs, and knew she traveled in exalted circles. He had a picture in his head of what women in New York must look like, and he'd mentally cut and pasted until he had a transformed picture of Sarah he could live with: a leather-miniskirted woman with her hair cut in some severe style.

It had been a defensive picture he'd created. If he had allowed himself to imagine her the way she always had been, they would have had to lock him up a long time before, driven insane with loss and grief. But then, their relationship might have only been first love, made more dramatic by the old tragic story.

It had also been real. True love, he'd thought then. These days, he wondered bitterly if such a thing existed at all.

Whatever. As he looked at her now, a pain squeezed his chest. She looked like his Sarah, only grown up—and adulthood had done good things to her. Her mouth was firmer and there was strength in her shoulders, knowledge in her eyes. Her body, almost boyishly thin in those days, had ripened to a delectable fullness at breast and hip. Funny. He would never have guessed she'd ever have much of a chest, but the cloth of her sodden T-shirt clung to the ripe slopes with uncomfortable accuracy. Frowning, he looked away.

She was the first to break the silence. "Success suits you, Eli."

A thread of anger wound through him. "Is that what we're going to do here, be polite?"

The old Sarah would have looked hurt over that. The woman who had taken her place regarded him steadily. "That would be my preference."

With an edge of bitterness, he said, "Well, all right. How are you, Sarah?"

If he had not been staring so hard at her, he would have missed the flicker of light in her eyes as her gaze fluttered over his mouth. He remembered suddenly how much she had liked kissing—kissing and kissing until he was mad with need for her.

"I'm very well, thank you," she said, her calm voice an almost violent contrast to the expression in her eyes. "You?"

"The same."

This time he let the silence stretch, wondering how deep the shell of civility went. As if he made her uncomfortable, she shifted to look out the window, but Eli didn't stop looking at her, at that smooth profile, dewed with remnants of rain, the full lips that had given and taken so much pleasure, the tendrils of hair on her shoulders. He drank in the details with a surprising thirst, and discovered an alarming fact. The spell she had always cast over him had not mellowed with age.

She crossed her arms defensively. "What do you want, Elias?" She looked at him, and he saw fire in those eyes now, a long-buried and very powerful anger. "A pound of flesh? To see me whipped in the town square? What?"

Revenge. The word came from a thousand dark fantasies

of seeing her father burn in hell, and later, Sarah with him. He wanted to make them suffer, as he had suffered.

"What did she look like, Sarah?"

If he'd hoped to shake her, he had succeeded. A rapid flickering of brutal emotions crossed her face—vivid pain and rage and sorrow. "I don't remember," she breathed, and bolted, opening the door and running out into the rain without a backward glance.

Watching her run away, Eli cursed and slammed his hands against the wheel. She would not run again. He would not let her.

This time Elias would have his revenge. All these years he'd waited for his chance, and at last fate had smiled. What better revenge on the man who had humiliated Elias Santiago than to make his daughter love him again?

Chapter Two

The rain had slowed by the time he pulled up in front of Sarah's parents' house. Mabel Greenwood sat on the porch swing in a blue cotton housedress printed with yellow flowers. He half expected her to bolt when she saw his truck, but her face just took on a pinched expression and she stayed where she was as he got out and headed up the walk.

He had never set foot on this property. He had been forbidden. It gave him a juvenile pleasure to do it now, to stride up that walk a proud and successful man who had proved them all wrong. He halted at the foot of the porch steps. Without preamble, he said, "I need to know where Sarah is staying."

"Don't, Eli," she said. "Don't open this wound."

"You can't open what never closed," he said, and was surprised at the vehemence of his words. "That wound has rotted and festered for a decade."

She made a disparaging sound. "You always did have a

flair for the dramatic. You and her dad both, putting her in the middle with your big words and melodramas.''

He said nothing, only looked at her steadily.

"Leave her alone, Eli. She's tired. She's lost. She doesn't need you barging in on her now. Neither one of you cared a whit for what Sarah felt about that war you were both so fond of.''

A faint heat rose in his face, for there was some small truth in her words. They had sometimes found fierce pleasure in that war, Eli and Sarah's father, in the way of men locked in mortal battle. It shamed him now.

"I don't want to start again,'' he said. "I just want to put it all to rest.''

Her mouth tightened. "No, you don't. You want her to suffer even more. To drag it all back out, where it's just gonna make her hurt all over again.'' Her eyes narrowed. "Don't you think she's paid plenty?''

"We have all paid. Sarah, me. Even you and your husband.''

"Not enough for you, though, is that it?''

He hoped the betraying flush did not show. They could never pay enough. "We all lost the child we should have had.''

"I don't trust you, Elias,'' she continued, ignoring his words.

"I'll find out where she is one way or the other.''

Mabel's eyes burned into him. "I never liked you,'' she said. "You were too fierce for my little girl. She nearly burned to death on that heat. You were too much for her and I didn't trust you to be there for her in the long run.'' She folded her hands and lifted her chin. In the gesture, Eli saw Sarah. "Truth is, I still don't much like you, but you might be the only one who can break through those walls. She's in the Gray cottages, by the Blumenschein museum. Third one from the top.''

Eli raised his chin. "I never liked you, either, Mrs.

Greenwood. You didn't believe enough in your daughter. You didn't stand up for her. But you love her, and I always knew that.''

Mabel Greenwood stood, hands in the pockets of her cotton housedress. ''Don't come back here again, Elias.''

He shook his head. ''No.''

Sarah was soaked by the time she made it to the cabin. She turned on hot water in the shower and steamed the chill from her bones. It was a shock to remember how cold the rain always was in the West.

When she was warm, she slipped into a pair of jeans and a comfortable old cotton sweater she'd purchased in Ireland on one of her first trips abroad. Carrying a cup of coffee for warmth and comfort, she wandered outside to sit on the bench below the vigas and latillas of the porch roof.

Twilight and rain had made the exuberant little garden a magic world, and after a moment Sarah went back in for a camera. It was an old favorite, a sturdy Minolta that fit her hand the same way the sweater fit her body—familiar and comfortable. Heedless of the water and mud, she waded into the middle of the flowers, careful not to injure any of them, and knelt close to look through the lens at the heart of a pink flower, studded with diamond drops of rain.

Instantly, tension eased from her shoulders. Through the lens of a camera the world narrowed to one thing—a thing made of color and light and shadow, contained in one frame. Quiet. Still. Manageable. As a young girl, she'd especially loved shooting flowers and nature, and hands. Small things. Tiny things.

And after the tumultuous past few hours, looking through her camera to a world of pink petals and gray rain was more soothing than any drug. Through the lens she focused upon a single raindrop with its upside-down view of the sky and porch, surrounded with the narrowly ridged petal. *Click, whir. Click, whir.* The world narrowed to these simple sounds and simple frames that created walls against the turmoil in her.

Buoyed, she moved along the fence to capture a blur of blue mountains behind the pink and white flowers; focused on the weathered wood of the gate; caught the ghostly shape of disembodied petals floating white upon a copper-colored puddle.

She heard the squeak of the unoiled gate, but a fragment of light slivered between a break in the mountains and the clouds, falling like a single finger over the edge of the porch, and she wanted to capture every inch of it.

"Just a minute," she said distractedly, sure it was Mrs. Gray, coming to check on her.

A moment before she reached the bottom of the shaft, the camera halted.

"Damn," she said, and scrambled in her pocket for a second roll of film, prying the lid off the canister with her teeth before she remembered this camera was not automated, and she wouldn't have time to rewind the film by hand and reload before the light changed. With a shrug, she clipped the lid on the film with her thumb, and tossed her hair out of her face. She turned.

And swore again, this time more forcefully. Eli stood just inside the gate, wearing a jean jacket over a simple chambray shirt, a pair of jeans and working boots with heels made for riding horses. His hair had been dampened by the rain, and the waves had turned to loose curls that fell on his collar. He'd hated those curls, which had a decided tendency to turn to ringlets, making him look like a fallen angel.

Her angel, she thought now with a piercing sense of loss. He did not move, only stood there, so tall and lean and beautiful, with a fierce expression on his face.

His face. The lines were too bold to be called merely handsome—the slash of strong, angled cheekbone, the hawkish nose and hard chin. Those were bones that made painters ache to run for their brushes.

But for a woman, the appeal was in other things. Above the cheekbones were eyes as seductive and dark as the mysterious desert night, fringed with lashes that gave him a startling beauty. In contrast to the harsh angles of chin and nose was a generous mouth with firm, full-cut lips. A mouth, Sarah remembered with a startled sense of heat, that could give amazing pleasure.

Defensively she raised her chin. "Now what?" Automatically she began to rewind the film.

"I came to apologize, Sarah." His tongue purred the slightest bit over the *r* in her name, and the sound struck her in some deep place.

"Fine." She lifted a shoulder and made to turn away.

"Wait."

She took a breath, steeling herself, and faced him.

"I was cruel, back there in the car. Seeing you again so suddenly is…" He frowned. "It's harder than I would have thought. I would like to see us put things to rest."

"As far as I'm concerned, there is nothing to put to rest," she said wearily. Numbness engulfed her, and with a part of her mind she realized the numbness was a defense. She could face her father, but she could not dredge up her past with this man without facing things she simply could not bear.

He stepped forward, his mouth hard. "Nothing? Was it so easy for you to just walk away?"

A thick pressure built somewhere in her middle. "Is that what I did? Walk away?"

"No, now I think maybe it was more like running. Just like you ran from my truck. Have you run all these years?"

She narrowed her eyes. "Who do you think you are to judge me after all this time? Do you think your opinion matters to me?"

"It matters." The velvet brown eyes turned liquid with

heat. The heat of fury and—Sarah realized with a shock—
the heat of desire. Desire that swept over her body in deliberately provocative gazes, touching her all over; desire
that kindled an unwilling answer in her flesh.

In that single instant she remembered the passion that
had once burned between them, a physical hunger so deep
that Sarah had sometimes felt mad with it. She remembered
it not with her mind, but with parts of her body, as if the
memories were written on her very cells.

Hormones, she told herself dismissively. What teenager
alive had not felt that kind of desire?

She stared at him, and he at her for long seconds.

At last he said, "So there is a little fire left in you. I
thought maybe they kicked it all out of you." With an
arrogant lift of his chin, he added, "You can't run forever,
Sarita—and you will have to face me before we are finished."

That voice, so rich, so close, so quiet, wrapped her as
intimately as any kiss, and Sarah felt a warning prickle raise
gooseflesh over her body. Backing up instinctively, she
said, "Leave me alone."

He stepped forward, and she willed herself to stand her
ground. He didn't stop until he was so close she could smell
his flesh, and it was a piercingly redolent scent—desert
wind and sun in his hair, spice and soap on his skin, hints
of starch in his shirt. Smelling it again after so long was
more powerful than even his proximity.

But she gritted her teeth and vowed he would not see
how he rattled her. She forced herself to keep her arms
down, instead of crossing them over her chest defensively,
and to show him he did not intimidate her, she raised her
chin and met his eyes.

As if he'd been waiting for that, he said quietly, "We
are not finished, Sarah."

For one long moment they were frozen like that, Sarah
staring up at him, her fists clenched, Eli standing too close,

his nostrils flaring with anger or arousal or both. Sarah found her eyes on his mouth. It was too close; she took in the bowed line along the top lip, and the square line of his chin. In the cool of the courtyard, with dusk falling gray around them, Sarah was far too aware of the heat of his chest, only millimeters from her body, and it was too easy to remember how that naked flesh had felt against her bared breasts.

"Go away, Elias," she said.

"You ran then. You're running still." With an exclamation of disgust, he backed away, then turned and simply left her.

Blindly, Sarah ran into the house and locked the door, as if against a monster. Then, weary from travel and the intense day, she buried herself in the covers of her bed, a pillow held firmly over her head, and went to sleep.

It was the most effective retreat of all.

Elias managed to avoid everyone when he drove into the ranch. His mother's house was brightly lit, and he saw people inside—two of his sisters, a brother, one of the grandchildren, Teresa, who was likely the focus of the obvious family meeting going on. He drove on by and up the mountain, past his grandmother's ancient but beautifully preserved Territorial adobe, past the fields and the plants. Finally the road branched into the dark forest, and he followed it up the hill to a clearing set in a meadow above the rest of the ranch, with views of the entire valley, clear to the mountains to the west.

The house itself was not elaborate. Aside from his truck, he indulged in few luxuries, preferring to redirect the bulk of his profits back into the business or into long-term, solid investments. It was an economic philosophy that had worked for him: Santiago Farms and Teas had netted a profit in the high six figures last year.

But he had wanted a home he could call his own, and

had contracted to have this one built, a simple adobe, made with authentic, handmade adobe bricks. Town ordinances required all new buildings to at least look like adobe, and because the real thing was very expensive, cinder blocks were often used in place of it, but nothing insulated against the hot suns and cold winter winds like the real thing. Worth every penny, in Eli's opinion.

The rest of the house was simply made, with wooden floors and exposed vigas in the living room. His only other major expenditure had been on the kitchen, which boasted every modern, gourmet gadget ever made. His mother teased him about it, saying it was just like a man to need electric gadgets to find a kitchen appealing, and he suspected there was some truth to it. Sometimes he liked cooking, especially exotic dishes with fresh vegetables and uncommon spices.

Tonight his needs were much simpler. He tossed his keys on the breakfast bar separating the living room and kitchen, took a plain American beer from the fridge and carried it out to the porch.

Standing there, looking out to the view of sparkling lights spread over the land, cold clarity moved into his mind, unblunted by memory or emotion. Sarah had come home, as he had known she would, eventually. So many years too late.

A rain-coated breeze blew over him, easing his tension. He let go of a breath and told himself it would be better to pretend he had not seen Sarah tonight. He'd built a life, as she had, and the sorrows were buried a long time in the past. No point to ripping open these wounds now.

But like a man who couldn't keep his tongue from a sore tooth, unbidden images of the last time he'd seen her rose up in his mind: the flashing lights of the police cars, red as blood against the night. The careless hands of the officers on him. Sarah's face, white and terrified, in the car.

A pained smile twisted his mouth. They'd thought they

were being so mature by coming home to face the music. They had run away to Albuquerque to get married, because Sarah had found out she was pregnant. It had been a move of great panic for both of them—not panic over the baby, but panic because they loved each other and wanted to be together and didn't know how to accomplish that. They had also known their families would make it nearly impossible to marry with permission. So they'd run away to elope.

But there, at the courthouse, with the blood work done and their hands clasped, Elias had thought of his mother and brothers, and Sarah had thought of her mother, and they could not go in. Together they had decided to go home and face their families, publicly declare their intentions—not out of a need for permission, which both knew they would not receive, but out of respect.

They congratulated each other all the way home. All the way up to the city limits, where a bevy of police had been waiting. They handcuffed Elias and took him to jail, charged him with statutory rape and alienation of affections. Garth Greenwood would have tried him for kidnapping, too, but someone talked sense into him, evidently.

While Eli waited—without bail—for his trial, he had hoped that Sarah, against all odds, would find a way to see him. Or at least get a message to him. He wrote to her, sending the letters to her friends and her parents, praying that somehow, fate would intervene on the side of their love, and one or two or three of the letters would go through. He tried to imagine her getting to the mailbox first one day, tried to keep a vision of her reading his letters foremost in his mind.

But a week passed, then another and another and another, with no word from Sarah. Day by lonely day his heart turned to stone. His family, furious over the trumped-up charges, would not speak Sarah's name, not even to tell him that she'd been sent away.

By the time he was released, the charges thrown out

when he went before the judge eight weeks after his arrest, Eli was well armored against the news that Sarah was gone, the baby with her. By then he had honed himself into an instrument of revenge, cloaked in hatred, and he poured himself into his goal. Somehow, some way, he would have his revenge on Garth Greenwood for stealing his woman, his child and his freedom.

Many things had changed over the years, but that single blue flame of vengeance burned as clean and hot as it ever had. At last the day had come.

For Sarah was not immune to him, and he had no doubt he could coax her back into his arms. A strange pain went through him at the thought—how sweet it would be when Garth learned of it!

Idly, he lifted his beer and drank, wondering if he was that cold-hearted, if his need for revenge was greater than loyalty to a memory. After all, Sarah, too, had suffered. She had likely believed Elias had deserted her, as he had believed her desertion, when in fact they had both been betrayed by fate.

In that light, his hunger for vengeance seemed almost evil. Sarah might be hurt again.

But as he considered that thought, his conscience stayed still. Dead.

Instead, a vision stirred. Sarah in the garden of cosmos, her jeans wet to the knees from the rain on the plants, her soft blond hair falling around her shoulders like a cape, her slim body animated and unselfconscious as she bent and clicked and shot her photos. He had not felt dead then.

Perhaps, a small voice warned, it was not revenge he wished for at all. Perhaps it was not his pride that was so wounded, but his heart, and it wasn't his pride that had never healed, but that broken heart. Maybe more than revenge, he needed a sense of what his sister the psychologist would name "closure."

No. He narrowed his eyes, lifting his chin as if in defiance of the night itself. Admitting he needed to finish it meant that he would have to admit how much he'd loved her, how much a fool he had been.

No. Love was for boys and fools. Love only caused pain. Anger and revenge were much more reliable emotions.

It was only two days before the news of Sarah's return spread through the family, and only hours after that when Teresa Benavidez, his troubled fifteen-year-old niece, sought Elias out in the office of the warehouse. "Hey, *tío*," she said in greeting. "You busy?"

He closed the file on his desk. "Never too busy to talk," he said. "What's up?"

She flowed into the small room—she always flowed or floated—and poured herself into an overstuffed chair. Her musky perfume drowned out the green scent of the rose hips being processed today, and her lips were painted with lipstick that was almost black. A fake nose-ring graced one nostril, since she didn't quite dare to actually get it pierced. Her mother—Eli's oldest sister—would kill her and she knew it.

Eli waited while she plucked at her blouse with dark blue fingernails and wiggled one foot, getting ready to say whatever was on her mind.

"I saw the family meeting the other night at Grandma's," he said when she still did not seem inclined to start the conversation. "Was it you at the middle of it?"

She rolled her eyes and popped her gum simultaneously. "It was stupid. I didn't even do nothing this time."

"Anything."

She waved a hand. "Whatever. Some girls at school got caught smoking and they said it was me who gave them the cigarettes." Her eyes widened in outrage. "I do not smoke."

Eli nodded.

Finally Teresa flowed into an earnest position. It was

always startling to see the overly painted, badly dressed girl move like that, like water or air, as if she were some magic being whose parts assembled themselves back in perfect order each time she moved even an inch. "I heard there's this photographer in town," she said. She put a finger in her mouth to snag the end of her gum and, talking around it, added, "Everybody says that she's real famous, that she does all kinds of magazine covers and all the biggest models."

A stillness went through Eli. He waited. "And?"

"Well—" Her gaze sailed around the room, and her shoulders shifted. "I heard you used to go out with her? And maybe you guys are still tight? Or something?"

"You mean Sarah."

A falsely guileless smile bloomed on her face, and it surprised him just as her grace did. Even though it was false, it was gorgeous. "Yeah! You know her?"

"I did." He plucked a pencil from the top of the desk.

"Tío," she cried. "You're not making this easy."

He let the eraser tap the desk, and sent the pencil upward through his fingers, then let it swing down in an arc and tapped the lead. "You want easy, Teresa, then talk to me. Don't play games. What do you want?"

The shoulders lifted, the eyelids fell, the head shifted. "Do you still know her? Are you guys, like, friends?"

"And if we are?"

"Then maybe you'd ask if she would shoot my portfolio?"

"Portfolio?"

"A modeling book." Now her gaze was open, almost painfully earnest. "If someone that famous and that good shot my portfolio, it would be such a break."

She was afraid, Eli realized suddenly, that he would make light of her dreams. As long as he could remember, Teresa had said she would be a model, and she was right:

a break like having a Sarah Greenwood portfolio of shots would take her a long way.

He pursed his lips, considering the possible consequences of asking Sarah for this favor. A small, dangerous part of him remembered the look of her mouth, moistened by rain, the way her sodden T-shirt had clung to the ripened slope of her breasts. A pulse of reaction jumped in his loins.

Dangerous.

But within that hard place in his heart he imagined something else: Garth Greenwood's face if he found Eli at his daughter's cottage.

He looked at his niece. "I can talk to her, but we have some bad blood between us. I don't know if she will say yes."

Teresa swallowed. "But you'll ask for me?"

He shrugged. "Sure." The worst Sarah could do was say no.

An almost feverish look of excitement lit the girl's large dark eyes. "Thank you." She jumped up, all legs and arms and hair, and kissed his cheek. "Tell me as soon as you talk to her, okay?"

He nodded. Still tapping his pencil, eraser to tip, tip to eraser, he inclined his head, watching her as she left. It looked as if fate, so unfriendly to the cause of love all those years ago, was more inclined to lend help for revenge.

A black-and-gray tabby slipped through the slats of the fence and ambled through the cosmos to join Sarah for breakfast. "Good morning," Sarah said, reaching down to stroke the big tom's arched back. "I saved you some bacon." She put the bits and pieces of meat on the wooden slats of the porch floor and grinned when the cat delicately nibbled them.

Every morning for the past three days the cat had arrived precisely at breakfast to beg a few scraps and wind around her legs. Sarah had asked Mrs. Gray if the tom belonged to her, but she'd only scowled. "That cat!" she had exclaimed. "He's a stray, and the worst beggar I've ever met. Just shoo him away."

But after years of being unable to keep a pet of any kind, Sarah found the cat a pleasing companion. She liked the benevolently sleepy smile he had when he lounged in a sunny spot in the garden, and his warm purring approval over her attentions. It was easy to please him.

When he finished his bacon, he sat back and looked at her expectantly. For a stray, she thought, he was certainly healthy. His fur was thick and glossy, though she sometimes pulled cockleburs from the hair on his belly. Aside from one nicked ear, he didn't have the scars most strays carried, like warrior knights, from all their battles. "That's all I saved," she said, spreading her hands as if he understood the concept of empty-handed.

Evidently he did, for he nimbly leapt into her lap and settled down to lick his paws. Sarah chuckled, and petted him lazily.

Her days since her arrival had settled into an agreeable routine. She awakened slowly and ate her breakfast here in the garden, then cleaned up and took a walk that ended up at her parents' house. She helped her mother with various chores or stayed with her father while her mother ran errands. Sometime in the afternoon she returned to her little house, where she read or watched a movie or simply sat in the garden and watched the sun set. Yesterday she had called an old high school friend, and they were going to meet for dinner today. Joanna, an art dealer, had often stopped by to see Sarah in New York, but this was the first time they had met on home ground since Sarah had left Taos.

The sound of footsteps on the flagstone path between cottages reached her, and Sarah glanced over without expectation. There were five cottages on the hill, and mornings were busy. Whoever it was on the path now was hidden by the trees and shrubby plants that landscaped the hill. She spied a jeans-clad thigh and a boot between a yucca and a huge sunflower bush. A rather nice thigh, actually. A shoulder, straight and clean, came into view below the branches of a Russian olive. Sarah's hand stilled as she waited for the rest, a dark head, a face hidden by sunglasses. Her fingers curled in the thick fur of the cat in her lap.

He stopped on the other side of the gate, his mouth sober, his hair glinting in the bright morning. "Hello, Sarah," Elias said.

She didn't move. Nor did she speak. On one level she did not quite trust her voice, because honestly, it was not fair that he could still be *that* unbelievably sexy. He'd been a beautiful adolescent, but many boys were beautiful. She knew some of his brothers had not aged so well as this— they had put on weight around the middle, and those sleek lines of cheekbone and jaw had softened with genial family-man warmth. Not Elias. He was as trim and sculpted as he had been at eighteen. And success sat well on him, lending an authority of carriage he had not held as a boy.

Sarah stroked the cat and waited. He had some purpose in coming here. Let him say it.

He took off his sunglasses, pursed his lips. "I have no right to come here after I was so angry the other night."

"True."

"But I have come with a request I promised I would make, and I wonder if you have a moment."

She lifted one eyebrow. "A request? How interesting."

He inclined his head. "Not for me. For my niece Teresa. Do you remember her?"

Sarah swallowed, thinking of the little girl who had ridden between them sometimes in his car, a beautiful little girl with a wild imagination, who made them both laugh. "Of course I remember her. She must be practically grown up by now."

"Not quite." He gestured at the gate. "May I come in?"

"If you promise this is really about Teresa. I do not want my day ruined with ancient history."

"Fair enough." He opened the gate and closed it behind him. As he crossed the courtyard, Sarah was snared as she always had been by the way he moved, straight and loose limbed, as comfortable with his body as a stallion.

He halted at the edge of the porch. In for a penny, in for a pound, Sarah thought, and gestured to the chair on the other side of the table. "Have a seat."

"Thank you." He sat formally, back very straight, and put his sunglasses on the table.

Sarah was glad of the cat, anchoring her in reality—his rumbling purr against her thighs, his big soft body under her hands. It was really almost too much to see Elias like this, in the flesh, grown and whole. It had the feeling of a dream, and she was afraid she might just start saying whatever came into her head. *Let's just let bygones be bygones and go have wild sex in my room, what do you say?*

Bending her head to hide her face, she said, "Tell me what Teresa needs."

"What?"

She raised her head and, to her amusement, saw that there was new heat in his cheeks, a genuine blush, and his eyes darted suspiciously away from the region of her braless breasts under the simple, light cotton tunic she wore as a robe.

Serves him right, her voice muttered nastily. For once, Sarah agreed with it. "Tell me about Teresa," she said again.

"Right." He folded his hands. "She wants to be a model. She asked me to come ask you if you might shoot a portfolio for her. I would pay you for your time."

Sarah took a breath. It was a delicate situation. The common misconception was that a girl needed only to be beautiful to be a good model, when the balance was actually far more complex. Often the strangest faces were the most photogenic, and the prettiest to the eye were rendered bland on the page. "What makes her think she'd be good at it?"

"I don't know. She's just always wanted it, since she was little."

"How tall is she?"

Elias frowned, and gestured to the middle of his throat. "Here…maybe five-nine? She's tall for a girl."

"That's good." She hesitated and then decided to simply tell the truth. "There's no way to know if she has even a little of what it takes until I see how she interacts with the camera, and how she looks on film." She met his eyes as honestly as she was able. "You are the only one who knows if it would be better for me to simply say no, or to give her a chance and maybe face the possibility that she is not going to be a model."

Something in his face moved. Softened, maybe. A little tension eased away from his eyes, and all at once there was a hint of the old Elias there. "She's in trouble," he said. "She's running with the wrong kids, maybe right on the edge of making some very bad choices." He paused. "I don't know if it would be better for her to keep dreaming, or know."

"When I was about fourteen," Sarah said, "a photographer in town for the summer took me under his wing and let me use his darkroom and his cameras. He walked with me all over town and helped me learn to see. I loved taking photographs before that, but it was John who gave me the passion." Sarah pressed her lips together in thought. "Maybe what I can do is have you bring her here and shoot a few good rolls of film, just to see. I'll give her those prints, and she can use my name, but if she has no real talent, I don't want to spend more time shooting her, because it will make me feel like a liar."

"That's more than—"

Sarah stopped him with an upheld hand. "You can pay me for my time on that one. And I am not cheap."

A hint of a smile touched his lips.

"If she has true potential, I'll shoot a professional portfolio for her, and since it would be my way of repaying my old mentor, I won't charge either of you for it."

"Fair enough, Sarah." He stood. "I did not deserve your consideration, and you offered it anyway. Thank you."

"You're right," she said. "You didn't deserve it. But that's no reason to punish Teresa."

He nodded. "When would you like us to come?"

The cat, spying something in the flowers, suddenly leapt off Sarah's lap, and she felt suddenly vulnerable. She crossed her arms. "I'm busy today, but we may as well get it done. Tomorrow afternoon, maybe two or three?"

"Two would be good," he said, his gaze on the horizon. "I'll bring her here. Should she bring anything?"

"Couple of changes of clothes, different colors. Maybe a hat or a scarf that she likes. That's really all."

"Okay." He didn't quite meet her eyes as he lifted a hand. "Fine. I'll see you then."

Sarah nodded, but he was already striding toward the gate, hurrying as if he had an appointment. He'd already gone through the gate when she spied his sunglasses still sitting on the table. She reached for them and simultaneously called out, "Elias!"

Eli could not breathe. The air was too hot. His blood pounded through his ears and he imagined he could hear the swish of it in his veins, like the river at spring runoff, the volume doubled, tripled. He thought his hands might even be shaking.

"Elias!" Her voice ripped through the stillness, oddly urgent, and he whirled, bracing himself—for he didn't know what.

For her. Coming toward him without hurry, her athletic

legs burnished and bare below a shapeless red tunic that had long sleeves and reached her knees and should not have been so alluring. But it was. The fabric was thin as water, opaque but somehow woven with shiny gold and silver thread that shone at every turn, every curve, as if she were clothed in nothing but spiderwebs.

The sight had been headily sensual as she sat calm and still in a chair, with a cat hiding half her body, but now she moved, and the cloth moved, too, shimmering around her waist, glowing down the front of her thighs. Elias stared, his chest tight, and it seemed the sun kissed the tip of each breast with a star of golden light, as if to focus his gaze upon that which he should not see. It was only a trick of the fabric, the fact that her breasts upturned—

"Your glasses," she said, holding them up.

Tendrils of hair escaped the loose knot into which her hair was bound, and fell down her neck. She lifted a hand to brush a wisp from her mouth and Elias thought it the most erotic gesture he'd ever seen, her fingers brushing over that cheek, her mouth parting a little, the soft gray eyes alive with humor—

His eyes narrowed. She knew.

With exaggerated care she put the sunglasses in his hand, and in a voice as husky and sensual as a spoonful of honey, said, "Close your mouth, Elias." Then she turned, walked back to the house and went inside.

For one minute he did not move, thinking in wild ways of following her into the dimness of those rooms, and tearing away that sinful fabric, and tasting that body he'd longed for so much, so long ago....

Fool.

He was a fool. With a frustrated groan, he whirled away and stormed back up the hill.

Chapter Three

Sarah walked to her mother's house at midmorning. It was already hot, but the clean, dry heat of the desert, which was all sun pouring from a cerulean sky. She loved being able to walk everywhere, even if—like today—it meant joining the hordes of tourists that crowded the sidewalks and breathing the fumes of a dozen oversize RVs waddling down the street. And her mood, which had been lifting a little with each hour she'd been home, was particularly exuberant as she strode up the hill.

She didn't lie to herself. She knew exactly what caused the feeling of triumph. Elias, staring at her as if he would catch fire at any second. Or melt in a puddle of lust. Thinking of it now as she passed a string of cinder-block adobe storefronts, Sarah chuckled to herself. Score one for her.

It was only fair. He'd been quite nasty to her that first night. He'd hurt her feelings and dragged out all kinds of insecurities and demons Sarah had no interest in plumbing. In ten seconds she had been reduced to the vulnerable, frightened, miserable teenager she thought she'd left behind a long time ago, and it had appalled her.

This morning it had been the adult Sarah and the adult Elias, and Sarah had won, hands down. It was a good feeling.

She spent most of the day with her mother, helping her to wash clothes and clean the house, then played a round of gin rummy with her father before he tired and wanted to nap. When she came out of the bedroom she noticed that her mother looked wan, too. "Mom, why don't you go lie down? There's nothing wrong with taking a nap when Dad does."

Mabel brushed her hair from her face. "Maybe I will. Are you coming back for dinner tonight?"

"No, I'm meeting Joanna for dinner at La Paloma."

"Joanna!" She smiled. "That's wonderful. I used to see her all the time when she was working at the gallery. How is she?"

Sarah flopped onto the couch, her feet in front of her, and lifted her hair to let the cool air from the window blow over her sweaty neck. "Very happy. She has a baby who is nine months old. She's going to bring him along." Sarah grinned. "I gather he's more or less the apple of her eye."

"She married an Indian, didn't she? Thomas something."

"Concha."

"Bet that didn't go over well with his people."

"I don't know." Sarah lifted a shoulder. "They're living on Indian land, and I gather the family is nearby, so it can't be too bad."

"I guess." Mabel's cornflower blue eyes gained a distant expression. "Things are so different now. When we were children we never thought of mixing the way you all have. We stuck to our own. All of us did."

Sarah sat up, feeling the familiar knot in her chest. Her parents were products of their times. She knew that. Most of the time she tried to accept it. "There had to be times you wanted to, Mom. Wasn't there ever a handsome Indian or Mexican boy you wanted to talk to?"

Mabel lowered her eyes, and Sarah suddenly felt Elias between them. "No," she said, and looked up. "But I understood what you saw in Eli the first time I saw him."

"I don't want to talk about that."

Her mother ignored her. "I was down in Penasco to see about some fabric a woman had there, and was about to drive home when I saw a girl who looked like you sitting on some steps. With a boy. Remember how his hair was so long? He was sitting there beside you with this...look on his face, and that hair was blowing like a piece of pure silk, as beautiful as anything I ever saw."

With a pang, Sarah remembered. The house, little more than a single room with a half kitchen, belonged to a young cousin of Eli's, and sometimes Eli got the key and took Sarah there so they had a place to just be together without driving all over the county. "I remember the place," Sarah said, and found to her horror that she had to blink hard.

"Have you seen him?"

Sarah lifted her face and lied. "No. And I hope I don't."

Mabel only nodded. Then she yawned. "I think I am going to go have a nap. You go on and have a good time with Joanna. Tell her I said hi." At the door to her bedroom, she paused. "Sarah, it's so good to have you home."

Accepting the olive branch, Sarah smiled. "It's good to be here."

She met Joanna at La Paloma, an old restaurant in an old hotel, once patronized by Mabel Dodge Luhan and her crowd in the twenties. Sarah arrived first, and when the waiter seated her by the window overlooking the street, she ordered a glass of merlot. When the wine came, she sipped it with a sense of decadence, and suddenly remembered the lunch on her birthday in London. It was only a little more than a week ago, but it seemed a lifetime.

And yet, again she heard the sound of many languages. German behind her. French at the table to her right. And around them all the mingled rhythm of English and Spanish and Indian inflections that she'd heard in London, the sound that spoke of home. She sipped her wine and closed her eyes, listening, doubly pleased when the sound of Spanish guitar, woven through with song, added its flavor. The air smelled of margaritas and roasted green chiles.

Home. She had not known the depths of her homesickness till she came back. Had not realized the desert was in her blood, that too many trees made her claustrophobic and she needed to rest her eyes on the mountains and the sky. Now that she was here, she didn't know how she'd borne being away for so long.

"Are you meditating?"

Sarah laughed and opened her eyes. "No." She jumped up to hug her friend Joanna, a tall, lovely brunette with yards of hair she wore long and loose. "I'm so happy to see you!" Between them, the baby, a fat, round-faced boy with straight black hair and rosy cheeks, laughed and caught a handful of Sarah's hair. "And I'm glad to meet you, too," Sarah said, kissing his forehead.

"Jacob," Joanna said.

He gave a happy shout and reached for her. Pleased, Sarah kissed his little palm, and when he giggled, took him from Joanna. "Hello, Jacob. Aren't you a doll," she murmured, and buried her face against his neck, smelling baby powder and fresh clothing and the pointed sweetness of baby heat. He gurgled and nuzzled her back. Sarah laughed. "Joanna, he's adorable."

Joanna inclined her head. "He doesn't often take to strangers like that. You should feel honored." She slid into the booth.

"Do you mind if I hold him for a little while?" Sarah asked. His soft, lumpy weight felt good.

"Of course not."

"I always have liked babies," she said, settling with him on her lap.

"I remember. I never did, until this one." She grinned. "And I'm making up for it now. I want about twenty more."

"Really?"

"Well, maybe three or four." She ordered a margarita from the waiter and leaned over the table. "So...how is it, being back after all this time?"

"I should have come back a long time ago."

Joanna nodded. "It gets in your blood. I don't know how anyone stays away once they were raised here." She dipped a tortilla chip into a bowl of salsa. "How is your father?"

"Okay." Sarah lifted a shoulder. "The doctors seem to think he shouldn't be as sick as he is. He's made a lot of changes in his health. He's lost the weight he needed to get off and he walks with my mother for a few minutes every day, but he's just languishing."

"How are things between the two of you?"

"I came home to make peace with him. He seems to want to make peace, too." She took a sip of wine.

"But—"

"But he wants me to forgive him, for the baby. He wants to talk about it." She set her mouth. "I don't want to go down that road. It's over and done with and there's no point."

"You don't forgive him?"

"No." Sarah said the word without apology.

Joanna sobered, looked at her son and back to Sarah. "In a way, I do understand, but it isn't going to do either one of you any good for you to hold a grudge."

Sarah bent her head, curling her fingers around Jacob's

plump hand, rubbing her thumb over his tiny fingernails. He cooed. "I know." She looked up. "I can't help it."

For a moment Joanna focused on something behind Sarah. Then she turned her attention back to her friend. "Have you seen Eli?"

She snorted. "About five minutes after I got here, believe it or not."

"Fate," Joanna said with a smile.

Sarah rolled her eyes. "Sure."

She chuckled. "Yeah, fate. He just walked in."

A spasm touched Sarah's stomach. She narrowed her eyes. "Not really."

"Really." She gestured subtly toward the other side of the room.

Reluctantly, Sarah glanced in the direction Joanna had pointed, and saw a waiter seating at a table a dark-haired woman in a luscious red dress. Eli waited politely as she was settled, then took his own seat.

"Good lord," Sarah said.

"My thoughts exactly," Joanna said with a faint purr.

He was elegantly dressed in a black suit that fit his trim form exquisitely, emphasizing his broad shoulders and lean hips. His hair was combed back from the chiseled face, and the smile he gave his dinner guest was charming.

Sarah looked back at Joanna, and found she had no words in her throat. Joanna lifted her eyebrows. "He's grown up nicely."

Sarah couldn't help it—she laughed, and made a fake coughing noise to indicate her agreement. "No kidding." She glanced over again, noticing with a pang of jealousy the way the woman leaned closer, eagerly, to tell Eli something. Warm yellow light haloed her hair and made her flesh look like cream. "Who is the date?"

"Jennifer Jaquez. She's a graphic designer. I think she's doing some work for Santiago Teas, designing new logos and labels and the boxes for the teas. They wanted something distinctive.''

"You know a lot about this."

"Thomas and Eli are good friends."

"Mmm." Sarah nodded. "Well, it doesn't look like a business dinner, now, does it?"

"You sound jealous."

"No. Just curious." She reached for a chip herself. "Has he ever been married?"

"No way. He's not the same man he was when you left, Sarah. You wouldn't even know him now. Not really. He never dates anyone very long, pours everything into his business—which is probably why it's so successful."

Sarah's throat tightened with tension and she scowled. "Let's talk about something else. I don't know that I've forgiven him, either, to tell you the truth."

"For what?" Joanna looked up, genuinely puzzled.

"He could have tried to find me. Write to me. Something. If I'd had one tiny glimmer of hope, I wouldn't have given the baby up."

Joanna went very still. She put down her spoon. "Sarah, you didn't...you can't mean to tell me you didn't know he went to jail."

"Of course I knew. He was arrested the night we came back to town, but he hadn't done anything." The expression on Joanna's face chilled her. "He didn't really go to *jail?*"

"Oh, Sarah—I had no idea you didn't know this. The old-boy network kicked in pretty good for your father. They couldn't make the charges stick, but Eli spent two months in jail waiting for his trial."

Sarah stared at her. "I didn't know." She closed her eyes to hide the sudden tears. "Oh, God."

Joanna touched her hand. "I'm sorry. I would never have said anything—it just never occurred to me that you didn't know."

For long moments Sarah could not speak as she struggled with a sudden rush of emotions—sorrow and regret and rage in equal proportions. "No wonder," she whispered.

"Sarah, he's coming to the table."

She barely had time to swallow a sip of water and arrange her features before he was standing there, smelling of some heavenly cologne, his jaw newly shaved. His eyes were dangerous, full of a hot, piercing light Sarah did not want to see. Did not want to feel.

"Hello," he said pleasantly, the tone so at odds with the dangerous look that Sarah wondered if it was her imagination. "Sarah, Joanna." His gaze fell on the baby. "Your son is growing."

Sarah ducked her head, taking refuge in the baby's hands, but Eli was kneeling, putting his face at a level with Jacob's, and reaching out a hand—that slim, beautiful hand, masculine and sensitive at once—to brush the boy's cheek gently. He wore a single carved silver ring on his right hand, and with shock, Sarah recognized it as the wedding band they had chosen. She looked at him.

His face was so close she could see a faint, tiny scar at the bridge of his nose where he'd been struck with a rock when he was ten and the individual pores of his jaw where his beard came in. His lower lip was faintly chapped from the hot day.

His eyes, boring into hers, were as fathomless as they'd always been, pools of unbroken darkness. She had no idea how long they stared at each other like that, with a baby between them, a plump brown baby they might have made, but she could not look away. Could not speak.

Abruptly he stood. "I just wanted to say hello," he said with an urbane smile. "Maybe you would both join Jennifer and me for dessert?"

"That would be great," Joanna said immediately.

"Good." Eli turned toward Sarah. "You and she will have much in common—she is also an artist."

"I'll look forward to it."

With a single nod, he departed. As soon as he was out of earshot, Sarah said, "Why did you say yes?"

Joanna's expression was sober. "For you," she said. "I had no idea there was still so much between you."

"There isn't," Sarah said fiercely.

"Oh, please."

"Joanna, don't do this. I can't stand it." She looked over her shoulder. "He scares me now."

"Maybe that's good. He isn't the man he was," she agreed.

"What do you mean?"

Joanna hesitated. "They say he lives to have his revenge on your father."

"And you're afraid he might take his revenge through me."

"Yes." The word was simple and chilling.

Sarah thought of the way he had looked this morning as he watched her come toward him, his eyes boiling, his lips parting, his arms rigid at his sides as if he controlled himself with only the most intense effort. And along her spine she felt her response, a tingling awareness that ached for expression.

"I'm not the girl I was, either," she said calmly, and knew it was true. "I'm not naive or innocent or prone to being carried away by passion." She shook her head. "I have no intention of allowing him anywhere near me."

"Not even for a curious roll in the hay?" Joanna teased. "Even with an old lover who looks like that?"

Sarah laughed throatily, remembering her urge this morning to take him inside. "Well, the thought might have crossed my mind. But it would be like curling up with a coyote. Too dangerous."

"Good."

Reaching around the baby playing with her necklace, Sarah picked up the menu. "Let's order. I'm starving."

* * *

Eli cursed his choice of restaurants from the moment he walked in and saw Sarah with Jacob Concha curled comfortably on her lap.

All day he'd thought of little but Sarah in her red robe. He'd thrown himself into his work, had even gone out and hoed in the fields, trying to burn away that vision of her in the water-thin cloth, the light kissing her breasts and thighs....

Nothing had worked. When Jennifer had called to ask him to supper, he'd jumped at the chance. She was beautiful, intelligent and lushly sexy. He did not, as a rule, mix business with pleasure, but there was an undeniable, enjoyable attraction between them, and he decided to throw caution to the wind.

Looking at her now, dark and lovely, made of a zillion soft, inviting curves, he knew he ought to be aching to tumble with her into a feast of sensual delights. He genuinely liked her as a person. She had worked hard to create her business, fighting family and friends to set up a competitive graphic arts studio in a town overflowing with starving artists.

But she'd had to wear red. Red that made him think of—

With controlled effort, he focused. "How are the plans for your new business coming along?"

Jennifer smiled. "You know, Elias," she said in a voice as pleasant as everything else about her, "I am getting the distinct impression you might be a little distracted tonight." She leaned closer, and he was afforded a dazzling display of cleavage that moved him not at all. "Is this about the blonde over there?"

Eli winced. "Sorry."

"Don't be. I thought I recognized her. Sarah Greenwood, right?"

"Yes. Jennifer, I really am sorry. I promise I'll be more attentive."

She laughed. "No, don't promise. We have been friends for some time and I have always sensed you were not emotionally available." She lifted one creamy shoulder. "But it was worth a try to coax you out. A woman never knows."

"Still, this makes me feel rotten."

"Don't." She touched his hand. "Being friends is good, too. And not to be vain, but I do not have trouble finding lovers."

He chuckled, as he was meant to, and took a deep breath, relaxing for the first time since he'd come to the restaurant. "I'm not emotionally available," he said honestly. "Probably never will be."

"Fair enough." She sipped her ruby-colored wine. "Is she the reason? That whole feud between your families?"

"Yes," he said without elaboration.

"What really happened to cause that war, anyway? I've never heard the story. Do you mind telling it?"

He smiled. "Do you want the facts or the romantic version?"

"Oh, the romantic one, please."

"Ah. Good choice." He leaned forward, donning an exaggerated Spanish accent. "Once upon a time, this land belonged to the descendants of the proud conquistadores, and their language and customs were Spanish, and all was well."

Jennifer chuckled. "Except for the Indians."

"Details," he said, waving them away. He smiled ruefully to let her know he was kidding. "Anyway, into this peaceful, abundant land came a horde of *americanos* who changed everything, took the land and changed the language, and would not go away.

"In those days, the Santiago family was proud and strong and rich. They held acres and acres of rich land and were respected throughout the country. Even when the *americanos* came in, the Santiagos made peace and kept on with their work, and did not even make trouble when an *americano* named Greenwood bought up the land nearby and made a cattle ranch.''

The waiter came with plates of steaming food: a steak for Eli, a large, exotic salad for Jennifer. Eli waited as the waiter poured a little more wine into their glasses, and he carefully cut a bite of meat, tasting it and nodding his approval before he went on.

''It happens that there was a young son of the Santiagos, a boy with a hot temper and hotter passions. He was so handsome all the mamas in the valley had their eyes upon him for their daughters, and there was fierce competition among the young girls themselves to catch his eye without angering their papas.''

Jennifer's eyes twinkled. ''Like a Santiago in this generation, no?''

''*Exactamente.*'' He winked. ''But it happened that the young Manuel had been smitten by his neighbor's daughter, the lovely, sweet Emily Greenwood, fresh to this land, as pretty as peach blossoms.''

He sobered, and wondered here, as he always did, what had really happened. ''The facts are simple from there. Manuel Santiago was accused of raping the Greenwood girl, and he was hanged one bright fall morning. The girl was disgraced and humiliated and killed herself that same night.'' He cut a precise triangle of meat. ''From that day to this, the war between our families has burned hotter with each generation.''

Jennifer inclined her head. ''You need to work on that ending a bit.''

He lifted a shoulder. ''There is no romantic way to say it.''

''The romantic part comes in with you and Sarah Greenwood. Falling in love as teenagers. Being torn apart by this old feud. Maybe it belongs to the two of you to heal that feud.''

"Never." The word was low and fierce.

"Too bad." She was quiet for a moment, then lifted her head. "It will happen again, you know. Somewhere down the line, in twenty or forty or a hundred years, another Santiago and another Greenwood will fall in love and the war will keep them apart."

"So be it." Across the room he saw Sarah and Joanna stand up, smoothing their skirts and gathering purses. He put down his fork, unable to pretend he did not need to look at her now. She wore a simple sheath, with a scoop neck and no sleeves, made of some unusual weave of silk the color of blue turquoise. It showed off her tanned skin, her flat belly, her long legs, and he liked it a lot.

"Are you still in love with her?" Jennifer asked.

Eli shook his head, very sure. "No." But with a sense of relief, he realized he could admit to something more base—lust. Yes, lust brewed like this in a man's veins, making him fill with heated blood that made him ready, made him hungry. Desire was a chemical thing, made of sights and smells and a need for release. It had nothing at all to do with love, which was soft and too complicated.

Yes, he would admit to lust. And he would use it.

Chapter Four

Sarah was acutely uncomfortable joining the party of two at their table, but Joanna had insisted. And to her credit, the beautiful woman with Eli did not seem to mind at all.

Joanna took the chair next to Jennifer, leaving Sarah to perch next to Eli, who only smiled politely as they sat down, and asked Joanna about her husband.

Sarah tried to relax, but her knee bumped his under the table, and she jerked back as if she'd been burned. She folded her hands in front of her and her elbow nudged his. She shifted again, but Eli shifted at the same second, and their thighs brushed for an eternity—skin sliding against gabardine in a slow, sinuous swish before Sarah had the presence of mind to pull hers away. When she looked at him after that, he only gave her a sultry, knowing expression.

He knew. He was paying her back for this morning.

The knowledge burned a little inside her chest before she realized what was happening between them was a full-blown war. With a decisive toss of her head, she met his eyes. If he wanted war, he would have it.

She relaxed a little, and crossed her legs, knowing he would be able to see her thigh, bare and tanned. She felt his gaze flickering over her neck, her arms, her breasts. She focused on the discussion that arose between Jennifer and Joanna, and joined in with the odd comment, but she never forgot she was at war with Eli. She felt his breath when he moved, brushing over her bare arm on the table, and she shifted to accidentally brush her knee against his.

But she knew she had lost when he stood. "Would anyone like to dance?"

Joanna gestured to her baby, sound asleep on her shoulder. "Sorry."

"I'd love to," Jennifer said, "but I have a sprained ankle."

"That leaves you," he said, as if he'd known the others would refuse. "Will you dance, Sarah?"

And heaven help her, she rose, chin lifted high, and met his eye. "Of course."

He held out his hand and led Sarah onto the dance floor, pausing for one moment as they faced each other. "I don't remember ever dancing with you," he said.

"I wasn't allowed to go anyplace there might have been dancing."

"Ah." He stepped closer. "And have you learned since then?"

"I guess you're going to find out."

"I suppose I am." He reached for her and Sarah knew a split second of panicky hesitation as his hand lit upon her waist, and hers fell on his shoulder—this was madness. Pure insanity.

But then he drew her into a loose embrace that didn't seem threatening, and she had to concentrate on following his lead. He danced as elegantly as he moved, with a simple, easy grace. It was impossible to remain aloof, especially with one of his palms burning against her waist and another against her hand. He smelled of cologne and wine.

He did not speak at all, and Sarah could think of nothing to say. It took every scrap of her concentration to hang on to her composure. His body, so lean and graceful, swayed tantalizingly against hers, and she stared at the place where his starched white collar met the vulnerable flesh at his throat, aware of her heart thudding and a slow, heavy pulse beginning to thrum low in her belly.

"You have learned to dance well," he said, and pulled her infinitesmally closer.

Sarah swallowed and could not look at him, suddenly and fiercely aware of his chest brushing her breasts. She kept their bellies apart, afraid to find he was aroused, afraid of what that sensation might do.

As if he noticed, he tugged her firmly against him, and bent to murmur in her ear, "Afraid, Sarah?"

She was thirty years old. She'd danced with gorgeous, compelling men in the most romantic cities in the world. She'd tangoed and waltzed with continental playboys. She was sophisticated and world traveled.

But when she felt Eli's body against the length of her own, thigh-to-thigh, chest-to-chest, a sensation of such desperate, sudden, shocking desire washed through her that she nearly went faint. She grasped his arm, but that only nestled them closer. Still, he did not relent; he danced, and her flesh moved against his, and his against hers, and when she felt the heat of him, all of him, she could not breathe.

"You win," she whispered, and looked up at him, trying to make him stop.

He bent his head, so close his beautiful lips were nearly brushing hers. She saw there was too much heat in his eyes, and his breath was ragged when he spoke. "What do I win, Sarita? A kiss?"

There was mocking cruelty in the words. She saw everything in those fleeting seconds while his lips poised over hers. Saw his rage and his pain and his piercing desire. Without thinking, she touched his face. "Stop, Elias," she whispered. "We'll destroy each other."

He closed his eyes, as if her fingers hurt him. "Your father already destroyed me," he said, so low she could barely hear. "He destroyed us both." His breath brushed her cheek, and when he opened his eyes there was such heat, such hatred, and so much hunger that Sarah could not look away. "We are ghosts, Sarita. Ghosts cannot hurt each other."

He turned a little, and his lower lip brushed hers, sending a wash of need through her—

Suddenly a flashbulb burst nearby. The moment was shattered. Sarah panicked. She pushed against him, frantic, and after a moment of holding her, he let go abruptly. She nearly fell in her haste to get away. She didn't pause to look at him. Breathing unevenly, she walked stiffly back to the table, murmured an apology and fled.

Out in the street, falling in with the flow of tourists, Sarah gasped for breath. She nearly ran for most of a block, drawing curious stares, which she ignored, only stopping when her lungs ached for rest. The night air finally penetrated, cooling the heat in her body and the turmoil in her mind. With a sense of despair, she sank down on a bench.

To the east, the mountains loomed as a dark shadow against a horizon of stars, and Sarah thought as she always did that it looked as if you could step from the top of the mountain into the sky itself, be instantly transported into a strange and wonderful world far, far away. Such a beautiful sky, glittering with a billion stars.

From a motel courtyard up the street she heard the sound of Indian drums, thudding into the air in a familiar and exotic rhythm. She simply sat there listening, her back against a cool wall, refusing to allow any thoughts to come into her mind at all. It was a survival skill she'd learned at eighteen, and she firmly believed it had saved her sanity.

She had been utterly powerless to halt the events that had
so transformed her life, and, like a willow, she'd learned
to bend with the wind. But the only possible way she could
do it was by not thinking. Not thinking about her father or
Eli or her baby.

She was good at it, this trick of not thinking. Tonight
she simply stared up at the blinking stars and forced herself
to make patterns of them. Little flashes of memory, loud
and in Technicolor, pushed their way past her walls, tiny
blips: Eli's hand upon her waist, the baby Jacob's soft
weight, a night flashing red. Each time, she clamped down
on it, boxed it, shoved it away.

After twenty minutes, the blips stopped. Peace returned.
The soft glaze of contentment in the night and the sound
of the drums had shoved away her tumultuous reactions,
and with a deep breath she stood up, smoothed her skirt
and walked home.

He couldn't get to her if she didn't let him. None of
them could.

Somewhere in the middle of the night, Eli bolted awake,
sitting up in his bed, a cry on his lips. It took long seconds
before he realized where he was or what time it was. When
he realized, he fell back on the pillows with a groan and
sighed. Outside the window, an owl hooted mournfully.

The dream that had awakened him washed back in, a
dream he'd had a hundred times, a thousand, over the years.
He was wandering in some strange place, opening doors,
stopping people in the street, looking under cars, into clos-
ets that magically appeared in front of him. Endlessly
searching. Sometimes he was looking for Sarah. Sometimes
he sought their child. The dreams went on and on, and in
them, Eli searched fruitlessly, endlessly.

The dream never lost its power to depress him. No matter
how many times it came, no matter how well-armored he

thought he was, it left a taste of ashes in his mouth when he awakened.

Now he shifted, looking out to the sky he could see through his window, and memories of Sarah rushed through him. This, too, was predictable. Her startled shout of laughter when something delighted her. The way she lifted her chin when something challenged her. The silkiness of her skin beneath his hands. The way she curled into him after they made love, warm as a cat, pleased and purring.

But now there were new images. The stunning heat of her against him as they danced. The challenge in her gray eyes—no longer the eyes of a child, but those of a woman who knew her power. And the dark baby in her arms, laughing up at her.

He curled into himself, as if protecting something vulnerable inside him. His sister had told him for years that he needed counseling to overcome his rage at the terrible betrayals he had undergone. Eli had scoffed, preferring to take refuge in his plan of revenge.

But in the darkness of the night, with sorrow on his tongue, he could not see how revenge would take these night sweats away. It seemed futile. Everything seemed futile. Dreams of honor or dreams of revenge—it didn't matter. They were all insubstantial, meaningless.

Knowing he would not sleep, that if he stayed in bed he would simply go over the same ground again and again, he got up and went to the kitchen. Taking an old herbal cookbook from his shelf, he flipped through the pages until he found a tea he had not tried to brew, something for which he had the ingredients, and got to work. By the time the sun rose, he felt like himself again, and in addition, he had a great new recipe for a spring tonic that was naturally sweet.

He also had to face the possibility that his actions the night before might lead to Sarah canceling the photo shoot. He waited all morning for the call. He dreaded it, dreaded calling his niece and dashing her excitement, and he felt guilty that his own actions would rob her of a chance she most desperately wanted—and only Eli could provide.

But the call never came. And he worried about that, too. By the time he went to pick up Teresa, his nerves were strung as tight as catgut. His sister Cynthia was waiting for him at the door of her expensive, rambling home. A slim, small woman with a smooth bob that ended at her chin, she was a marriage counselor with a thriving practice. Her husband, a mechanic, never seemed to mind that she made in a month what he brought home in a year. Aside from the troublesome Teresa, their lives were as close to perfect as any Eli could imagine.

"I hope you know what you're doing, Elias," she said, her arms crossed.

"She'll never know until she tries. I think she has a good shot."

"I'm not talking about Teresa. I'd just as soon she put aside her obsession with being a sex object and move on to something that might utilize that brain of hers, but she has to make her own choices." She gestured him into the tiled hall. "I'm talking about you and Sarah Greenwood."

Eli affected a bland expression. "She's a photographer, Cynthia. Teresa wants pictures."

"Whatever. I think you're opening a Pandora's box, and I certainly hope you don't let anyone else in the family know who shot the proofs. I'm not interested in fighting that battle again." She called over her shoulder, "Teresa, Elias is here. Hurry up."

A muffled answer came down the stairs, and Cynthia gave her brother a smile. "She's been up there all morning, trying to decide what to take with her. I loaned her some of my hats."

"This session is just between us," Eli said to reassure her. "I've already heard Mama on this subject when she found out Sarah was back in town." He glanced at his watch. Quarter till two. "Teresa, the bus is leaving in two minutes."

Cynthia put her hand on his arm. "Are you really at peace with all this now? It isn't painful to see her?"

Eli rolled his neck. "I'm okay."

Her eyes narrowed, but Teresa chose that moment to fly down the stairs, her feet barely touching the steps. Her face was scrubbed clean, as instructed, and she wore a simple green floral dress that made her skin glow. "Good choice," Eli said. "That dress looks great on you."

"I have others," she said, lifting a bag with several hangers sticking out of it. In her other hand she carried a straw hat. She bent to kiss her mother. "Wish me luck."

"Good luck, baby."

Teresa beamed at Eli. "Let's go."

"You don't even look nervous," he said on the way out.

"Nervous? Why would I be? One of the most famous fashion photographers in the nation is going to give me a shot at a portfolio! This is a great opportunity."

Eli chuckled. "Good for you, *hija*."

Traffic was heavy on the main drag, but they parked at two minutes to two, and Eli helped Teresa carry her things down the steep, bricked path to the cottage. The sun beat down upon them with fierce, high-altitude weight, scorching hot, and Eli found himself wishing he'd stopped long enough to change into a cooler shirt. Sweat trickled down his back.

He took a breath as they rounded the last tree before Sarah's cottage, and Eli thought himself well braced for the sight of her. She sat on the porch in the cool shadows, wearing a crisp, cotton shirt, safari shorts and sandals, her hair pulled back into a short, neat braid. She looked like an ad for upscale travel to the islands—cool, wealthy, in control.

As Teresa reached the gate, Sarah stood up and moved smoothly forward. "Hello!" she said warmly. "You must be Teresa.'' She didn't bother to even glance in Eli's direction. "Come in."

Teresa grinned. "I remember you!" she said with surprise. "You used to give me Tootsie Pops and told me there was a store in Oregon that would give you one free if you found an Indian chief on the wrapper."

Sarah laughed. "That's amazing."

"I've never eaten one since without looking for the Indian."

Eli found himself annoyed at being ignored. "Where shall I hang these?" he asked, lifting the clothes in his hand.

"Hmm." Sarah reached for them. "I'll put them in my room. She can change in there."

Deliberately he held on to them for a moment, hoping to force her to react to him. See him. Instead, those cool gray eyes flickered over him as if they'd never met, much less shared one hell of a hot half hour the night before. It was as if it had never happened. Nice trick, he thought, and let the clothes go.

She put them away and returned with two cameras hanging around her neck, and another in her hand. "Let's go to the studio. I don't have the lights that I would in a professional studio," she explained, "so we're going to use natural light today, just to see how well you come across on film."

"Cool," Teresa said.

Eli trailed behind the women into the long, open room, and waited while Sarah positioned Teresa by the long panels of glass brick that formed the north wall. He wandered to the south end of the room and leaned against the window, watching them. It was impossible to tell how Sarah felt about Teresa's potential. She was matter-of-fact as she lifted the girl's chin, inclining her head. "You have good bone structure," she said. "A great mouth."

Teresa smiled. "And don't forget, I'm tall."

"Yes. That is a plus, but it isn't as important to print work as it is to runway." She stepped back, shot a fast series of shots, lifted her head. "You're very short for a runway model, believe it or not."

Teresa made a surprised face, and Sarah caught that, too. "Good," she said. "We're just going to do some very casual things right now. Soft things, to match that dress. I want to see how you do with the camera itself."

"Okay."

Eli watched from his post on the other side of the room as Sarah talked gently, asking questions about Teresa's life and friends, her ambitions, interspersing it with directions. "Lift your chin...give me a smile...tell me about your boyfriend—oh, yeah, that's good." She shot a lightning-fast series, and grabbed a different camera.

As he watched, Eli imagined her doing this in a crowd of people, with crews for lights and makeup and food, the models skinny and young and gorgeous. He liked the air of competent calm she exuded, and liked imagining her giving orders to all those crowds, coaxing the best shots from the models.

But he also remembered the passionate calm she'd brought to her camera work as a young woman, when she would set up a shot and wait for two hours for the light to be exactly right. She used to shoot the same thing—a particular tree, a glass of milk, a rock in a puddle of water—from seventeen different angles. Then she would sit and wait for the light to change, and do another series of shots.

The sun beat down on his neck, and he moved to sit in a sling-back chair tucked into the corner. From here, there was a wide, blue-and-green view of the valley, the colors washed out by the fierce afternoon sunlight.

"That's great, Teresa," Sarah said, rewinding the camera in her hand. "Why don't you go put on something with a harder edge, and come back. I want to try something."

Teresa hesitated, looked at Eli. "Harder edge?"

"More grown up," he said. "Something sexy, maybe."

"Oh!" She looked disappointed. "I don't think I have anything like that."

"I anticipated that. There's a black dress on my bed. It might be a little tight, but it laces. Fix it however you need to." She flipped the top of a film canister open. "On your way back, grab the purple bag off the couch, will you? And don't worry about shoes."

With a happy little giggle, she ran off to do as she was told. At the door she paused. "This is *fun!*"

Sarah grinned, the most open, honest expression he'd seen on her face since her return. "Sometimes it is."

The girl ran out, and as if she carried all sound waves with her, the room went silent as a vacuum except for the fine motor whir of the cameras rewinding, then being re-loaded. She worked automatically, without looking at him.

He ached to ask if she thought Teresa had potential, and to avoid blurting it out, pointed at the southern window. "Great view. I bet it's great in the evening."

"Yes. I've wondered several times who might have built this originally, who painted here."

He nodded, his eyes on the view. "I remember your landscape work. Have you worked with this view?" he asked without thinking, then backtracked. "Sorry. Didn't mean to get personal."

"That's a logical question to ask a photographer," she said. Her voice was still as cool, as matter-of-fact as if he were a complete stranger. She clipped the last camera closed and brushed a wisp of hair from her face. "I haven't worked from this window. The grade is too deep for the camera, and the glass would cause reflections, but I have done some shots from the gate, just outside. It has the same view."

"Do you do any art photos now, or only commercial work?"

The pale gray eyes fixed on the distant landscape. "I

haven't wanted to," she said, almost bemused, "until I came home. The light here…it's a cliché to say that people come to Taos for the light, but it really is different. It changes every minute, and the colors, the quality—it's just not like anywhere else." She brought her attention back to the room. To Eli. "Have you traveled much?"

It might have been an opening to friendship, but somehow her tone made clear it was the sort of small talk she made on a set with any bystander. He folded his hands. "I have to travel on business now, but I never stay away for long." He paused. "I have never wished to leave. This is my home."

"Mine, too," she said, and smiled wistfully, as if she would not be able to claim it.

Teresa came back, sparing him a reply. Eli swore without thinking, and his niece giggled. "What is that?" he asked.

"It's mine," Sarah said.

Hers. Eli stared, trying not to imagine how that bare little dress would look on her. It was a black leather minidress with laces up the front, and left Teresa's shoulders and arms bare. The neatly curled hair had been teased into disarray. "You like it?" she said, tossing her head. Big gold hoops shone at her ears.

"Absolutely perfect." Sarah took the purple bag and gestured for Teresa to sit down. "We're going to do some hard glamour shots. Major makeup time."

"Cool!" Her eyes widened as she saw the contents of the bag. "Oh, wow. Look at all of this. Is all of it yours?"

"Heavens, no. I rarely wear much makeup, but I have spent a small fortune figuring out how to get special looks, and a stylist doesn't always have what I need, so I keep this with me. Everywhere."

"Yvonne will die when I tell her."

"Be still and let me do this."

Curious, Eli watched Sarah transform his young, fresh-faced niece into a steamy siren. In the black leather mini, with her hair teased all around her face and the makeup lending a good six or seven years, Teresa looked nothing like herself. "Your mother will kill me when she sees these pictures," he said.

"Part of the game," Sarah said with a wave of her hand. "Her book should have a little of everything." She put a stool in the middle of the room, and bid Teresa sit down. "I have to shoot with the light over my shoulder for this, so I'm going to need you to work a little more formally this time. We're going to do some different moods—maybe some haughty poses, and then some really sexy ones. The trick is to make yourself into that haughty person, think about things that make you feel arrogant. Maybe pretend I'm that person you feel superior to. Then—" she glanced over Teresa's shoulder to Eli "—we're going to do really sexy. Should I make Eli leave, or can you do it with him behind you?"

Teresa shot a glance over her shoulder. "I can do it even if he's watching."

"Scamp," he said, and settled back in the chair.

Chapter Five

In the long, light-drenched studio, Sarah worked with a sense of growing excitement she kept carefully hidden under a professional demeanor. She'd been delighted to see that the girl had excellent bone structure, with high cheekbones, smooth brow and a straight, delicate nose. The camera loved the way the light caught on those planes. Teresa also had the right eyes, very large and dark and expressive, and best of all, she had The Mouth. Models paid a lot of money to plastic surgeons for lips like this, a kind of mouth that was natural in Teresa's face.

Millions of girls were pretty and had the right features, but went utterly dead in front of the camera. Teresa loved it, played to it, drew up a dazzling array of emotions, from coquettish to sultry to little girl; from pensive to mischievous to gleeful and giggling. Sarah would wait to say anything until after she saw the contacts, just to be sure, but long experience told her Teresa had what it took. Sarah even had some ideas of the best way to develop a "look" that would make her stand out in the crowd of model wannabes that crowded New York every season.

She carefully hid her feelings, however, sending Teresa out to change once again, this time into a Western-style jean jacket with silver studs. Sarah draped her with turquoise and strands of liquid silver. "Perfect," she murmured to herself. "Let's do this outside, with the adobe and the vigas and flowers."

She shot several more rolls outside, wishing the light had already gone golden, but that would not happen for several more hours. Still, it was a good background, the freshness of the cosmos reflecting the freshness of the girl. Teresa, exuberant, did a laughing little dance in front of the flowers, and Sarah captured it all. Behind, in the overhang of the porch, stood Eli, and he was an excellent, blurry addition, suggesting a fantasy of the mysterious Western man.

Impulsively, she zoomed in on him. He leaned negligently against a carved post, staring off into the distance, one foot crossed over the other. With the camera's eye, she narrowed in on his carved face. *Click.* On his neck, brown and long at the opening of his simple dark blue jean shirt. *Click.* On his right hand, one thumb tucked into a belt loop of his jeans. *Click.* On his long, lean legs. *Click.*

She realized he was looking at her through the lens, and wondered if he knew she was shooting him. Between them, Teresa jumped and danced and played, and Sarah pretended that was what she was shooting. He wouldn't be able to tell that she was focusing on his face, on his sober eyes and beautiful mouth. She pressed her finger down hard. *Click, click, click, click, click.* Something swooped through her belly, and with a tight sense of warning she lowered the camera. He didn't look away.

Sarah did. "I think that's enough for today," she said, and glanced at her watch. "I have to be somewhere for dinner."

"With your father?" Eli said, his mouth twisting the faintest bit.

She lifted her brows. "Yes."

He shook his head with faint disgust. "Go get your things together, Teresa."

"Okay. What do you think, Ms. Greenwood?" she asked. "Any hope for me?"

"I'll let you know when I've developed the film." She wanted to be cool, but couldn't resist pushing a hank of Teresa's heavy dark hair over her shoulder. "I will say it was an excellent session. Even if you don't have what it takes to make it in New York or Hollywood, there is no reason in the world you can't do some catalog work, especially if you wanted to play up an ethnic look. It's very big right now." She grinned. "You're a natural, after all."

"Really?" It pleased her more than Sarah expected. "Oh, thank you!"

Touched, Sarah added, "I'll get the proofs done tonight, and no matter what we decide about a whole portfolio, you should have some good shots to put in your book. I'll help you pick out the best ones."

Teresa went to change, and Sarah took the last of the film out of the camera, suddenly nervous to be with Eli alone in the courtyard. He came closer, stopping just short of joining her. "A good day's work," she said, rolling the small cold spools in her hands.

"Thank you, Sarah, for doing it. I expected you all morning to call and cancel."

She jerked her head up. "Why?"

But even before she met the depth of his gaze, she remembered standing in the circle of his embrace, feeling his chest move, when they danced last night. The memory, safely shut off until this moment when his nearness brought it back, rushed through her, lighting little fires against her inner wrists and under her breastbone. "Oh," she said softly.

"Oh?" he repeated. "Just 'oh'? You forgot until now?"

There was something lost about him, standing there with his hands at his sides—something that looked vulnerable and perplexed. Sarah was filled with an unaccountable sense of protectiveness. "Eli," she said quietly. And could think of nothing to say after.

"How did you learn to do that?" he asked.

She didn't know what he meant and shook her head, frowning, wishing she could answer, because the question was earnest.

"You run, but you really escape. You turn it off. Everything." His voice held a raw note. "I have this dream, sometimes, when I'm—" He shook his head. Closed his mouth hard. "Never mind."

She stepped down from the porch. One step, but it brought her so close she could whisper to him, so close she could again smell his skin, unsullied now by cologne. Only the scent of Eli, a smell of desert winds. It gave her such a deep sense of pleasure, pleasure blurred into a thousand images, imagined and remembered that she thought nothing for a moment, but simply grasped the feeling and breathed it inside her.

Then, because she knew he needed an answer, she said, "I stop looking at everything and look at just one thing." She had a camera in her hand and held it out to him. "One square of the world."

He hesitated, looking at the heavy black camera for a minute, then took it from her in a rush, as if he were afraid he might lose courage. A fleeting impression of his long hand snagged in her brain, a single snapshot of him that she could manage.

Lifting the camera, he looked through the lens. "Just focus on something," Sarah said. "Turn that wheel right there." She illustrated by putting her hand on his, then stepped back as he seemed to focus on the pink and white cosmos, then maybe the rolling blue mountains visible over the gate.

He turned to face her. She could see only his mouth, carved like one she'd seen on a Renaissance statue in Italy, a mouth sensually full and richly shaped, but disciplined, too. Firm. She wondered what he saw through the camera.

"One gray eye," he said, as if he'd heard the question. "With very long eyelashes. There is a charcoal color on the edge of the iris, which looks like a crystal." A faint frown traced his brow and he lowered the camera, as if to affirm what he saw, then lifted it again. "I never saw that before, that charcoal."

She gazed at the impersonal blueish lens, staying still. He said nothing, but the lens moved once, then again. She couldn't tell what he examined. It didn't matter. It seemed a small enough gift to give him, after...after everything.

"You have little lines around your eyes now," he said quietly.

She laughed. "Thank you for pointing that out."

He didn't return the smile, only moved the camera again, stepping back as if to see her whole body. "And you have breasts now."

"A gentleman wouldn't admit to looking at a woman's breasts."

"A gentleman wouldn't admit it, but he would still be doing it." He lowered the camera for a moment. A ghost of a smile hovered around his mouth.

A thread of connection rose between them in that moment, an almost visible link that had somehow survived the violence that had separated them. Sarah felt it, a many-fingered root in her heart, wounded but still intact. And she saw by the dawning recognition on Eli's face that he felt it, too.

Teresa came outside, her face scrubbed clean, her hair tied in a loose knot at her neck. "I'm ready!"

Eli gave Sarah the camera back. "Thank you. I'll remember your trick."

Sarah nodded.

"Thank you, Ms. Greenwood," Teresa said. Her arms were full of clothes. Eli took some of her burden and Teresa stuck out her hand. "I'm very grateful."

"My pleasure."

"Thank you, Sarah," Eli said, though he didn't try to shake her hand. As he passed through the gate, he turned just a little. "Give my regards to Garth, eh?" His lips turned up in a bitter, knowing smile.

Sarah did not let him goad her. "I will, Elias."

Her father was not well when Sarah arrived. The day had been very hot, and now a wind had begun to blow, kicking up dust and pollen, leaving the smell of ragweed in the air. Garth sat in his recliner, wheezing, his cheeks flushed an unhealthy mottled red, and kept his inhaler at the ready.

"Damned wind," he muttered. "Need a good thunderstorm." Irritably, he flipped through the channels with his remote, so fast she couldn't even tell what he was looking at before he flipped again. It drove her crazy.

"Why don't you look in the listings, Dad? Find something that might take your mind off things."

"I don't want to."

She suppressed a smile. "How about if I look for you?"

"Go ahead."

Calmly she leafed through the newspaper guide. "Let's see. There's a lot here—a good western on TNT. Reruns of 'Bewitched.' You always liked Samantha."

"What channel?"

Sarah told him and he punched the numbers. It was a very old episode, in black and white, but finding it seemed to please him. He put the remote down. "You know why I liked her?" he said. "Because she reminds me of your mother when she was young."

"I can see that." Sarah smiled. "That's a pretty sweet confession for a grouchy old cop."

"She's pretty, your mom. You look a lot like her now."

"Thanks. People actually tell me I look like you, though."

"Is that right?" He pulled his mouth down, studying her face. "I reckon you do, a little."

Sarah looked back at his hard chin, the straight, bold nose she'd inherited and hated as an adolescent. As she'd grown older, she'd grown to like the way it changed her ordinary, all-American face into something just a little different, a little surprising. She patted his arm. "A lot, according to Jerry Wall. I saw him on my way up here this afternoon." Jerry was one of her father's pals from the department. "He said they're ready for you anytime you want to get back to it."

"Desk job," he said disdainfully. "Don't want it."

"You aren't well yet. Maybe a desk job will look better when you've had some time to heal."

His face closed. "Maybe."

"I'm going to help Mom get supper on the table. You need anything?"

A wind gusted against the house, with a brief, hard *whoof* and a scattering of tiny pebbles against the window. Garth started wheezing and fumbled with his inhaler. "No, thanks," he said, breathlessly. "I'll wait for supper."

In the kitchen, Sarah asked Mabel, "What's with Mr. Cheerful tonight?"

"Ah, they gave him those darned steroids again. They make him grouchy." She lifted a pan of steaming spaghetti noodles from the stove and carried it to the sink where a colander waited. "And the wind's not helping. Surely you remember how grouchy he gets when it's windy."

Sarah took cloth napkins, washed to a flannel softness, from the drawer. "I had forgotten." From the next drawer she counted out forks and knives. "Isn't there any other way to treat him besides the drugs?"

"For your father?" Mabel rolled her eyes and shook the noodles, then turned on the water in the sink to rinse them. "I keep telling him he ought to try some alternative therapies, but he won't have it." She roughed her voice. "'Nobody's gonna mumbo-jumbo over me.'"

"Stubborn should be his middle name." Sarah chuckled.

"Look who's talking!"

Genuinely surprised, Sarah halted with plates and silver in her hands. "Me? I'm not stubborn."

Her mother hooted. Carrying the pot of noodles to the table, she said, "Who would not wear anything but six inches of dangling earrings when the school made them against dress code?"

Sarah put the plates on the table, smiling in spite of herself. "That was a matter of principle."

"Ah. Who painted her room three inches at a time until it was the checkerboard she wasn't allowed to have?"

Her smile widened. "Again, personal freedom."

"And who dated a boy behind our backs for three years no matter what?"

Sarah halted. "Low blow, Mom."

Mabel scowled. "Don't you start, too. It's been more than a decade, Sarah. Don't you think it's time a person could actually say his name in your presence?"

She thought of Elias standing by the gate this afternoon, his mouth twisted into a parody of a smile. "No."

"And you aren't stubborn at all, are you?"

Startled, Sarah let go of a small, surprised shout of laughter. "Okay. Maybe a little." She stuck her head around the door. "Come on, Dad, time to eat." She looked at her mother. "I still don't want to talk about it."

"Like father, like daughter," Mabel said, but let the subject go.

Unfortunately, Garth's irritable mood led right back to

it. Over the last of his spaghetti, he said, out of the blue, "Sarah, do you think you're ever going to forgive me?"

Sarah put her fork down carefully. Of course it wasn't out of the blue—he'd likely overheard the conversation between her and her mother. She said again, "I don't know how many times I have to say this. I don't want to talk about the past. Not any of it. Why is it so hard to respect that?"

He pursed his lips, a sure sign he was digging in his heels. "It seems important, Sarah. We need to get it out in the open."

"Why? What possible good will it do?" She found herself pushing away from the table—ready to flee if necessary—and took a deep breath. "I'm here. Isn't that enough?"

"It haunts me," he said. "Some nights I lie there for hours, going over and over and over it, wishing I'd done—"

"Done what?" she asked sharply. "Let me marry Eli? Let us have our baby?" He looked appalled, and she smiled bitterly. "Not even in your regrets does it ever go that far, does it, Dad?"

"Sarah, that's enough," Mabel said.

But there was such a river of clean hot anger running down in her now that Sarah couldn't stop. "You've been trying to knock my walls down since I got here. I keep telling you to stop, telling you that you won't like what's behind them. If you want to heal this relationship, you have to leave the past alone." She stood up, vaguely aware she was breathing hard. "You want me to forgive you, but the bottom line is, I can't. I haven't forgiven myself." She threw down her napkin, slapping her palms down on the table to lean over him. "You want to talk about sleepless nights? I have a few to tell you about. You want to hear about those?"

Her mother's voice, anguished, stopped her. "Sarah, please. Sit down and finish your supper."

She didn't move for a moment. Then, afraid she might weep, Sarah said, "Give me a minute." She went to the bathroom and washed her face with cold water, over and over until the bright red river of anger had subsided.

You're a piece of work, her voice said with a faint sneer. *Have a fight with a sick man just to make yourself feel better.*

She looked at herself in the mirror, seeing the sad line of her mouth, the grief in her eyes. She'd rather eat rocks than fight with her father, go over that old, old ground again. But she simply could not abide a discussion of their crimes against each other.

When she went back to the kitchen, she said quietly, "I'm sorry I lost my temper."

"My fault," her father said gruffly. "I'll stay out of your business if that's what you want."

"Thank you."

"So, how did Jerry look?" he said, taking up another roll. "Did you tell him he should come see me?"

Sarah accepted the offering, in spite of the lights flashing red against a black night in her memory. "I did," she said, and picked up her fork. "He said you should go see him."

"Maybe I will."

It was almost eight before Sarah returned home to start work on the contact sheets. She'd developed the film before leaving, and it hung in neat strips in the roomy darkroom. Flipping on the safelight, she put on an apron and turned the radio to a classical station. The vinegary scent of chemicals filled her head, and the cocooning darkness and silence gave her a sense of calm.

Positioning the negatives on color print paper, she quickly made a series of contact prints, and when they were dry enough, flipped on the light to take a look. Her earlier suspicions proved true—Teresa had the mysterious something that made a good model. The camera devoured her face, her form, and the girl was able to express emotion in every crook of her elbow, the tiniest gradiations of smiles. The glamour shots in the black leather dress were stunning, and there were a few in the courtyard that showed promise.

She turned off the lights and slid a strip of negatives into the enlarger. Working purely on instinct, she made enlargements of several shots, in various moods and poses, so she'd have something the girl could show off to her friends. The last was a shot of Teresa in the courtyard, laughing, her black hair tumbling down the arm of the jean jacket, with the Southwest landscape lending an air of the mysterious. As if to emphasize the unknowable, Eli stood in the background, sober and straight and beautiful.

She made the enlargement, put the paper through its steps and left it in the water bath, a soft sense of anticipation in her stomach as she moved on to the next set of negatives.

Even Sarah, queen of denial, had to admit the real reason she was making enlargements was for this—for what she was about to do.

Taking a deep breath, she pulled the strip through the lens, watching as the images shifted from a dancing, leaping Teresa to the man in the background. To his face, a face made by the gods to torture women, she thought wryly. She focused the image, until his dark eyes stared right through her, until only those eyes filled the white square at the bottom of the enlarger. Eyes so beautiful, so haunted, so lost.

Haunted. For a moment she rested her head against the cool metal of the machine, taking a deep breath. She wasn't sure she wanted to see him that clearly. If she did, she would have to admit to things she had never claimed, even to herself.

No.

She pulled the focus back so his whole face and part of his shoulders were in the frame. How many times had she ached to have something like this of him, to remember him, think of him? With a feeling akin to fate, she turned off the enlarger light, took out some paper and positioned it, then made the exposure. She put the paper in the developing tray, watching as his face emerged once more, those large sober eyes piercing her heart.

She finished in a rush, then stood there in the darkness for a moment, a fierce, strange emotion blooming in her. She didn't stop to think as she made the enlargements of the entire series: his face, his neck, his hand in his belt loop. That Italian Renaissance mouth.

As the images emerged, a whispery breath moved on the back of her neck, blew over the nerves in her breasts and along the front of her thighs. She watched his mouth emerge from the developer, and a swallow flew in circles in her belly. The shot of his hand, so long and brown and beautiful, made her think of the way he had once moved that thumb over the tip of her breast, along her lip.

By the time she finished, she had seventeen shots of Elias Santiago drying on the line, in comparison to twelve of Teresa. Her hands and knees felt shaky. Her heart thudded and her hips were soft and her breasts ached.

Suddenly struck with the absurdity of being aroused by pictures, she laughed. "Yeah, Greenwood," she said aloud. "You're so calm and cool it's frightening."

Not.

With a resigned smile, she took the shot of his face from the line and held it. "I loved you more than the sun," she said to his image. "More than breathing." She'd thought she would say more, but the words jammed in her throat, and she found that single declaration was all she could manage for now.

Eli's brother Miguel came to see him that evening. Two years younger than Eli, he was a clean-cut capitalist who ran the production angle of the factory. He looked troubled when Eli opened the door. "Miguel, come in," he said. "Is there a problem at the factory?"

"Not with the factory." Miguel accepted the invitation and moved into the living room, taking a seat on the edge of a chair. In his chinos and pale pink cotton shirt and with his razor-cut hair, he looked like an ad in *Golf Quarterly*— Miguel adored the sport, as a matter of fact.

He folded his manicured hands. "I have been hearing rumors, Elias," he said.

Eli took two bottles of soda from the fridge—Miguel did not drink spirits—and sat down on the couch. "*Elias,* huh? Am I in trouble?"

"You will be if Mama finds out you've been hanging out with Sarah."

Somehow, he'd suspected the news would get out. "How did you know?"

"Pete Pacheco saw you with her at La Palmona the other night. Dancing."

"So what? We're all grown-ups now."

"That isn't the point, and you know it. It almost killed Mama when you got arrested, and she'll never forgive Sarah for that." A sullen look settled on his mouth. "Neither will I."

A burst of fire lit in Eli's chest, and he took a swallow of his soda to quell it. "This family is as much to blame as theirs. If it weren't for this stupid war between us all, none of it would have happened."

"How can you just forget about 150 years of bad blood, Eli? What about all the Santiagos who've been killed or hurt by Greenwoods?"

Bitterness soured the taste of soda on Eli's tongue. "And we know all their names, don't we? Every one of them has been repeated over and over to every new child, every generation. Manuel and Luis and James, Alonzo and Rita." He gave his brother a fierce look. "The Greenwoods have their own list of names, too. And what's the point, Miguel?"

"The point is honor."

"Honor." He shook his head. "There's no honor in any of this." He thought of what Jennifer had said the other night. "Don't you see, Miguel, that it has to end? We can't let this go on for another generation."

"Is that so?" Miguel narrowed his eyes. "You think I don't know how you burn for revenge against Sarah's father? You think anyone doesn't know how much you hate him?"

"That's not a family vendetta," he said. "It's personal. Me against him. Not against his family."

"Ah, I see. So if you managed to make the old man jump off a cliff or something, that won't bother his family any. And we can go on to heal this long war."

Eli jumped up, propelled by things he couldn't—or maybe wouldn't—name. A nerve in his eye jumped. "No." He turned to face his brother. "But maybe they will understand."

"You're blind in this, brother. I will tell my children of this war, and will remember those names to them so they are burned on their hearts, as they were burned on mine." He stood up. "As your name is burned on mine, as the latest victim in this war." He lifted his chin. "And I'll tell you something else, Eli. I pray you *will* finish that vendetta—and that you will punish Sarah along with her father. Because I hate her more than him. She stole more than he did—she stole a child of our blood, sent it away into the world, where we can never claim it, where the child will never know that his or her face belongs to a proud and ancient family." His eyes, shiny with emotion, narrowed. "I curse Sarah for that."

"Miguel," he said softly, holding out an imploring hand, "that hate will eat you up. Give it to me—this is not your battle."

"It is," he insisted. "It belongs to all of us, Eli, because you belong to us, because that baby belonged to us."

The phone rang, and Eli looked at it in surprise. Few people ever called him here, and not so late, either. With a frown, he said, "Excuse me," and answered it gruffly, fearing bad news.

Her voice sounded thin. "Eli? This is Sarah."

At the sound of her voice over the line, sounding so much the same as it had in the past, Eli was no longer a man in his own house, arguing with his brother. He was seventeen and drunkenly in love, waiting by the phone for Sarah's call, standing guard so no one else would pick it up.

He ducked his head, curling around the phone in an unconsciously protective gesture before he realized what he was doing. "What can I do for you?" Despite his best effort, his tone was husky, and he felt his brother look at him.

"I made the contact sheets tonight, and I just wanted to tell you they are very, very good. If you want to bring Teresa by tomorrow, I'll show you, and we can set up a schedule for shooting her portfolio."

Relief whooshed through him. "Ah, that's great news. Thank you." He tried to avoid glancing at his brother, but his eyes darted guiltily in his direction anyway. "Tomorrow, maybe? I'll have to call her and see what's going on. Can I call you in the morning?"

"That would be fine."

A humming silence spun between them, and Eli tried to imagine where she was standing in the cottage, and what she was wearing. He visualized her in the kitchen, wearing the thin-as-water red tunic; feeling slightly winded, he thought of her breasts moving beneath it. "Thanks for calling," he said quietly.

"My pleasure," she said, her voice warm as velvet, and hung up.

Eli put the receiver back with a sense of loss. For a minute he was lost in his vision of her in the dark, silent kitchen, the silver-and-gold threads of that tunic shining along an arm, a buttock, a thigh—

"You are a fool," Miguel said.

Eli raised his head and made his face blank. "What are you talking about?"

His brother only stared at him, his eyes burning bright, then he gave a single shake of his head. "I am finished with it."

"You're jumping to conclusions, *hermano*."

"Lie to yourself, Elias, but don't lie to me."

"Who do you think you are to come to me like this, like I am a child to be scolded? You have not lived my life. You have not been in my heart." His throat tightened. "You don't know, Miguel."

With a dismissive, angry wave of his hand, Miguel said, "You're going to do what you want no matter what I say. But do me a favor, huh, Eli? Keep it private, so I don't have to worry about my mother." He left, his head held at a self-righteous angle.

Eli watched him go. Always, Miguel had been the one to take the moral high ground. Everything to him was black and white, right and wrong, up or down. Nothing gray or in-between. And he expected the rest of the world to fall in behind him. Miguel was the one the priests loved when they were children, the one who made the best grades, dated only the nicest girls. It had been that high code of honor that made Eli choose him for his position in the company—Miguel would see to it things were properly run, that there was no waste, that employees showed up on time and did not stand around gossiping too long past their break time.

Oddly, that old code won Eli's younger brother a respect, made it easy for others to obey him. No one could ever accuse Miguel of playing favorites, and it was never difficult to know exactly what he wanted.

But Eli doubted his brother had ever been touched by passion. For anything—a song, a sky, a beautiful face, an exquisite kiss. He'd never been mesmerized, for weeks or months on end, by a woman who seemed to have hung the stars. He'd never known the belly-deep yearning for the taste of a particular woman's flesh—

A cold sweat washed down his spine. Not a woman, a girl. Eli had loved a *girl*. The girl who had been destroyed. The girl he would avenge, along with his lost child and his broken dreams. The woman did not matter. He had to remember that.

Chapter Six

Eli made arrangements to pick up Teresa at a friend's house the next afternoon. He'd not said anything to her about Sarah's announcement, choosing to let Sarah see the girl's pleasure firsthand.

To his annoyance, when Teresa came down the walk from her friend's front door, she was dressed in her usual attire: jeans at least six sizes too big, cinched with a belt she let hang down to one side, a cropped shirt that showed far too much of her tummy, the ghastly Frankenstein makeup the girls were adopting these days, and her fake nose-ring.

It embarrassed him. "Why are you dressed like that? This is a professional meeting and you look like a gang-banger."

"I do not!" She slumped in her seat. "Anyways, what does it matter? If she had good news, she would've told you on the phone."

"Not necessarily." He put the truck in gear and backed

out. "And it doesn't matter if the news is good or bad. She offered a valuable service to you, and you aren't going over there looking like that."

"I'm not changing."

"Then I'll take you home."

She gave him her best adults-are-insects glance. "Fine. Doesn't matter to me."

For a split second he felt mean for withholding information that obviously meant a lot to her. But if she was going to make it in the world, even if it wasn't the modeling world, she would have to learn to respond to stress in more appropriate ways. "I'm disappointed, but it's your choice." He turned in the direction of her house.

It wasn't far, but for the entire drive they had a contest of wills. Teresa sulked silently, and Eli resisted the temptation to give in and tell her the news. Without a word, he pulled up in front of her house.

Teresa did not move, only stared through the front window with her arms crossed. At last she sighed noisily. "Fine. Let me change and I'll be right back."

"Don't forget to wash the makeup off."

"We'll be late!"

"Sarah won't mind."

Within a few minutes she was back, barefaced, dressed in a normal pair of jeans, still baggy but decent, and a crisp blouse that looked as if it had never been worn. He wondered when girls would start wearing tight pants again, and felt a twinge of pity for boys growing up now.

Sarah was not waiting outside for them this time. They went in the gate and knocked on the front door, but she came out of the studio. He had braced himself on the way down the hill, but it was still like a fist to the gut to see her anew, every time. She wore exotic clothes today—a filmy skirt and a tank top he thought might be tie-dyed or something. No, not tie-dye. "What's that material in her blouse called?" he asked Teresa quietly.

"Batik, silly."

"Right." Batik. In dark and light blues that brought out the golden hue of the flesh on her arms and the faint golden freckles on the upper swell of her breasts.

"Come on in," she said, smiling at Teresa. "I made some prints for you."

They followed her into the room, where several large photos had been thumbtacked to a pasteboard display.

"Oh!" Teresa breathed, and moved forward. "I can't believe this is me."

Even after watching the session yesterday, Eli was a little startled by the images scattered over the board. The images were like magazine ads, which he supposed was the point. The ones in the garden looked like something for selling perfume, a young girl's scent. The ones in the black leather mini made Teresa look like a dangerous femme fatale— maybe a vodka ad. And in the soft green dress she'd first worn, she looked like spring and hope and innocence.

He looked at Sarah. "They're very good, aren't they?"

"Yes."

And it was only then that he realized there was something different about her today, an almost palpable shine, an exuberance of spirit that gave a glow to her eyes and skin. It had been this quality, more than anything else about her, that had captured him. A small puff of yearning burst in him. He looked away. "I didn't tell her what you said. I wanted you to do it."

Teresa turned, her entire body a rigid line. "What?"

Sarah laughed, and her hair fell back from her face in a gold-and-yellow tumble. She grasped Teresa's arms. "Don't look so worried!"

"But I am!"

"I can't promise anything, Teresa," Sarah said. "But I've worked with a lot of models, and it would be an honor to work with you, to shoot a portfolio for you."

"Really?"

"Yes. But there's something I'm going to want in return."

"Anything."

Sarah smiled, and there was gentleness in the gesture. Eli liked her suddenly for being so kind. "I want you to agree you won't go to New York until you graduate from high school."

"New York?" She said the word as if it were Atlantis.

"Yeah. You have a lot of talent. And I really have no doubt that, especially with my connections, you could have a career there tomorrow. But I've seen too many girls get lost there. Or something happens, and they can't work anymore, and they don't have anything to fall back on. If you will agree to finish high school—and agree to give some thought to what else you want to do with your life—I will shoot your portfolio, and send it to my friends, and help you get summer work between now and graduation."

"She needs to talk to her mother," Eli said.

"Of course. I'd also like to talk to her, if you think she will."

Eli hesitated. "Probably not the best idea." He couldn't help smiling over that. "She knows we're here, but it sticks in her throat."

Some of the radiance faded from her face at this news. "I'm sorry to hear that." She shook her head. "But I'm also not going to let it bother me. What do you say, Teresa, do we have a deal?"

"Oh, yes!"

"Good."

Eli said, "Do you have the contact sheets? I'd like to see the rest of the shots."

"Sure. In here." She moved toward a door that stood open, and for the most fleeting seconds, the light shone through her skirt. Eli saw the neat outline of her legs, all the way up her thighs, before she moved into the doorway.

Teresa followed, and after a moment Eli moved toward

the door. He'd never seen a darkroom, but imagined it would be a small space. He halted just outside, letting the two of them exclaim over the work. Sarah's back was to him, and he found his gaze on the skin exposed between her shoulder-length hair and the scoop of her top in back. She turned, as if feeling his touch. "It's a pretty tight squeeze in here. I'll bring them out."

She handed him a sheet of paper with tiny pictures on it. "You'll need the loupe," she said, and put it in his hand. "This group is particularly nice." She pointed to a series near the bottom of the page, and Eli dutifully bent his head to look at them.

But at the edge of his peripheral vision was a far more compelling view. She was half a foot shorter than he, and she stood rather close to point at the shots. Near his elbow was the loose neckline of her blouse. He caught a glimpse of breasts restrained only by a breath of gauze and lace, breasts tanned as far as he could see.

He imagined there was no tan line, anywhere, and the image caused an instant, deeply painful arousal.

You're a fool, his brother's voice said in his head.

A fool. He nodded curtly and gave her back the prints, moving away to look out the window at the serene view of blue hills and green fields.

It was so easy, when he was away from her, to think in objective terms. To tell himself he wanted to have her to get revenge. But when he was with her, he forgot all that. He forgot everything except the way she made him feel, the things she roused in him.

"Elias!" Teresa said. "Look at yourself, *tío!*"

He turned in time to see Sarah turn bright red. Not a little girlish flush, but a deep, painful red that burned on her chest and chin and forehead. She murmured a protest, and lifted a hand as if to confiscate the photos from Teresa, then firmly clenched her hands together behind her back.

Her chin lifted and she tossed her hair back from her face in a gesture he remembered as defensive.

He met her gaze for a moment, then smiled faintly. "Did you take pictures of me, Sarita?"

She lifted a shoulder. "You were there." As if this explanation eased her, the bright color began to fade.

"Do you mind if I see them?"

She did mind. He could see that much, but after a fleeting hesitation, she said, "Go ahead."

Teresa leapt toward him with the grace of an airborne scarf, landing as lightly as a cat. Her mouth held a secretive little smile, and he lifted a brow in censure. She thought it was romantic; he would have to set her straight about that.

Still, he took the pictures, curious what could be in them that would so embarrass Sarah. At first he saw nothing to account for that flush—he even saw why she had snapped it, maybe impulsively. It showed him standing against a post, staring straight at the camera. The light was good, his pose strong.

The next was a close-up of his face, and he did not like what he saw in his eyes. Too much emotion. Too much of what he'd been thinking at that moment.

In a slightly defensive tone, she said, "My father destroyed all my pictures of you."

He raised his head. "So you wanted one to remember me by?"

The flush returned, but the pale gray eyes met his with a kind of honesty that had been missing till now. "I...don't know," she said. Then, "Yes."

He swallowed, and gave the sheaf back to Teresa without looking at the rest. "You should be more sensitive, *hija*."

Teresa's grin only deepened as she nodded. "Okay." She whirled around to face Sarah. "So when can we get started? Will we shoot a whole book? Will some of these shots go in it? I can hardly wait to show Yvonne! She'll just die of envy."

Sarah chuckled, and Eli could tell she was glad of the distraction as she moved to the board. "Bring her with you one day, if you like. Most girls seem to enjoy it." She took the photos down. "These copies are yours, to show your friends—and your mother, so she'll know what you're getting into."

"Really?" Teresa squeaked, and flung her arms around Sarah's shoulders. "Thank you so much! I'm so happy!" She put the pictures against her chest. "We aren't going to work today, are we?"

"No," Sarah said. "But there's no reason we can't get moving very soon."

"*Tío*, it's up to you—I don't have a job, so we can come whenever you want." Teresa looked at Sarah. "My mom won't let me come without him."

"Sounds like she wants to take good care of you."

"I guess. *Tío*, can I go? Yvonne only lives up the street. I want to show her."

Impossible not to be drawn into that exuberance. He grinned. "Sure. I'll call you later and let you know what we worked out."

Sarah watched Teresa dance through the courtyard on her way up the hill. "She's like a gazelle. I've never seen a young girl who was so graceful."

"You were," Eli said. He didn't look at her.

Oddly pierced, she said, "I'm flattered you think so." To change the subject, she gestured toward the patio. "Let's go get something to drink and we can work this out."

He glanced at his watch. "I have a meeting in a half hour, with the graphic designer for our new boxes, but it's just right around the corner."

Sarah remembered the beautiful woman he'd been with the night they'd danced, and a pang of jealousy bit her.

Brushing it away with annoyance, she nodded briskly. "It shouldn't take long."

She led the way across the hot courtyard and into the main room on the other side. A swamp cooler pumped moist, cool air into the rooms. "I am really not used to the heat here yet," she said, smiling. "Do you mind if we do it in here?"

A faintly ribald grin turned his mouth into a seductive masterpiece; the effect trebled when he lifted one dark brow. "I wouldn't mind."

She shook her head, chuckling. "You know what I mean."

"This is fine," he said, and settled in a chair by the table. "It's nice in here. How long are you staying?"

"I rented it for a month, but Mrs. Gray said I can stay as long as I want." She opened the fridge. "Do you want tea or pop?"

"Tea would be great—if it has sugar."

Sarah grinned. "One of my weaknesses, I'm afraid. No fake sweeteners for this girl." She took tall blue glasses from the shelf, filled them with ice and poured tea for both of them. Eli simply sat there, his hands resting on his thighs. Afraid the silence would get awkward, she said, "I haven't decided if I'm going to actually stay here or go back to New York."

"Really?" The word was polite, uninterested.

Sarah carried the glasses to the table and set them down. "Are you hungry? I have some chips or fruit or—"

"This is fine, Sarah."

"Okay." She sat down, right on the edge of her chair, and leaned her elbows on the table. "My schedule is very flexible, so I guess we need to just work out what's best for you."

He did not answer right away, and Sarah looked up to find his luminous eyes moving on her, over her face, down her throat, lower still. And as if his gaze were a touch, she became urgently aware of her flesh, all of it, her bare arms and the skin along her shoulder and the part of her chest above her tank top.

"What?" he said. "I wasn't listening."

But when he met her gaze, Sarah found it was her turn to be lost, lost in a velvety depth of fathomless eyes. She imagined simply leaning forward to kiss him, and the vision caused a bolt of hunger to press through her body, unwanted and impossible. "Eli, can we do this?" she asked suddenly.

"I don't know," he said quietly. "Maybe not. Maybe there is too much history."

She lowered her head. "Maybe there is."

"I didn't know where you had gone, you know. They locked me up for almost eight weeks before they threw the charges out—and by then, you were gone."

"I didn't know. Joanna told me the other night. I had no idea it went on that long." She raised her head. "I'm so sorry. You don't know how many times I've gone back in time and not called my mother to let her know we were coming home."

"Me, too."

Their hands lay on the table, separated by mere inches, and Eli moved his suddenly, putting his index finger against her ring finger. "But once done, nothing can be undone."

A vision of a small red face flashed over her imagination and with a breathless sense of panic she straightened, pulling away from his touch, and the depth of communion between them. Too dangerous. She tossed hair from her face. "You're right. It's all water under the bridge now."

"No use crying over spilt milk." His eyes glittered.

She let herself find a faint smile. "May as well let bygones be bygones."

"*Lo que pasó, voló,*" he recited with a grin.

"No fair," she protested, as she had always done. "What does it mean?"

"'What happened flew by.'"

"Ah."

For the smallest moment, neither the past nor the future meant anything to Sarah, only now, with Eli before her, playing an old game with her. And she saw in his eyes the same grateful ease.

Before it could shatter, Sarah reached behind her and took a calendar from the counter. "Let's get this figured out so you aren't late to your meeting. I have several ideas about this—the best way to build her portfolio—and some of them will require different times of day. Are there times that are better for you?"

He shrugged. "Unless I have meetings, there are not too many bad times. You spend the mornings with your mother, yes?"

Her mother, not her father. Sarah let it slide. "Most of the time. She likes me to have dinner with them as often as possible, too, but I don't always want to."

"So, you tell me. What's best for you, Sarah, in terms of light and your vision of this work?"

Forced to decide, Sarah said, "Let's just play it by ear. Maybe come tomorrow in the morning, and we'll shoot some sweet shots. I'll see if I can rent the studio lights I need around here somewhere. Once I get them, we can do a long session maybe on the weekend or something." She made notes to herself as she talked. "I think," she said, musing aloud, "that I'd like to do a series at the pueblo if we can get permission, and at the Martinez hacienda. The Southwest is very popular, and she has a great ethnic look that might be a huge boon to her."

"Okay. You let me know. Sunday is better than Saturday. I have meetings all day Saturday." He stood up. "Tomorrow, then? What time?"

Sarah remembered her wish that the light had gone golden the other night. "Let's do it in the late afternoon.

Bring her over about four-thirty, and plan to be here for a few hours. I'll feed you."

"No," Eli said. "I'll bring food. You shouldn't have to cook."

"Oh, I don't cook. I would have fed you pizza."

"You don't cook at all?" He seemed amazed.

"No," she said, unapologetically. "I've never had to learn, and I don't like it much."

"Did you just eat out all the time?"

She laughed. "You seem to find this incomprehensible."

"I don't know any adult women who can't cook."

"Now you do."

He inclined his head, smiling. "I guess so. So, anyway, I'll bring food. What else do you need? Clothes, film? Let me pay you for your time."

"Thank you, but no. This is my way of repaying my own mentor. Just bring food and Teresa, and I'll take care of the rest."

He spread his hands in acquiescence. Sarah's mental camera snagged on the frame of his palm, cupped as if to receive a blessing. She imagined putting a kiss in it, or a flower, as people did in the hands of saints. The foolishness made her smile, and shaking it away, she got up to walk him to the door, following him out into the white-hot sun beyond.

He stopped next to the tall cosmos and turned to say, "Tomorrow, then."

Irresistible, Sarah thought. "Wait one minute." She bent over to pluck a perfect white cosmos, leaving a long stem with a ferny leaf. Her nails were short and she couldn't quite sever the stem, and she made a little noise, embarrassed again.

She felt him move closer, and a moment later a touch lit on her spine, just above the top of her tank top. Two fingers, maybe three, that brushed over a single bone of her back, once, then again before they were gone, so fast she wondered if it might have been a cabbage moth.

Plucking the flower free in a rush, she straightened to give it to him, but he had come closer, and her bare arms brushed his chest as she stood up. It was a simple touch, her arm across his shirt, but it somehow lit a flurry of tiny lights through her body.

She forgot the flower as she looked up at him, his black hair shining, the harsh sunlight making deep shadows of his eyes, but illuminating every centimeter of his mouth. He swayed even closer, and she stared at that mouth, her heart pounding. She went utterly still, waiting, poised, wondering if he would kiss her.

A harsh, soft breath whooshed from him and he took a step back, his eyes unreadable.

Sarah swallowed, and held out the flower. "For your buttonhole," she said, and realized he didn't have one.

But he gravely accepted it, and lifted it to his nose to smell it. The delicate white petals brushed his hard brown cheeks, and his lush black lashes swept down, lending another softness to balance the hawkish nose.

Sarah caught her breath, feeling sunlight on her crown and heat on her arms and a rush of yearning for Elias Santiago that had nothing to do with who either of them had been. It was the mature, knowing hunger of a woman for a man she felt instinctively could please her.

It had been so long since she'd felt such a thing that she took one moment to let it move in her, let it awaken those long-numb places that had given up on desire. She let her gaze stroke the feathery lashes and sweep down the arch of his cheekbone, and imagined softly kissing all of those places.

He lifted his eyes, and their eyes locked over the petals of white flower.

"Thank you," he said, and his voice spoke a thousand volumes.

Sarah could not bear to look at him for another second. "See you tomorrow," she managed to say in a far breathier voice than she would have wanted, and headed back to the house.

"Thanks," he repeated, but she only lifted a hand as if he were just a friendly acquaintance. In a moment she heard his boots on the stones as he left.

Inside, she closed the door and put her back against it, as if to keep out a demon. The only trouble was, the demons were all inside her.

Chapter Seven

A routine developed over the next few days. It wasn't much different for Sarah than what she'd been doing since she returned home. She spent part of each day with her parents, part of it alone—sometimes reading, sometimes walking out on the backroads, sometimes simply sitting without movement or thought in the shadows of her porch, gazing at the mountains. Usually the cat sat with her, as if he lived with her now. He was a good companion.

The photo sessions simply gave a small new dimension to the days. Teresa was a good subject and so overjoyed to be participating that it would have been impossible not to enjoy the work. Sarah looked forward to the sessions each day.

This morning as she sat eating chunks of watermelon from a bowl—a substance the cat had approved most heartily, to Sarah's amusement—she let herself think of Eli's presence at those sessions. He stayed out of the way, often bringing a book that he read sitting on the porch, his long legs stretched out before him. By unspoken agreement, they had settled into an oddly formal, courteous relationship that protected them both against a breach from the past that might make the sessions unbearable for one or the other.

She plucked a cube of red fruit from the bowl, broke it in two and gave the cat under the table half of it. Teresa and Eli would be coming over in just a little while, and she supposed she needed to get up and get ready, but it was pleasant to sit here lazily in her robe. She had thought she might miss the hustle and bustle of her old life, but she didn't yet. Her agent had called the day before, agitated and hurried, to urge her to settle her affairs and get back to work. She had mildly refused, and didn't feel a twinge of regret. From the other side, her parents were hoping she'd move back, but she wasn't ready to commit to that, either.

Licking sweet juice from her thumb, she wondered if she was going through some kind of early midlife crisis. People often did at thirty, didn't they? She needed to know what she really wanted.

But maybe in order to know what the future held, she would have to first deal with the past. The thought whispered through, the most gentle of suggestions, but Sarah recoiled violently. She swung her feet down and stood, briskly dropping another bit of watermelon for the cat, and bustled inside.

The past could just stay buried.

In the cool, dim bedroom with its multipaned windows and thick walls, she picked out a simple sundress to wear for the day, and shed her robe. For one instant, as she stood there dressed only in her panties, she felt suddenly awash in the awareness of her body. Her skin. Her breasts, touched by cool air. Her stomach, bare only to her. Her thighs. It was a startling sensation and she paused, closing her eyes to see if she could locate the source of it.

Bubbling up from the well of her subconscious came the

memory of a fresh and vivid dream. She stood with Elias in a vast field of sage that scented the air. It was night, with a moon spilling a half cup of light over them. They were both naked, facing each other without touching, and in her dream, Sarah had ached for his hands to stroke her the way his eyes did, ached to reach out her own palms and press them to his lean limbs, to his hard brown belly.

Standing nearly naked in her cool bedroom, Sarah felt herself brimming with the bone-deep yearning she'd felt in the dream. She imagined him standing before her, those luminous eyes touching her—

A knock sounded at the front door, and, jolted from the sensual suspension, Sarah cried, "Just a minute!" She tugged a camisole on, then the dress, and rushed into the other room.

When she flung open the door to find Eli standing there, she felt disoriented, as if her dream had called him. Her mind flashed a vision of him standing naked before her—

She smoothed her hair. "I'm sorry—I wasn't quite ready. Come on in." She backed away from the door in her bare feet, trying without success to calm the flutter of her hands, flapping at her sides like wings.

He came inside, letting the screen close gently behind him. He wore a simple white cotton shirt with a collar, the long sleeves rolled to the elbow. Under his arm he carried a newspaper.

Sarah halted, stung by the look of him, and the message of her dream. She wanted to touch him, to make a bridge over the gulf of things they couldn't say, and run across it into his arms. She wanted to kiss his mouth and taste his neck, and feel his naked body pressed into her own. The wish was so unreasonably insistent that it took long moments for the expression on his face to register.

"What's wrong?" she asked. "Where's Teresa?"

"I haven't picked her up yet. I wanted to see you alone for a moment." He bent his head, took the newspaper from beneath his arm and, after a second of hesitation, held it out to her. "Page four," he said.

Frightened by his manner, Sarah moved forward to take it. His hand touched hers, as if offering comfort, and she shivered, the dream hazing her senses. She turned away and opened the paper.

"Oh, no," she breathed. "Will they ever let this die?"

There on page four was a quarter-page photo, a crisp, clear black and white of Sarah and Eli dancing at the restaurant. It wasn't clear that they were dancing, however, so it looked as if they were embracing, and on the verge of a kiss. The tag line enigmatically read, "Will the feud be healed by our own Romeo and Juliet?"

That was all. No explanation. None was needed for insiders—and the only people who would care would be furious. She looked up, stricken. "Our parents..."

He closed his eyes briefly. "I know. I don't even want to go out in the street today."

The phone rang—stridently, it seemed to Sarah. She looked at it urgently, then back at Eli.

"Don't answer."

She stared at him, torn, but in the end, she let the phone go on ringing until it finally quit. Before it could ring again, she rushed over and took the receiver off the hook. "How will we explain this to my father? To your mother?"

He had not moved from the door, and he only shook his head. "There is no way. It will just have to be borne, let die." With a sudden curse, he stormed across the room, folding his arms as he stared at the landscape. "How many generations will it take, do you think? How many more children will have to endure this curse?" He turned to look at her, a burning in his eyes. "How many more will have to lose everything, as we did, Sarah?"

"I don't know." She sank onto the stool by the counter and put a shaky hand to her temple, thinking of her father.

He would be apoplectic by now. Her mother would be angry with her.

It roused all the old feelings—the guilt and the insecurity and the fear, and along with it, a sense of stubborn rebellion. But all she could do was utter a soft swearword.

Then Eli was standing beside her, and his hand lit on her bare arm, his fingers curling gently around in a gesture of strength, as if to give her courage. "You and I have paid enough, I think. More than enough."

"I can't bear to have it all start again," she said, and lifted her head. "Maybe I should just pack my bags and get back to work. That would stop the rumors fast enough. Give you some peace." Unnerved by his nearness, she stood up and moved away.

But he didn't leave her alone this time. He came behind her, not touching her, but his body warmed her back, her buttocks, her legs. "Don't run, Sarah. Not this time."

She whirled, her anger finding a clear target. "I didn't *run* the first time. I was hauled away and hidden in a dreary, bleak home for unwed mothers. It was like something out of a gothic movie, and they kept me there without communication with anyone I knew or loved for nearly seven months. And then they took her away, and expected me to just come home without a whimper, as I'd always done." She stared up at him. "I waited and waited for you to come for me."

He jerked back, as if an electrical shock had gone through him. "Don't you think I tried?"

"You know, that's what I always used to think, that you probably had looked and just weren't able to find me." She narrowed her eyes. "But now I think you were probably so furious by the time you got out of jail that you didn't even bother."

He opened his mouth, closed it again, and with stiff dignity backed toward the door. "I'll tell Teresa this is a bad day for this. We'll finish the rest later."

A lump in her throat made it impossible to speak. "Then it's true, isn't it, Eli? You didn't even look."

He bowed his head. Nodded.

Sarah bit her lip to keep from calling him back as he left. "I'll call you," she said.

"I'll be waiting."

With an acid burn in his gut, Eli left the house. There was a roar in his ears, and sorrow in his chest, and a pain of yearning in his groin that he'd almost grown used to now. When he reached the gate he hesitated, feeling somehow that this was all wrong, that they were still responding to old patterns. He was reacting from shame and anger. She was responding to betrayals.

Vast betrayals. And he'd just dealt another. The shame of it burned in his chest, and he stopped at the gate.

What did he want? Apart from family or work or obligations of any kind, what did he want?

To kiss her. Touch her. Explore what had been and what still was.

"Eli, wait."

He turned to see her coming off the step, her hair loose on her shoulders, the thin cotton of her dress swirling around her legs. Her big gray eyes looked haunted and sorrowful.

"Sarah…" he began.

"Wait a minute." She halted before him, and he saw her mouth working before she finally shook her head, as if to clear it. "I'm sorry. I overreacted."

"Overreacted?" he echoed. "No, you didn't. It's a wonder you haven't murdered us all, Sarah." He raised his eyes. "I am ashamed that I didn't look for you."

She shook her head. "Let's not go over all that, okay? What we're doing with Teresa is at least a step in the direction of healing. Let's go on with it."

He said nothing for a moment, searching her face for the

desire that had been there when he first came into her rooms. It was submerged now under her masks. He wondered what it would take to bring it to the surface again. "That dress is almost as bad as your robe," he said, without thinking.

A puzzled frown crossed her brow, and she looked down, smoothing her palms over her thighs. "What's wrong with it?"

A lot was wrong. The way the slim straps seemed too loose and threatened to fall down her shoulders. The way the thin yellow fabric both hid and illuminated the underswell of her left breast, the bend of her waist; the way light reflecting up from the ground showed the inner line of her thighs.

He had been quiet too long, and she raised her face to seek her answer, knowledge dawning on her cheeks.

A tight fist of need drew up in his belly as he stood frozen, wanting to press his mouth to every golden freckle on her breasts, all the way into the hollow between, wanted to stroke that inner thigh, kiss drunkenly those parting lips. "I'm sorry, Sarita," he said roughly, and brushed a finger over her cheek.

She took a breath, and he saw that there was a faint sheen of tears in her eyes. "If you make me cry, I will never forgive you," she said.

With iron will he forced himself to step back. He put his hand on the latch, cold and rusted under his palm, an anchor to sensibility. "I'll be back with Teresa in a little while."

"Maybe," she said, "you should come a little later. Give me some time to go talk to my parents. Maybe you should talk to your mother, too."

"You do what you have to." He grinned ruefully. "You only have your parents. I have all my siblings, uncles, aunts, everyone. Maybe I'm the one who should go to work in New York. Get me a camera."

A smile touched her mouth.

When he had the gate firmly closed between them, he said, "Maybe we should talk a little, Sarah. Not everything. Just—" He didn't know what he meant. "Clear the air a little."

Fear blossomed wild in her eyes and she clasped her hands so tightly together he could see white on the knuckles, but she gave him a single, jerky nod. "Maybe."

There was no point to avoiding the inevitable. Sarah braced herself with a good strong cup of coffee, then walked to her parents' house.

But to her amazement, there was no one there. The car was gone, so they weren't out for a walk. She let herself into the house and peeked into her father's room: the bed was neatly made, with the cat curled in a ball on the pillow.

Odd. Sarah went to the kitchen to see if there was a note from her mother. There was not.

A terrible fear touched her—maybe there had been an emergency. Maybe the phone call she had ignored this morning had been from her mother. Urgently, she called the hospital, but the woman who answered the phone assured her Garth had not been in. They hadn't seen him in several weeks.

Puzzled, Sarah stepped out on the porch. The neighbor, an elderly woman with a black-and-silver cap of hair, was bent over her flowers. "Mrs. Hernandez," Sarah said, "did you see my parents this morning?"

"I saw them get in the car about an hour ago, but they just waved, happy." She shrugged. "Nothing wrong, I hope?"

"I guess not."

Sarah went back in and scribbled a note of her own. "I was here and you weren't—see you at dinner."

Back at her cottage, she hoped to find a note taped to her door, or some other indication of where her parents might have gone, but there was nothing. She found herself pacing the long living room, back and forth, like a caged tiger, restless and anxious.

Blips of memory flashed in her mind, dredged up by the strange events of the morning. She remembered the night Eli had been arrested, remembered praying there would be no mistakes, that they would not shoot him there in the street. *Blip.* Her father's roaring when he discovered—the first time—that Sarah had been sneaking out to meet a boy from the Santiago family. *Blip.* Her mother, weeping and red eyed, but silent as Sarah was loaded, numbly, into her father's car and driven three hundred miles to the unwed mother's home.

She blinked at the regular flashes of memory, regular as a metronome. Memories she had not allowed to surface in many, many years. Memories she'd buried so carefully she'd thought they would never be unearthed.

Desperate to stop them and the dangerous flood of emotion they carried with them, she grabbed a camera and went out to the garden, trying to find calm in the single frame. But as she bent over a white cosmo, she saw the delicate petals against Eli's face, his mouth, and a sword went through her heart.

She put the camera down and sat on the step. *Thought you were so grown up, didn't you?* said the nasty little voice in her head. *You're really in control now, aren't you?*

"Oh, shut up," she said aloud. She considered going out to the plaza to shoot pictures of tourists, just for the heck of it, but she was afraid she might run into someone on the way. Someone who would have seen the picture. One of her father's policeman friends, maybe, or her mother's bridge partners, or any one of the Santiagos who still hated her.

Stuck now, aren't you?

No question about it. And it was a reprise of the old melody—she was stuck between her wish to please her parents and her wish to make her own decisions.

At last she heard Eli and Teresa on the hill, coming down to the cottage, and she jumped up with relief, until a nasty thought occurred to her: what if her parents came by and found Eli here?

No.

"I have an idea," she said as they entered the courtyard. "Teresa, I'm going to teach you a little about the way the camera works. The Hacienda has some interesting light and angles, especially this time of day. What do you think?" It was something she'd been meaning to do, anyway.

"Kill two birds with one stone?" Elias asked, lifting a brow.

She tried to think of a cliché to go with it, and was too flustered. She simply gave him a rueful smile. "Yes."

"Sounds good to me." He lifted a wicker basket. "I even brought a picnic."

"Oh!" Sarah was absurdly pleased. "Well, let me get my bags, then, and we'll go."

"Sure you want to venture into the world?"

Sarah lifted her chin defiantly. "Hey, I'm a famous photographer, remember? What are they going to do to me?"

He smiled, giving light to his dark eyes. "And I am a wealthy, successful entrepreneur." He held out his arm gallantly. "What can they do to me?"

Sarah's heart lifted. This Eli she knew. "Who would have believed we'd come so far?"

Teresa looked from one to the other. "What in the world are you two talking about?"

"It's an old story, *hija*. I'll tell you when you're older."

"Whatever." Her tone said adults were beyond comprehension.

Eli put the basket into the back of the truck. "It's going to be crowded, but it's not far."

"I'm skinny," Teresa said, "but I'm claustrophobic. Can I have the window?"

Sarah grinned. "Shameless greed," she said, and

climbed in. To her dismay, the truck was a standard shift. Demurely she put her knees to one side and tugged her skirt down over them, but Eli gave her a wicked grin as he put his hand on the stick shift. No matter how far she moved, it wouldn't be quite far enough to avoid the brush of his arm against hers, or the teasing brush of his fingers below her skirt. "Sorry," he said.

She gave him a look, and he chuckled.

And in that instant she was aware of several things. A lot had changed between them over the past few days, especially this morning, and it gave her a vast sense of relief to discover they could play verbally like this.

The second recognition was that she was as giddy and breathless as a girl on her first date. She was thrilled to be sitting next to him in his truck, going on a picnic.

And for once, the knowledge gave her no sense of alarm. She simply let the happiness and anticipation exist in this moment, attached to nothing. Only now.

She voiced the third thing aloud. "I feel wonderfully wicked."

He laughed. "You know what? Me, too."

"What's wicked?" Teresa asked.

Eli and Sarah exchanged a glance. "Never mind," Sarah said.

"Hey, did Eli show you the new tea boxes?" Teresa said. "Is there still a picture in here, Eli?"

"There is a color copy in the glove box."

"Is this what you've been working on?" Sarah said, taking the sheet Teresa gave her just as Eli pulled in to the parking lot of the Martinez Hacienda. He parked under a tree, and Teresa exploded out.

Sarah moved more slowly, looking at the color copy of the new art. A bright border with a southwestern geometric pattern banded the sides, and a stylized botanical garden graced the top. This one looked like chamomile.

Her marketing eye picked it apart, and it was with genuine pleasure she said, "Eli, I love this!"

"The borders will be the same on all the various mixes, just done in different color combinations. Each box will be printed in a color to coordinate with the botanical drawing—this one is yellow and white to go with the chamomile flower. This oval will be on the front of every box." He pointed to a stylized drawing of Taos Mountain, with fields of herbs spreading down from a wealthy-looking adobe hacienda. Santiago Herb Teas, Taos, New Mexico was printed in a circle around it. "I'm really pleased," he added. "I didn't even really know what I wanted, but Jenny managed to figure it out."

"It's gorgeous. I hope you've given her a giant bonus."

Eli smiled and plucked the sheet from her hand. "We'll see first if it brings us the market share we want."

Teresa popped back at the door. "Are you guys coming?"

"So impatient!" Sarah said, but slid out.

They paid their admission to the old hacienda, and wandered into the first courtyard. Sarah spent a few moments showing Teresa how to operate the camera, then gave it to her. "I want you to spend one roll shooting anything you like, anything that catches your eye," she said. "People, shadows, rocks. Whatever. Just look through the lens and don't be afraid to take a picture that might seem strange."

Teresa showed the first hesitation she had displayed. "Anything?"

"Yes." Sarah tucked the strap around her neck. "Play. That's all. Just have fun."

"But what if I waste it?"

Sarah chuckled. "It's only film. There is much more where that came from."

Teresa shrugged. "If you say so." She moved slowly away from them, her dark head gleaming in the noonday sun. Sarah could see the girl felt uncomfortable at first, but she quickly forgot about them.

"I remember," Eli said conversationally, walking beside her through the courtyard, "when you saved all your baby-sitting money for film. Took you a week to get enough for one of those little packs, and you'd shoot the whole thing in two hours on a yucca."

Sarah grinned. "I learned a lot from yuccas."

"Yeah?" He gestured to a bench in the shade and they sat down. "Like what?"

"How to get clean, sharp focus. Those little curls on a yucca leaf are so small it took a very steady hand to get it right. Depth of field, too. That was hard." She pursed her lips, remembering the stillness of desert evenings and a stand of yucca. "They still appeal to me. I like the way they're shaped."

"Me, too," he said. "It was yuccas that made me start thinking of the teas. You remember my grandmother? That shampoo she makes from yucca root?"

"Yes."

"Well, I was out at the grocery store one day, and there were these two old guys in the tea aisle, laughing about the herb teas. They were joking about the teas they would make from all the weeds in town. Weed tea. They thought it was so hilarious."

Sarah turned to watch his face. His eyes were fixed on the horizon, remembering. "I went home and saw all that land that was good for nothing but weeds. Too dry for most crops. No grass for cows. Only sheep and goats like it. And the yuccas and the sage." He grinned. "So I was thinking of the yucca shampoo, and thinking of asking my grandmother how to make it, how maybe we could put it in bottles to sell. And there were two women in her house, getting her summer tea. She had all those specialty teas, you know, for summer, winter, spring. Teas for a cold and for heartache, and—" He lifted a shoulder. "Everything."

"A tea for heartache? Really?"

"And one for love, and one to ward off the evil eye."
He chuckled, clicking his boots on the tile. "I decided not
to sell those. Love potions could be dangerous."

"Love tea is a great idea, Eli!"

"No. She told me she would not make those for people
if she could not see into their hearts to see their real trouble.
She would only make the tonics."

A pair of sunburned tourists in shorts and fishing hats
posed in front of the well to have their picture taken, and
Sarah watched them idly. "I was so excited the first time
I saw your teas, Eli." She smiled at him. "They were in a
grocer's in Manhattan. A sort of arty little place, with all
natural foods and that kind of thing." She remembered
standing in the narrow little aisles, hearing the rain outside.
"There it was—Summer Tonic, by Santiago Teas."

"Did you know it was our tea?"

"Not that minute, but once I picked up the box and saw
they were made in Taos, I did."

He leaned on the wall. "Wow, I really never imagined
seeing them in New York."

His pleasure was so deep it made Sarah laugh. "Did you
think you ship them out around the country so people can
put them in storage, or what?"

"No." He inclined his head, grinning at her. "It's just
amazing, that's all. To think something we make here is
sitting on a shelf in somebody's house in a city I might not
ever see."

"I guess it is amazing when you put it like that. I started
seeing them all over after that. They're very popular in
some places."

"That's good."

"Will you ever go public with the stock?"

His dark eyes glittered. "You making an offer?"

"I am."

"We'll see." He lifted his chin toward Teresa. "She's back for more. What did you shoot, *hija?*"

"Oh...all kinds of things," she said.

Sarah wondered what mischief she'd find on the film when she developed it. There was no mistaking that expression. She would find out soon enough, she supposed. "Let's get a few shots of you here, shall we?"

"Then we can have our picnic," Eli said.

"Good plan."

Chapter Eight

After they left the Hacienda, Eli drove without thinking to a bluff overlooking the Rio Grande gorge and the tiny silver ribbon of river below. A gnarled stand of cottonwoods cast dappled shade over the ground. He was out of the truck and reaching for the picnic basket before he realized his mistake.

Sarah stepped out of the truck, smoothing her skirt, and stood right where she was, staring at the landscape. After a moment she looked at Eli with an oddly stricken expression. "Why here?"

He ducked her gaze. "I come here often," he said. "I forgot—"

"You *forgot*, Eli?"

It wounded her, and with regret Eli reached for her, feeling her arm slip from his fingers as she stepped away.

"It doesn't matter," she said. Stiffly she moved through long grass that had found life in the shade of the trees. Her camera swung from her hand.

He left the basket and ran after her, catching her shoulder to halt her retreat. "Sarah, that isn't what I meant. I had to try to forget. I kept coming here, so I would have other memories, besides…" Besides the two of them, entwined in a wild rush of passion. There was no need to say it aloud. "You have not had that luxury, to put other things in place of what…where…" He stopped. "I'm sorry. I did not mean to hurt you."

She stared off to the ragged break in the land, sudden and deep, that was the gorge. "I know," she said, and for one tiny breath of time, put her hand over his and raised her eyes. "I know."

They were so close. Her chin was uptilted, her hand trusting over his—it would have been the right thing to bend just a little, and kiss her. He hesitated a moment too long, however, and she moved away. Returning to the truck, he got the basket and Teresa fetched the blanket for them to sit on.

Eli had brought sandwiches—turkey and chicken—a bowl of black olives, oranges and pears, and a large chunk of sharp cheddar cheese. There were bottles of exotic juice to wash it down with, guava pear, raspberry-strawberry, others.

"You should have brought lemon tea," Sarah said, teasing him. "Santiago sun tea."

"Teresa is off sugar," he explained. "She picked out the juices."

"Off sugar, huh?" Sarah frowned. "You aren't dieting, are you?"

"No. I just think sugar is bad for your skin." She held up a bottle of juice. "This will make you healthier. That's what my mom says."

"She's right."

The girl could never be still for long. She ate a sandwich and a little cheese, then, taking an apple, asked if she could borrow the camera again. She wandered toward the gorge, stopping now and then to shoot a picture.

"With that camera in her hand, she reminds me of you," Eli said, his eyes on his niece. "Always with that camera, shooting the sky and the ground and everything." He looked at her, smiling gently. "Everything."

She gazed at him oddly, a faraway expression in her eyes.

"What's wrong?" he asked.

She shook her head with a smile, lowering her eyes. "I don't know. Ghosts, I guess."

Ghosts. The ghosts of the pair of them. They had come here often, and made love. He wondered if it was that she remembered, the feeling of their joined flesh, the fury of their youthful passion, the glory of their discovery of one another. His body responded all too willingly, and to distract himself, he picked up an orange. He tore into the thick skin, releasing the fresh, sharp smell. "Did you talk to your parents this morning?"

"No. They weren't home." She gave him a rueful twist of her lips. "Thanks ever so much for reminding me. I had forgotten."

He chuckled. "My apologies." He separated a section of orange and held it out to her. "Do you remember the Spanish?"

"*Naranja.* One of my favorite words." She took the section from him. "I love the way it feels in my mouth."

With deep shade from the cottonwoods above them, they smiled gently at each other across time, and in the space between breaths, a door that had been closed tight suddenly swung open. Eli found himself staring not only into her eyes but beyond, seeing the whole of her soul, and the past. He felt it, too, as acutely as if he'd been locked in a stuffy room and someone had flung open a window to allow a breeze to waft through.

And in that moment, falling into her eyes, into her soul,

Eli reached out and touched her face. It was a hesitant touch, only the tips of his fingers against her cheekbone, then her jaw. A wisp of hair blew against his wrist. He wanted to speak, to somehow express the sense of wonder that filled him, but there were no words to capture it, so he only gazed at her, and at last took his hand away.

But she didn't shy from him this time. Her open gaze stayed on his face. "I loved taking pictures of you," she said softly. "Your face has changed some, but your eyes are exactly the same."

He was aware of his heart thudding harder in his chest, and of the blood moving through him, rushing and hot. But he found he could speak quietly, without revealing himself too much. "Your eyes have changed more than anything else about you."

"Have they?" It seemed to startle her.

"There was always laughter in your eyes then. A secret. Now…" He paused, trying to think of what he meant. "Now there is wariness."

She lifted one shoulder in a jerk that showed it mattered to her. "I was very young then. Life teaches you to be careful."

"Life is not always as hard on people as it has been on you."

A flash of pain crossed her face, and she closed her eyes. "That's not true. There is always something that takes that youthful wonder away." She looked at him. "Something."

"No, Sarah. That isn't true. What if your father had welcomed me? What if we had simply been able to marry and have our child? If that had happened, there would not be so much sorrow in your eyes now."

"Is this what you wanted to talk about?" she whispered. "That's too much. I don't…I'm not sure I can talk about all of that, Eli."

"One part of it, then." Impulsively he reached for her hand, taking it into his own and looking at the slim length of her fingers lying against his palm. "It was cruel to make you give her away, Sarah."

She bowed her head, and her hair fell forward in a curtain to hide her face. "It was me who did it."

He shook his head, but she couldn't see him, so he reached out with one hand and pushed her hair from her face, cupping his palm around her jaw. There was a surprising fragility to the bones. "You were betrayed. By all of us."

The gray eyes turned cold. "Which does not excuse my own betrayal." With an abrupt move, she pulled free of him and stood, brushing at her skirt. She strode toward Teresa, and Eli could not help watching her, his heart thudding with regret.

As he drank in the way the sunlight glazed her arm, kissed the crown of her pale hair and illuminated the shapes of breast and hip and legs, he knew he was doomed. He wanted her. Maybe he loved her still.

But until now, he had not seen how deep her pain went behind those rigid walls that kept him out. Kept the world out. And he feared if he tried to breach them in order to free her, the resulting emotions might destroy her.

Eli dropped Sarah—firmly hidden behind her walls of careful politeness—at her cottage, and took Teresa home, mentally bracing himself for the confrontations he knew were brewing. The entire family had probably seen the newspaper photo by now.

His sister's car was in the driveway, and, coward that he was, he didn't stop the engine. Teresa looked at him curiously. "Aren't you coming in?"

"Not today," he said.

"Is there something going on? You've been kinda weird all day."

"I'm sure you'll hear about it soon enough." The front door swung open, and Eli swore as his sister came out of the house, as small and fierce as a crow. "Probably three seconds."

Cynthia came directly to his window and crossed her arms. "Elias, how could you?"

"How could I what?" he snapped. "Dance with an old girlfriend in a public restaurant?"

"Not just any old girlfriend, and you know it. I've been fielding calls from your brothers all day. They're ready to get a posse together and string you up by your boots, and here I am, aiding and abetting you by letting you take Teresa up there to get her pictures done." She narrowed her eyes. "If that's even what's happening."

He waited until she wore her tape down, and said mildly, "It isn't my fault some photographer thought that would be a grabber."

"Mom, you aren't going to make me stop now, are you?"

"I don't know yet." She glared at her brother again. "You could have been more careful."

"Mom," Teresa said, "you can't—"

"Go inside, Teresa. This is none of your business."

"It is, too, my business. It is if this stupid old war ends up making me give up my portfolio."

Eli touched her hand and lifted his chin toward the house. "Let me talk to your mom alone."

With a last, worried glance at her mother, she obeyed, and Eli waited until she was out of sight. "Don't punish her when you're angry with me."

She took a deep breath and put her hands on the side of the truck, imploring. "Eli, don't you remember how awful it was? All that fighting over it, and the punishments and the craziness? This family doesn't need to go through that again. We've barely healed all the wounds from the first round."

The brutality of his anger, sudden and hot, was blinding. "It has nothing to do with the family! Only me. My life."

"And your life has no bearing on ours? That might work somewhere else, but it doesn't work here. Family is life, Elias, and you know it."

He clenched his jaw and looked away from her. "I've worked hard for this family."

"Oh, Eli, I know." She reached through the window and put her hand on his arm. "But you can't do this. Not for us, but for you."

"I'm not doing anything," he said, and both of them knew he lied.

She slammed her hand on the door. "Damn it, Eli, at least be honest with me."

Mute, he met her eyes. "I have to go, Cynthia." He put the truck in gear. "Thank you for your understanding."

As he drove out to the ranch, the argument lay like a rock in his gut, and he wondered if it might be easier to duck everyone, go spend the night in a hotel somewhere. But there was work that had to be done—he had calls and orders to make, and reviews on the quarterly earnings, and he had worked too hard for too long to slack off now.

The ranch was long and narrow, shaped like Italy, only it ran uphill. His mother's renovated house sat just inside the gate that marked the property line. Beyond it were the fields of herbs, dissected neatly by a road that led to the production plant. In the distance sat his grandmother's two-hundred-year-old house, the base covered with a blur of red blossoms.

Eli drove to the plant, waving to the field supervisor as he passed, and parked in his spot among the other cars and trucks in the parking lot. As he got out, he smelled freshly mown peppermint, and beneath that, the faintly cloying odor of ragweed, blowing in from the east.

His brother Miguel was busy with a machine as Eli came in, but Eli would have had to be blind to miss the daggers Miguel shot in his direction. He ignored them and went to his office without incident, taking mail from the basket where his secretary had left it. She left early on Thursdays, to volunteer in her child's third-grade class, and Eli found her notes, along with an agenda for the afternoon and next day, on his blotter. A lot of phone calls, he saw.

He closed the door, hoping it might be a deterrent. For a little while it worked. But first Miguel, and then on his heels his mother, showed up to express almost exactly the same sentiments his sister had. With his brother, he was dismissive.

His mother deserved more. "Sit down," he said, when she showed up.

A small woman with a trim figure and black hair only now showing streaks of silver, she said in Spanish, "I don't want to sit down." She always spoke Spanish, even though she was utterly fluent in English. She simply felt Spanish the superior language. Her children, and more often her grandchildren, spoke back to her in English, but it never dented her resolve. "I want you to tell me what you're doing with that girl."

Eli wanted to placate her, and spoke back in her favored language. "Mama, it wasn't what it looked like in the paper. I saw her at La Paloma and danced with her, that's all."

"How can you want to dance with her after all the sorrow she caused you?"

Her aim was true and deep. He simply had no answer, not one that would make sense. For the truth was, Sarah *had* been a source of misery and sorrow in his life. But she'd also been the source of his greatest joy, a fact his mother would not understand. "I don't know," he said quietly.

Her shoulders sagged. "Ah, Elias, she'll tear you up. I can't stand to watch it happen again." She pressed a fist against her chest. "Not a day goes by that I don't think of that baby."

He pressed his mouth together, thinking of the vast sorrow he'd glimpsed in Sarah's eyes this afternoon. "It's the same for Sarah. How much worse for the mother than the grandmother, eh?"

"If you start with her again, Elias, you'll be dead to me. I mean it."

"Don't you dare threaten me," Eli said in a low, hard voice. His anger rose, and as if buoyed on it, he stood up. "I am no boy to be ordered around at your whim, Mama. I am a man, and will choose my own life."

"You are a selfish man," she said. "Don't care about anybody but you. We tried to warn you back then, but you wouldn't listen, would you? And here you are again, after everything I said came true, going to do it all again."

"Stop it," he said through gritted teeth. "This has to end, or it will just keep happening over and over and over. You have to forgive her. I have to forgive her. There has to be peace, or this curse will ruin anything we ever try to build."

She lifted her chin and glared at him. "I'm so glad your father is dead, so he doesn't have to see this." Haughtily, she turned on her tiny heel and left him.

Eli let go of a breath and leaned back in his chair, closing his eyes. At least that part was over with.

Sarah found a message from her mother taped to her door when she got home. "Gone to the mountains," it said. "A day or two and this will blow over."

In spite of herself, Sarah grinned. It was one of her mother's classic moves—find a way to get around the problem first, then, and only then, deal with it. But in this instance it was probably exactly the right call. Her father loved to fish, and they had a cabin on a small lake not far away. A day or two of fishing would blunt his fury, and maybe even let it all blow over.

At the very least, it delayed the argument, gave Sarah some time to think of how she would respond if her father came unglued. She'd worked hard to smooth their relationship, and hated to think of all that hard work coming undone over a silly photograph.

But it had become more than just a photograph, hadn't it?

A thunderstorm was moving in over the southwestern mountains, and the air temperature dropped along with it. Sarah changed into a pair of jeans and a shirt, and washed some greens for her supper, trying to distance herself from that thought.

But it haunted her. Her dream hung in her mind, casting a sensual haze over her whenever she thought of it. And today, when he touched her, when they talked, she had seen they were not aloof from each other. The embers of their old relationship were starting to crackle.

She took her plate to the couch by the south windows so she could watch the storm come in as she ate. It was beautiful and dramatic, moving in fast with dark gray clouds and flashes of lightning, and at last the rain itself, pouring hard from a slate-dark sky that covered all hints of day. Sarah curled up in the chair and watched it fall, a glass of wine keeping her company.

What a day, she thought absently. The wine was smoky and rich on her tongue. The rain pounded so fiercely at the windows that it was a long moment before she realized there was the sound of a knock buried in it. With a little jolt of worry she glanced at the door, hoping it wasn't her parents, come back already. She didn't want to deal with it.

With a faint sigh she put the wine down, padded across the room in her bare feet and opened the door.

It was Eli who stood there, his hair dripping, his face wet. The white cotton shirt stuck to his chest and arms, transparent against his dark skin, and his eyes burned as he stared at her.

A bolt of pure, undiluted hunger filled her, rushing

through every cell, making her body ache. She might even have made a little sound, part fear, part need.

Without a word, he came in, put his cold hands on her face and kissed her.

Sarah made a soft, mewling cry. His mouth carried the flavor of rain and a decade of yearning, and Sarah reached for him to brace herself, keep herself from falling as she met the raging hunger of that kiss, those lips, the tongue that plunged into her mouth. She caught his upper arms, and felt the tenseness of muscles there beneath wet cotton.

He backed her against the wall and pressed his body into hers, kissing her face, her chin, her throat, her mouth again. The sound of rain, the smell of it on clay walls and hot earth, came in through the open door, and with it a wind bearing raindrops that sprayed over her face and her hair. His clothes were wet, but they warmed as he pressed into her, warmed with the heat of his flesh and the heat of her own, and Sarah arched into him, put her arms around him, pulled him closer, overwhelmed at her need to absorb the taste of Elias, remembered and not remembered, darker than it had been, seasoned with years and lost dreams and a thousand moments of yearning.

She gasped and pulled him tighter, a blinding, dizzy hunger in her, a thirst so deep that the more she drank the more she wanted. She clasped him tight, drinking of that fierce flavor, and slid her hands down his back and over his buttocks in a gesture that would have been too aggressive for a sixteen-year-old, and pulled him tightly against her, feeling the crush of his chest and the thrust of his arousal, and her own agonizing need to somehow meld with him. Their breath came in tearing gasps, gathered like a swimmer's bid for air, without halting the rhythm.

Eli, she thought. And a dozen images pushed into her mind, of times between their last kiss in the car, with police lights flashing their red doom, and now, when she would have given a limb to be in his arms this way. She felt tears on her cheeks, and a faint fine trembling in her arms.

She slid her tongue against his and remembered lying in a narrow cot, aching for him. She arched her body closer to his and remembered awakening—for years—in a strange bed and realizing anew that Eli was gone. His long, graceful hands gripped her, and she remembered the long fingers of her daughter—

All at once, Sarah shattered. Her weeping was no longer a soft, silent thing, but great gulping sobs that ripped through her chest and throat. The fine trembling in her fingers and wrists turned to bone-cracking shivers that rocked her limbs and her spine.

As if he knew, as if he understood, Eli only gathered her into him, wrapped his long arms around her and enfolded her completely, his head bent into her neck while she buried her face against his wet chest and wept. Twice she tried to raise her head, tried to find some trick to pull herself back under control, and twice he simply held her more tightly, stroking her hair, her back, his face close against her neck.

She wept as if she were grieving, wept in a way she had not since she was a small child.

And when she was finally hiccuping to a stop, Eli settled with her on the floor and pulled an afghan from the couch. He kicked the door closed and leaned against the wall, pulling her close into the cradle of his arms and holding her while the rain fell and darkness began to gather.

Safe in the circle of his embrace, Sarah simply rested, listening to his heart and his breath, smelling the familiar scent of his skin. She closed her eyes and let go of a shuddering breath.

She didn't know how long it was till she finally stirred. She thought she might have fallen into a stupefied doze, lying against him that way. Her body had begun to protest the position with an ache in her hip and a stiffness in her shoulder. She raised her head. "You must be frozen, Eli."

His eyes, those fathomless, bottomless, beautiful eyes, were liquid. "No," he whispered, and brushed hair from her face.

"I'm sorry," she said. "I don't know—"

"Shh. It doesn't matter."

She put her hands on his face, as she'd longed to do all day. She opened her palm to feel his jaw, the coarseness of male flesh, and spread her fingers over his high, slanted cheekbones. She looked at his mouth, and very softly kissed it, closing her eyes as the firm, rich mouth touched hers. "Thank you," she whispered.

He swallowed. "I came here to make love to you," he said roughly.

She nodded.

"But that would be too much for us now, I think. Will you give me a cup of tea instead?"

Sarah smiled. "I happen to have some very fine tea here. Santiago Farms."

"Good." Gently he stood up, and helped Sarah to her feet. "I'm sorry I upset you."

Sarah just shook her head, sensing the emotional storm could all too easily circle back with the slightest encouragement. "Let me get you some tea." She frowned, looking at his clothes. "You're so wet. Go in there and take off those clothes and wrap yourself in a blanket. I'll put them in the dryer."

He cut her a wicked glance, waggling his eyebrows. "If you wanted me naked, all you had to do was say so. I aim to please."

Sarah laughed, thankful that he could make a joke to ease the tension between them. It made her remember, suddenly, the long, heated struggle they had faced to keep their passions under control when they were young. For months they'd hovered on the precipice, afraid to jump, but aching for it. More often than not, it had been Eli who had pulled them back before they went too far, and often it had been with a joke. "Go," she said.

She put water in a heavy blue teakettle and set it to boil, then took cups and spoons and tea from the cupboard, wondering what else she had to go with it, suddenly wishing she had the cooking skills to whip up the pitiful ingredients of her cupboard into some nourishing, gorgeous creation. There was a half sleeve of saltines, a jar of peanut butter, two cans of soup. One cookie at the bottom of a bag.

As she tossed the bag into the trash, Eli came out, carrying his clothes. He'd wrapped the bedspread around him, awkwardly, leaving one gleaming brown shoulder and arm free. A fist of new desire struck her.

"I'll just put the clothes in the dryer," she said.

"That's what I thought we were doing."

Sarah took the jeans and shirt, hurrying away so she wouldn't have to look at that delectable shoulder. After she tossed the clothes into the dryer, she scurried back to the center of the kitchen, and promptly forgot what she was doing.

"Tea," Eli said, settling on a stool by the counter.

"Right." She blushed, even though she tried not to, tried to act as if she'd had attractive men in her rooms a million times. Which she had. Well, at least half a dozen.

But none of them had been Eli, half-naked and tempting as a river god as he leaned on the counter and tucked the blanket around his waist. "Aren't you cold?" she asked, thinking she would fetch the afghan for him.

"Not at all," he said evenly, but Sarah caught the wickedness glittering in his eyes.

She put her hands on her hips. "You're teasing me."

"Me?" He put one long dark hand against his chest, that chest that was no longer boyishly thin. This was a man's chest, with dark hair lightly scattered from one nipple to the other, and muscle-sculpted, lean, hard curves. "Is it working?"

She met his laughing eyes. "You've grown up, Elias."

His gaze traveled over her. "So have you, Sarita."

The teakettle whistled and, relieved, Sarah rescued it. "I was just looking for something to go with the tea, but I'm afraid the pickings are very lean." She put the mugs on the table and poured hot water into them. "That cooking thing again."

"Career women," he snorted in mock disgust.

"New York living," she corrected him. "Who needs to cook when there's food on every corner?"

"Did you like it, Sarah? Living in the big city, traveling all over the world?"

She stirred sugar into her tea and settled on a stool opposite him. "I did," she said. "It was exciting, at least at first. There's so much movement, so many people, all of them so different. It's amazing."

"I can see that it would be. This—" he gestured, as if to include Taos "—must seem very slow in comparison."

"It is," she said, and frowned. "But I missed it, that feeling of a day lasting forever. And as small towns go, you have to admit Taos is more cosmopolitan than most."

A shadow crossed his eyes, and he ducked his head. "In some ways."

And finally, here was the opening. The right moment to bring a little more of this out of the shadows. "It's hard to imagine how even my father pulled locking you up for eight weeks."

A bitterness touched his mouth for a moment, then was gone. "Not so hard when you think of how much he wanted me out of the way, so he could separate us." He snapped his fingers. "He had friends on the bench, friends all over. Eight weeks was more than enough time."

"I hate the idea of that happening to you," she said, thinking of him sitting in jail, all alone. "Did you know he'd sent me away?" she asked suddenly. "Or did you think I had deserted you?"

His face went still. "At first I waited for you to come, somehow. I knew you would be watched. I knew it would be hard, but every day I thought there would be a letter or something. Maybe you would send a friend to tell me you couldn't come." He took a breath. "But you were gone. I didn't know until I got out."

"Someone in your family had to have known what happened."

He lifted a shoulder. "Probably. But they are no more blameless than your father."

She gave him a wry grin. "No one in your family had me falsely arrested."

"No, your father did that, didn't he?" He touched her hand, his expression a little lighter, but still sober.

"Yes." She wanted to add more, wanted to tell him—what? That day by day her heart had tightened a little more, and a little more, and a little more until it was as black and dry as a grape that had lain too long in the sun to even be a raisin. No life in it at all. "Yes," she repeated quietly.

His hand fell upon hers. "I'm sorry."

"Even if you had wanted to find me, you wouldn't have been able to. He wanted us apart, and he won." She thought of her father, trying now to make that right with her. "Now he wants to bring it all out in the open. He wants my forgiveness for making me give up the baby."

The baby. It was the first time she'd said it out loud in context, ever, and a strange twist pinched her heart.

But Eli said only, "And have you granted it?"

She met his gaze squarely. "I might be able to make peace with him," she said firmly. "But I won't forgive him. I can't."

"Neither can I," he said, his thumb moving on her fingers.

Sarah looked at their joined hands, and realized she had turned hers to hold his fingers against her palm, instinctively seeking comfort. His hand felt right. He felt right to her, sitting in her kitchen, even all these years later. "Eli," she said quietly, "are we starting again?"

"I don't know."

"Maybe it's only nostalgia."

"Maybe." He looked at her gravely. "Maybe we only need to say goodbye in the right way—finish it on our own terms."

"It scares me," she whispered.

"It should," he said without humor. "My family hates you. Your father still hates me. Nothing has changed."

"Except us," she said, feeling a weaving of hope and despair. "We've changed."

"Have we?" His smile was sad. "If we were different, would our families matter so much to us?"

The dryer buzzed suddenly, loud and annoying. "There are your clothes," she said. "I'll get them for you."

There was something intimate about taking the shirt and jeans from the dryer, still redolent with the scent of his skin. The smell made her want to bury her face in the clothes, inhale it deeply, but of course she did not. She shook them efficiently, remembering when she had longed to do such mundane tasks for him. It made her smile as she gave the clothes to him.

"What?" he asked.

Sarah grinned. "I was remembering when I couldn't wait to make a home for you. Cook for you and wash your clothes, be there waiting when you came home. Somehow, the fantasy has lost some of its appeal."

He stood up to take the clothes, affording her a full view of that naked chest, and a rush of hunger pushed through her. A rush of need, to feel him, touch him, explore him.

What would it hurt? A voice whispered in her mind, and she nearly reached out to put her palm against that bare flesh, against the hair lying silkily across it, then clenched her fists.

"Sarah," he said in a low voice. "Come here."

Chapter Nine

She simply stared at him like a wild creature, half starved, half wary. Her big gray eyes shone nearly silver in the quiet, rain-tinted light coming from the windows, and he saw her catch her breath.

"Come here," he said again, coaxing her closer, holding out one hand.

The rain made the only music, pattering on the roof and windows, thunder rumbling through, low and distant, like drums. And still Sarah only stood there, holding his clothes next to her chest, poised between running away and coming closer.

Her eyes never wavered as she took a step, then another, stopping to put one hand on his chest, lightly. He forced himself to be still, wait for her to make the next move. All day he had been aching for this. All day. All year. All decade.

Sarah, touching him.

"Eli," she whispered, imploring.

He stepped closer, took the clothes from her hands. She resisted a little, then let go of the material. He heaped the clothes on the stool and reached for her. Gently. Only his hands on her shoulders, close to her neck. He brushed his thumbs over the shelf of her collarbone. "Do you remember when we first kissed?"

A little of the fear bled away from her eyes, and a hint of a smile brushed her lips. "Yes."

"In the gym," he said quietly. "Some kind of dance after school."

"The Halloween dance."

"Really?" He grinned. "It took us two months?"

"It was forever." Her lids fell a little, and he saw her gaze on his chest. With one finger she brushed his chest hair, and it was an erotic siren on his nerves. He forced himself not to react. "I remember holding hands with you, but I was really nervous and my hands were sweating, and I was afraid you would be so grossed out you wouldn't ever want to hold my hand again."

Her finger drew a circle over his chest, small, then wider. Eli dared move his hands a little, stroking her shoulders. "I liked holding your hand."

She lifted her face, meeting his gaze, and he saw again the charcoal band around her irises. "Your hair was so long then. I wanted to put my hands in it so badly."

He dared to inch a step closer, let his hands slide down her back until they rested in the dip of her spine. "What I remember is daring myself. Standing there wanting to kiss you, trying to get my courage up." He grinned. "I'd get so close, then get scared."

She grinned. "And in the end, I kissed you."

"Yes. I was glad." He bent a little closer. "This time you can be afraid and I'll be bold. It will be another kind of first kiss."

Worry flooded back into her face. "Eli," she said, "I don't think it's a good—"

He closed the distance between them and took the rest of the words from her lips. Earlier, he had acted without thinking, like a starving man eating too much too fast. Now he could lean in gently, capture those soft, vulnerable lips. Now he could taste them slowly, remembering the texture, the pleasure, the slide and slant and fit of their mouths together. It was a chaste and simple kiss, one he did not prolong, but it made him a little giddy, and he laughed.

She pulled a little away. "Are you laughing at me?"

"No." He slid his hands under her shirt in back, so he could touch her skin. It was smooth and surprisingly muscled under his palms. When she didn't object to that, he slid his palms around to her waist, letting his thumbs glide over her stomach, right in the hollow of her belly button.

In return, she lifted both hands to his chest and spread her fingers over it. "You didn't have chest hair when I knew you."

"I was a boy then." Her slow exploration made his body hum, and his voice was a little ragged. "Now I'm a man."

"Am I bothering you?" she asked in a hushed voice.

"No." Daring a little more, he bent to kiss her again, this time more hungrily, opening his mouth, drawing her in. It was a slow, narcotic kiss this time, deep and then shallow, tongue to tongue, then tongue to lip, then lip to lip and over again. Her hands slid over his torso, up and down, then over his arms, growing more restless, but he did not move his own hands for a long time, simply let them rest there, on her belly and sides, while he kissed her. When he heard the slight hurried harshness of her breath, he circled her navel, dipped inside, angled his hands till he could feel the ridges of her ribs.

She did not bolt, only lifted her arms to his shoulders, giving implicit permission. He pulled the shirt up slowly, eased it upward. She pulled away from the kiss to let him pull it over her head, and as he closed his eyes he saw the dazed, drugged look in her eyes before she moved in, taking his face in her hands to pull him into another kiss.

There was an aggressive, needful edge to the kiss now, more urgency. A gilded dizziness hazed his mind as he lifted his hands and cupped her breasts, letting go of a groan as she sighed against his mouth. He stroked her nipples with his thumbs, and then he could not be slow anymore, and sought the clasp, front or back, that would get rid of the barriers between them.

He found it, and nearly broke it in his need, and at last her bare breasts flowed into his palms, a luscious weighty softness, the tips pearled to tight knots. He breathed her name, and bent, then knelt when he could not reach her, pulling her into his lap, her legs straddling his waist.

And only then did he open his eyes, and let himself see what he'd felt, her narrow tanned shoulders, the freckled golden upper slope of her breasts that he'd glimpsed beneath her shirt, and lower, the startling paleness of flesh that had not seen the sun at all. He slid his hands over her ribs, cupped her breasts tenderly in his hands and bowed his head to take the crown into his mouth.

She moaned, and the sound gave new heat to his need. A wisp of memory swirled through and he suckled hard, electrified by the extraordinary taste of her, the uneven pebbled texture, the sweetness against his tongue. The world narrowed to this, to the sound of Sarah's breath as he teased and roused her. Urgently he used his hands to pull her hips tightly against him, needing the weight of her against him, and when she gladly met his thrust with pressure of her own, he let his restless hands move again. Up her back, into her hair, over her arms, down her sides and across her belly.

And his need to see her—see that it was really Sarah, not some dream or wish—made him pull back and look at her. At her passion-clouded eyes, and the look of her mouth, slightly open, at her shoulders and breast and belly.

His hands moved with his gaze, reinforcing his knowledge that the moment was real.

"There isn't another man like you anywhere, Eli," she said. "That scares me."

The murmured declaration sent a pain sharp as a hundred razor cuts through him. So many wounds. Small and large. He moved his hands a little on the flesh of her stomach, and a new texture caught his attention, a thin, papery scar on the side of her belly. Startled, he looked down. "She left a mark on you."

"Yes," she said, and he felt her withdraw suddenly, ducking her head away from him.

"No." He caught her. "Don't. Let me see it."

She closed her eyes as he traced the branching faint scar with his fingertips. Soberly he shifted and put his mouth to it, and the ache in his lungs grew so sharp he could barely take a breath. "I wish we knew where she was."

"Eli, don't!" she cried, and pushed him away. She scrambled backward, lifting her arms to cover herself, wounded betrayal in her eyes. "Don't."

"Sarita," he said, reaching for her.

She ducked away from his grip, and hurt rose in him. "Stop running, Sarah!" he cried. "It isn't going to suddenly not be just because you pretend it never happened."

The walls were going up fast. Eli saw them, in the rigidness of her shoulders, the lift of her chin, the cold bleeding of all life from her eyes. "Not it," she said distinctly. "*Her.* And don't you dare try to force me to talk about it. I won't. Ever. Do you understand?"

"She wasn't only your child, Sarah! She belonged to me, too."

She turned her back. "I think it's time for you to go."

He bent to pick up his shirt, and angrily flung his arms into the sleeves, stomped his legs into his still-damp jeans. "This is not over," he said. "You will not push me away like this. Do *you* understand?"

She whirled, clasping her shirt to her front. "What are you going to do, Eli? Give me truth serum? Tie me up and torture me?" A tiny, sharp smile curled on her mouth. "I don't know why I never saw how much you and my father are alike. He wants to force me, too, and neither of you will."

The ultimate insult. "Why did you even come back?" he said, and left her.

Sarah's parents returned home Sunday afternoon, and, glad to have an excuse, Sarah called Eli to reschedule the photo session set for that afternoon, the first one since their encounter in her kitchen. Eli's voice was as cool as her own as he replied that he understood her need to see her father.

Then he abruptly shifted direction. "Teresa is worried, Sarah, and with some reason, that she is not going to be allowed to complete this work. There's a lot of pressure on my sister. I'd like to get this done quickly, if we can."

Sarah frowned, holding the receiver against her ear. "I hate that she might pay the price for all this," she said. "If I have Sunday dinner with my folks, I should be finished by mid to late afternoon. If it's a problem for you to stay, I can borrow my mother's car and meet Teresa in a neutral spot."

A long pause marked the air between them. "You'd rather I stayed away?"

"No, I—" She sighed. "I guess I'm uncomfortable with you right now."

"Don't worry, Sarah," he said with more than a hint of harshness in his words. "I have managed to be civilized once or twice in my life. I'll be there at four."

He hung up. Sarah rolled her eyes. Perfect. It should just be a bang-up afternoon. First her father, then Eli, both sulking. It annoyed her, and as she walked up the hill to her mother's house, she wondered why she had ever put up with either one of them.

It was the best possible attitude with which to confront her parents, she realized, opening the gate. A few days ago, when she'd first learned of the photo, she'd felt guilty and uncomfortable, as if she'd done something wrong. Today she felt less like the girl she had been than the woman she'd become on her travels. The attitude was reflected in the tilt of her head on her shoulders, in the broad swing of her arms. She thought of a warrior goddess charm that a friend had given her, and felt the invisible weapons and shields cloaking her.

The scent of barbecued meats reached her, and Sarah followed the smoky smell to the backyard patio. "Hi," she said cheerfully. "Got any hot links on that grill?"

Her father, a spray bottle of vinegar water in one hand, a long spatula in the other, looked up. "You betcha. Also some trout done just the way you like it—in foil with lemon."

"Must have had some luck at the lake, then," Sarah said. She kissed his balding pate and sat down across the table from him, where the shade of the flowered umbrella would protect her from the noonday sun. "Where's Mom?"

"She ran to the grocery store for some pop."

Critically, Sarah noticed the high flush on her father's face, and checked the size of his ankles, noting with dismay they were swollen. "You still aren't feeling well today, though, are you?"

"I'm fine," he said gruffly. He lifted the lid of the barbecue, a converted fifty-gallon drum he and his buddies had made. Savory-scented smoke billowed out, and he poked the sizzling meat with his spatula, turned a couple of hamburgers and squeezed a shot of vinegar water into the coals for good measure. Carefully he closed the lid and cleared his throat.

Sarah folded her hands, waiting.

"Saw the picture in the paper," he said.

"I assumed you had."

"Didn't you take enough of a beating the first time around?" He lifted one graying eyebrow with that superiority she'd always hated. "Have to go back for seconds?"

With effort, Sarah stalled her anger. What had she expected, after all? That her father would miraculously change his attitude? Taking a deep breath, she said, "I danced with him. That's all. It was the night I went out with my friend Joanna." Even as she said it, she wondered why she lied. There had been more than dancing, even that night. "It was nothing."

Garth narrowed his eyes. "I see him around, you know. Driving that fancy truck like he's some big man around town, and I won't lie to you, Sarah—I still want to throw a rock at him. Slap that cocky grin off his face."

"It wasn't enough that he sat in jail for two months for a crime he didn't commit?" She sighed and held up her hand. "No, don't answer that. I really don't want to argue about this. I want to forget about all of it."

"You know about the jail, huh?"

"Joanna told me."

He scratched a spot above his eye. "You aren't going to believe me, but that shames me now. It was wrong."

Inexorably, he and Eli seemed determined to drag her into the past, whether she wanted to go or not. "Dad, please. Drop it."

"I don't think we can. Not till you and I work out what's still lying between us."

Sarah looked away, fixing her gaze on the smudges of blue and green and splashes of yellow that framed the backyard.

She lifted her chin. "Fine, Dad. Let's talk." She faced him, her heart hard. "Talk away. Tell me how much you hate Eli and how bad you feel about everything that happened to me. And then," she said, "I can tell you that nothing you say is ever going to change any of it. It still happened. It's still there—and I'm never going to forget about it if you don't stop bringing it up.'' In exasperation, she lifted a hand. ''You can't tell me you would have done things differently.''

''I can, Sarah.'' His voice was gruff. ''I would have changed a lot of things. I wouldn't have had that boy arrested and I wouldn't have sent you away.''

''Oh, really? And how would you have prevented me from seeing Eli if you hadn't?''

''I don't know. But it wasn't right.'' He shot a silvery spray of water into the air. ''Maybe I couldn't have stopped you. But then I wouldn't have had to sit here every damned day for twelve years wondering if my daughter was ever coming back.'' He pursed his lips. ''Wondering if I'd ever have a chance to make it up to you.''

Tears sprang to her eyes and Sarah bowed her head to hide them.

''I really thought,'' he went on, ''that I was doing the right thing. I was trying to protect you. We just wanted you to have a better life than getting married and having a baby so young, with a boy who barely had five cents to his name.'' He paused. ''Aren't you ever glad, Sarah? Glad that you got out of here and saw the world and made a name for yourself?''

Sarah had clung to her anger for so long that it frightened her to feel it sliding away under the reasonable, relentless force of words—not only her father's, but Eli's, as well. ''I don't know,'' she said finally. ''I wouldn't be who I am now if my life had gone differently. Who's to say what the right path was?''

''We all make mistakes,'' he said.

''Yes,'' she replied, feeling more of her tension slip away. ''I guess we do.''

The screen door slammed, and Mabel came down the steps, looking sunburned and healthy. ''It was a zoo out there, I swear it was! And everybody in town had to stop to talk about that damned picture.'' She put a six-pack of cola on the table. ''I'll sure be glad when something else comes up to take its place.''

Sarah sighed. ''Amen.''

''Everything all cleared up?'' Mabel asked.

Garth looked at Sarah. ''For now.''

''Good. Let's eat.''

The evening photo shoot passed without incident. Eli brought a book with him and kept his nose in it the whole time, and by now Teresa was growing so facile at delivering what Sarah asked that they were finished in two hours.

''Did you develop my film?'' Teresa asked near the end.

Sarah shook her head. ''I haven't had a chance. I'll do them tonight or tomorrow, so you can see how they came out. How did you like it? Do you feel as if you learned something about being in front of the camera?''

''I think I'd like to try doing it in the studio—just to see how you see.''

''We can do that.'' She knelt to take advantage of a glissando of light over the girl's brow.

''Today? Maybe you and Eli?''

Sarah stood. ''No, I don't think so.''

Teresa lowered her voice, casting a careful glance toward the shadows of the porch to make sure Eli was still there, reading. He was. In a theatrical whisper, she said, ''Did you guys have a fight, or what?''

''Not at all.''

It clearly wasn't the answer Teresa hoped for. ''What happened to you guys, anyway?''

''What do you mean?'' Sarah shifted the cameras in her hands.

''You know, back then. When I was little.'' She inclined

her head. "I remember how happy Eli was then, when he was with you. It was like going to the circus."

The words transported Sarah back in time instantly. Gilded afternoons, riding with Eli in his beat-up old car, the wind blowing through the windows, little Teresa belted in between them. A fierce sense of nostalgia filled her for a moment, bittersweet and yearning. To be so young and optimistic again!

"I got pregnant," Sarah said, baldly. "My father had Eli arrested and sent me to an unwed mothers' home." She stood up and moved to a cabinet on the other side of the room, unwilling to see Teresa's face.

"That's so sad!" Teresa cried. "What happened to the baby?"

Sarah swallowed. "I gave her up for adoption."

Stunned silence met this announcement. Sarah felt a quick press of regret move in her. Now even this one hitherto sympathetic Santiago would take up the torch and hate her along with all the rest. She took a breath. Maybe with good reason. That was the real killer—Sarah knew her actions had earned that hatred.

She was so deep in thought that she jumped when Teresa touched her arm. "It must have been terrible for you," she said, and tears glimmered in her wide brown eyes.

Without thinking, Sarah lifted the camera and shot a fast series of pictures. "Those will be priceless."

Teresa backed away. "I don't want to use those pictures. You keep them."

With shame, Sarah saw what she'd done. Impulsively she reached out and captured Teresa's hand. "Wait." She swallowed. "I'm sorry. I've kept people at arm's length so long that I sometimes can't even recognize kindness when it's right in front of me." Her throat went tight. "It *was* terrible."

Teresa's lip trembled. "And all this happened because of that stupid feud?"

Sarah nodded.

"It makes me so mad!" Teresa cried. "I can't stand thinking of that, of your baby and all of it. It's terrible."

"I wish it had made me mad, Teresa. Anger is a much more powerful emotion than despair." She wondered suddenly if it was appropriate for her to be discussing such things with Teresa, and let go of the girl's hand. "I'm sorry. I shouldn't worry you with any of this."

"I like it."

"Old gossip." Sarah managed a weak smile.

"Maybe." There was suddenly in those expressive eyes a very old soul peering out. Then it disappeared in the impish, sly smile of a young girl. "Maybe not old, huh? You still like him. I can tell."

Sarah couldn't help a swift glance over her shoulder. Through the windows she could see Eli, leaning against the wall, his face tipped up to the sun. The sight of his long brown throat made her want to—

"Sometimes," she said, looking away, "you can't put things right, no matter how much you want to. I made a big mistake," she added frankly, maybe for the first time. "And I have to pay for it."

Teresa only looked at her, gears whirring plainly. But the girl didn't share her conclusions.

Suddenly Sarah remembered something she'd been thinking about since her return to Taos. "Listen, there is something I'd like you to do for me."

"Name it."

Sarah took a piece of paper from her pocket. "My father is very ill and he isn't getting better. I want to find out if your great-grandmother might have a tea for him." She took a breath. "I can't ask Eli—he hates my father. And I can't go myself because it means going on Santiago land." She grinned. "I'm not crazy about getting shot."

Teresa chuckled. "Miguel might cut you up in little pieces."

"Really? He's the worst one?"

"Yeah," she said apologetically, and shrugged. "He hates your guts."

Sarah laughed. "Don't mince words, sweetie."

"Sorry." But she laughed, too. She looked at the paper Sarah had given her. "You just want me to give this to *Bisabuela* Octavia, and ask her to make a tea for him?"

"Yes. I've written down his symptoms."

"I don't know if she reads English, but I can read them to her." She rolled her eyes. "At least she'll *speak* English. My grandma won't. She's stubborn."

Like Sarah's father. Like Eli. Like Sarah herself. "It seems to run in both our families."

Teresa folded the paper and stood up.

"I still think you should try to make up with my uncle," she said wickedly, and rushed out before Sarah could answer.

Sarah stayed in the studio, watching them through the window as they left. Watching Eli move, so free and fluid, in jeans that fit like a soft, worn glove against his narrow hips. Watching his sober face as he carefully avoided her gaze.

And all she could think of was the taste of his flesh against hers, the press of his rain-flavored mouth, the glide of his hands down her back. The way he'd held her when she cried.

Somewhere in the region of her chest she felt the crumbling of the mortar that cemented her careful walls together. For days the bricks had been falling, until there was almost nothing left. She felt as rawly exposed as a bird without feathers, vulnerable to everything.

And for one long moment she thought longingly of her old life in New York. None of her friends there knew she'd given up a baby for adoption. None of them knew about the ancient war her family had with another one. No one knew anything but what she told them.

Maybe she ought to just pack her bags and leave. Explain to her parents that she couldn't face all this, that—

No. The one thing she couldn't do this time was run away. If she started running again now, she would never stop.

But even with that rational voice in her head, panic threatened to overwhelm her. She had to get out of here. She rushed into the main house and dialed the only phone number she knew. "Joanna," she said when her friend answered, "I'm stuck here. I don't have a car. I'm losing it. Please come get me."

Joanna didn't even hesitate. "I'll be right there."

"Tío," Teresa said when they drove away from Sarah's, "I want to go see Great-Grandma."

"What?"

"Don't take me home. I want to see Great-Grandma."

Stirring from his dark mood for the first time all day, Eli looked at her. "I know that expression. What are you up to?"

"Nothing." Her face said otherwise.

"I hope you aren't meddling in things you don't understand."

"Like I'm some little kid who can't see what's right in front of her. You treat me like a baby."

"What's right in front of you?" He turned into the graveled driveway that led to the farms, his nerves acutely aware. "Did Sarah say something?"

"No."

The answer was too fast, too urgent for Eli's taste. "I mean it, Teresa. Don't interfere. This isn't some game. I don't want you to get hurt."

"It isn't me who's hurt," she said.

He parked in front of his grandmother's house. "What's that supposed to mean?"

"You would know if you would just open your eyes and

look," she said, and opened the door. She jumped down
and turned back. "But just like all guys, the only thing you
care about is how you feel."

Exasperated, he leaned over to catch the door before she
could slam it. "You want to tell me what this is all about?"

She tossed her head, and he saw in the gesture a thousand
years of women stubbornly asking men to read their minds.
"No. Figure it out." She slammed the door.

Perplexed and annoyed, Eli watched her cross the grass
to his grandmother's house. What had he done to deserve
that?

He'd been planning to go home, maybe read awhile, and
catch up on some paperwork, but suddenly the idea of going to his lonely house and spending the evening alone held
no appeal. On the other hand, he was hardly fit company.
He ran through the possibilities in his head—he could call
a friend, go to a bar and have a drink with one of his
brothers, visit someone....

No. "Damn her!" He slammed his hand on the steering
wheel. What he wanted was to go to Sarah. Not with any
nefarious secondary purpose, though God knew he wanted
her. Needed her. But right now, he just wanted to be in her
company.

He hated himself for it. With a curse, he flung the truck
into gear and backed out. This had to end. It had to stop.
He needed to make love to her, to see what still lived between them—or find out if it had died. He needed to talk
to her about the baby, because the two of them had shared
a terrible, life-altering loss that had never, ever been allowed to heal. He wanted to know if this pain would go
away if he held her.

Teresa's words haunted him. *Just like all guys, the only
thing you care about is how you feel.*

When he got to the end of the driveway, he turned right
impulsively, driving north without a goal. The wind coming
in through the windows was warm, scented with evening,

and the fields of sage glowed a soft gray-green on either side.

Teresa was right. He had been considering only his own feelings. Clearly, Sarah would not or could not manage what was happening between them. And what did he do? Pushed her harder. Further. Forced her to acknowledge not only the growing passion between them, but the past as well, even when he suspected she would crumble to dust if he pushed too far.

He needed someone to talk to. Someone who was outside the situation, someone who had no personal stake in the outcome. Someone who would just listen. And he could not think of a single possibility. For the past ten years he'd been so completely focused on business that he'd had little time for friendships, and in all honesty, the members of his large family met his friendship needs. He thought of Jenny, the graphic designer with whom he'd become friends, and nearly pulled over before he realized how odd that would be.

Finally he thought of Thomas Concha, who had been his friend since high school, a man already settled and happy in his life. There had always been something calm about Thomas, too, a reasonable nature balanced with a strong sense of the absurd.

Feeling better, he took a right at a forked road that led to the reservation, and followed the winding roads through the lush, green plains that belonged to the Taos. Though the pueblo was famous and drew a huge crowd of tourists each year, few families still lived there. Many others had built homes on the outlying lands owned by the nation, land spreading out from Taos Mountain in undulating fields. He passed ranch homes and trailers and adobes, and finally took a smaller road that led to the Conchas' spread, nestled near the creek, with tall cottonwoods shading an attractive, brand-new adobe with a Spanish tile roof. In town, such a house would be worth a million dollars. Out here on Indian land, no movie star in the world could touch it. The thought made Eli smile as he got out of the truck.

A pair of shepherds came barking around the house, and redoubled their cheerful greetings as they recognized Eli. "Hey, guys," he said, letting them lick his hands. He heard voices and followed the sound to the side of the house, to a place beneath the trees where a wide patio lay, lit with candles against the dying day. At one corner a three-foot wall met a kiva-style fireplace that provided warmth and cheer in the spring and fall.

Three people clustered there. Joanna sat on a bench against the wall, her long tanned legs stretched lazily out in front of her, and Thomas sat in a chair by the wooden table. The other head, even from the back, was instantly recognizable, and Eli swore under his breath. He froze, unable to manage this last bit of bad luck. How was it possible?

Joanna caught sight of him. "The finger of fate strikes again," she said with a smile in her voice. "Sarah, look who's here."

He saw her shake her head, slowly, and then she stood and turned around. Eli saw she held the baby, dark and plump and sleepy, in her arms. "We don't seem to be able to avoid each other very well," she said, as much to the others as to him.

"I'm sorry," he said, raising his hands. He backed up. "I'll go. I was just…" He stopped, unable to think of what he'd been doing. Why he had come.

"Don't be silly, Elias," Joanna said. "We're all adults here. We've been friends for too many years to stop now. Come sit down. Sarah won't mind."

Across the damp-smelling grass, with a cool breeze from the creek blowing toward them, Eli looked at her, waiting. She did not have to speak, and she knew that; he saw her waver, shifting the sleepy baby closer as if to shield herself.

"I don't mind, Eli," she said.

So he moved forward, trying not to smell her skin as he passed, and took a chair on the graceful patio with his friends. The older dog, heavily black along his back, with only a little gold along his muzzle and in spots over his eyes, settled on his foot. Sarah sat back down on his left side.

The night fell cool around them, with hidden crickets whirring in the grass, and the slowing calls of birds, and the faint near-clatter of the flat cottonwood leaves. Thomas was learning to play guitar and picked out some country songs he liked, then Joanna took the instrument and played ballads, singing in her strong voice from Simon & Garfunkel and mournful Joan Baez. It made Eli smile. "You were born too late," he said to her, grinning through the dark. "You would have been happier singing in a park somewhere, with love beads around your neck."

She threw a tiny twig at him. "Shut up, Eli."

"Instead she had to make up some causes," Thomas said. "Can't waste that crusading spirit."

"You, too," she said, and threw another twig.

"Now see what happens?" Thomas said with a twinkle in his eye. "She gets married, has herself a baby and gets all soft. Probably be fat as a cow by next year."

Joanna only smiled serenely and put a hand over her belly. "Won't even take until next year. I'll be fat as a house by Christmas."

"Another baby?" Sarah exclaimed. "That's wonderful!"

"Congratulations," Eli said. Without thinking, he turned and rubbed the back of the baby Sarah held. The boy slumped, oblivious, his little mouth spilling clear saliva to her blouse, in the deepest of sleeps. "I can see why you'd want more. This one is a charmer."

"He sure loves Sarah," Thomas commented. "Followed her all over, lifting up his arms until she held him."

Sarah absently rubbed her chin lightly over the baby's head, a faint smile her only comment.

Till now, Eli had been able to keep everything at bay, taking pleasure in the comfort of friends, in the pleasure of feeling at ease with himself in the soft darkness. But looking at Sarah now, with the baby so happily slumped against her, brought everything back. He knew she was aware that he looked at her, but she didn't acknowledge it, only brushed her fingers over the tiny ones pressed against her breast. Candlelight gave a halo of light to the crown of her head, and spread a burnished line over the curve of her cheekbone and mouth.

A mournful feeling awakened in Eli. A feeling that said this should have been his, this quiet, this small comfortable gathering, the baby asleep, the bed waiting inside to hold him and the body of his wife.

He looked at Thomas, and his old friend stood up, touched his wife's head lightly and said, ''Me and Eli got man's business,'' in a mockingly macho voice that made the women smile.

Grateful, Eli followed him inside.

Chapter Ten

Inside, Eli accepted the cup of coffee Thomas poured for him. It smelled faintly of cinnamon. He poured in some milk and drank a little, remembering a Mexican chocolate drink his grandmother had often made for him when he had had a bad day at school. With the chemist portion of his brain, he wondered if cinnamon held some soothing quality, or if it maybe jolted the mood centers of the brain.

"So tell me," Thomas said.

Eli sank into a ladder-back chair and could not think how to go on. Words rose to his lips, then dissipated, none of them quite right. "I have barely slept since she came back," he said finally. "I think of her every minute."

"And you don't want to."

"Would you?"

Thomas pursed his lips. "Maybe not." He sipped his coffee, considering. "But maybe there's a reason."

"Yeah?"

Thomas chuckled.

"It's stating the obvious, but maybe you still have feelings for each other, huh? Not so strange. She came here to talk about you, you came here to talk about her." He lifted a shoulder. "Maybe you should talk to each other."

"She won't talk."

"At all?"

"She runs from the hard things."

"So start with the easy ones."

Eli blinked. "Oh."

Thomas slapped his shoulder, laughing. "Man, you always take things so seriously. Everything isn't that hard, you know. Gotta learn to just take one little step, then maybe another if the first one is okay. You don't have to do everything at one time." He winked. "Even back in high school, you did this number...what if, what if, what if, and you called it all down on your head. She got pregnant, her father locked you up, she got sent away and everybody lost everything."

Eli looked at him.

"Maybe this time you should think more about what you do want, instead of everything you don't." He cracked a grin. "You worry too much, man."

Eli gave him a rueful smile. "I have to think about this."

"Nope." Shaking his head, he reached over and took the coffee cup from Eli's hand. "That's your trouble, thinking all the time. Act, Elias." He gave the name its Spanish incantation, and said again, "Act."

Eli wondered if he had the courage. If he could face rejection if it came, if he could bear to lose her again. Once had nearly killed him. And he was older now, more set in his ways. He did not bend so easily anymore.

But suddenly, sitting there in the friendly kitchen made by a man and the wife he loved, Eli knew that was what he wanted. Another chance. A chance to build a life like the one Thomas had built, a life with children and a wife and the peace he knew some people found.

No. Not just any wife. He forced himself to take the next step in his self-examination. He wanted to find out if Sarah could still be that woman. Until he knew, he would never be free.

With a quick nod, he moved toward the patio. His heart pounded unevenly as he crossed the kitchen's clay tile floors, and passed through the living room with its broad, dark windows, then moved through the glass doors that led to the patio. There was an odd weakness in his elbows as he stepped into the darkness.

He looked at Joanna hard, and without a word she stood up. "I'll be right back."

Which left him standing alone in the cool night, alone with Sarah and a sleeping baby. He wanted to tell her what he thought about when he saw her with this baby, that he wished it was their own child, that he wished they'd had the chance...

But he remembered what Thomas had said, and started with something simple. "Will you let me drive you home, Sarah?" But that wasn't quite what he wanted. "Or maybe we could just take a drive?"

She raised her head. "Yes. I would like that." She paused. "The drive, I mean."

He held out his arms to help her with the baby, a weighted mass of unconscious child that swayed like a sack of sand. Eli held him close, smelling lotion and baby sweat, and he couldn't help putting his head down to the rosy cheek to inhale. "He smells so good."

Sarah bent and pressed a gentle kiss to the baby's head. Her hair brushed Eli's nose, and it seemed she lingered a heartbeat longer than she needed to, leaning close to both Eli and the baby. Then she ducked away without looking at him. "I'll wait here."

There was a deep, somehow comfortable quiet between them as they drove back toward town. Sarah sat with her hands folded in her lap, neatly seat-belted in the passenger seat. Eli did not invite her to move over, and she did not offer. "Do you have a preference?" he asked.

Sarah paused to think about it. "No, not really."

"I know a place," he said, and seemed to sit a little straighter, the decision made.

He took a side road away from the main body of town, going deeper into the rich blackness of a desert night. "There are so many people here now," Sarah commented, amazed at the pockets of lights that diluted the darkness. Mostly very expensive houses, on large tracts of land.

"It happened slowly for me—a house here and there, another little bunch. It must seem very strange to you."

"Yes."

Wind blew through the windows, smelling of rain, and along the ridge of mountains to the west, branches of lightning flickered silently and were gone. Sarah found herself relaxing, almost against her will, and let go of a breath she didn't know she'd been holding. She put her head back against the seat. "This is nice," she said. "It makes me remember—" She stopped, embarrassed, afraid the memory would ruin this careful peace between them.

He reached over the seat and took her hand. "Remember what?"

She turned her hand over to accept the offering of his touch. "Remember when we drove around all evening, just driving and driving, all over."

"Those are good memories for me."

The musical sound of his voice, warm and beautiful, added to her sense of well-being. "Me, too."

The truck bumped and bucked a little over the rough track. "Hang on," he said. "We're almost there." He drove a little farther, then turned and parked. "Come on," he said. "Let's sit outside, watch the storm come in."

Aware of a tingle of anticipation and worry, Sarah got out. Eli pulled the seat forward and grabbed a striped blanket, then walked to the end of the truck and pulled down the gate. Sarah followed more slowly. He waited for her.

When she joined him, he said, "Thomas said you came to talk to Joanna about me. I went to talk to him about you. He said maybe it would be better if we talk to each other."

"That depends on what you want to talk about, Eli."

"Nothing important." He tossed the blanket into the bed. "You used to be my best friend, Sarah. Maybe I'd just like to know if that might still be true."

The admission pierced her, and like nothing else could have, drew forth her honest response. "I missed you for years, Eli. Such a long time. It was like losing an arm—and what I missed the most was being able to tell you things. I've really never had another friend like you, ever since."

He bowed his head. "Same here." Gracefully he leapt into the back of the truck, and turned around to give her a hand.

Sarah jumped up, chuckling over the sparkling-clean rubber bed liner. "I can tell this is a hardworking truck," she said, tongue in cheek.

He laughed. "Oh, yeah. Much as I paid for it, I'd never fill it with a real load." He sat with his back braced against the cab and gestured toward her. "Come sit with me."

A pulse jumped in her belly, but she did as he asked, sitting down beside him. Only their knees touched, but it was enough.

"Are you cold?" he asked, lifting the blanket.

"Not at all."

He turned his face up to the sky. "How long do you think till the rain gets here?"

Sarah looked up. Ominous clouds boiled up to the west, racing toward the east, but in front of them was still a lot of star-studded sky. "Maybe two hours."

"You *have* been away a long time." He looked at his

watch, then the sky. "I say maybe forty-five minutes. Probably less."

"It's a bet." She breathed deeply, feeling the night and the cool air fill every corner of her lungs. "So, tell me, Eli. What matters to you these days?"

"Hmm. Good question. Work, mainly. I work a lot." He turned his head, and faint light played over his high cheekbones. "You?"

"Not much of anything anymore, somehow. That was the biggest reason I came home. I was just wandering all over the place with no purpose."

"You know what I think? You need to put your art back into your life."

She snorted. "I take pictures all day."

"Not that kind. Art, like you used to do."

Sarah thought of the kind of work she had done when he knew her. "I do miss it sometimes, the still lifes and landscapes."

"I still have some of your old ones."

"Really?" A rush of warmth went through her. "Like what?"

"There's one of a blue jay on a sunflower."

"I loved that picture!" Sarah exclaimed.

"Me, too. There's another one of a man with a cigarette, and my own favorite—one of a rose against a stucco background. There's sun on half and shadows on half. It's a great photo."

"I'm surprised you didn't tear them into pieces."

He shrugged. "I thought about it."

Sarah laughed, nudging him with her elbow. "That was not the right answer."

He braced his elbows on his knees, and gripped one wrist with the other hand. "Should I lie?"

"No. Just be kind."

"You changed the subject."

"I did?"

He leaned a little closer. "You always do when it comes to art or babies."

"I don't mean to." Her gaze fell on his mouth, not far from her reach if she wanted to sway a little, incline her head just the smallest bit. And wasn't that what she wanted? Wasn't that why she had agreed to "go for a drive"?

He looked at her, as if letting her decide. Sarah put her hand on his crooked elbow to brace herself. Then she swayed, and inclined her head, and brushed a kiss over his mouth.

"Is that what you want, Sarita?" He didn't move, his dark eyes suddenly liquid. "To kiss me?"

"Yes," she said simply, and kissed him again, shifting so she could reach him more easily. He tasted of cinnamon and coffee and a thousand lost dreams, a flavor that was nostalgic and promising at once. She paused, and lifted her fingers to touch his lips.

"I love your mouth. I didn't know how much when I left here. I didn't know it was so rare."

He said nothing, only slid his long, slim hand beneath her hair, around her neck, and kissed her again. Heat and restraint mixed in his touch, in the firm but loose way he held her. As he kissed her, in that way that he had, so intensely and skillfully at once, Sarah tasted all the seasons that had passed while they were apart, tasted the falling leaves of autumn, and the wood smoke of winter, and the dampness of spring. But most of all, she tasted summer, the summer that was now, with both of them in it, and the summer of their lives—their youthful days together.

It made her feel supple and strong, that taste, and she wanted to give it back to him. She sat down again, then leaned back, pulling him with her, so their arms and hands would be free, so they could touch each other. He came with her, and they flowed into a single twining vine, outstretched on the bed of the truck, the blanket below them, their legs tangled, their arms embracing, their torsos pressed close.

Sarah made a sound of pleasure, a sigh and a cry together, without ever taking her mouth from his, for she couldn't bear to stop drinking of his kisses. But she raised her hands to his thick, wavy hair, renewing her memories of the way it slid through her fingers, and she clasped his head, so she could shape her palms to his skull. She moved her hands down, over his neck, his shoulders, down his back, to his hips, and all the area between, touching all of it.

As if he had the same need, he opened his hand and gauged the shape of her chin, her ear, her neck. He touched her shoulder, her arm, her breast, her waist, her thigh.

He raised his head then, to look at her, touch her face. Twice it seemed he might speak, but he did not, only passed his fingers across her brow, kissed her, touched her chin, kissed her, moved lower. He held her gaze as his hand fell upon the buttons of her blouse, and he began to open them, one by one. Only when he could not reach the last one did he look away, so he could find it, and undo it. He pushed the fabric away, and put his hand around her breast, encased in ordinary cotton, then raised his head to look at her again. "It feels like a dream to touch you," he said, his voice raw.

Sarah ached at the stillness of his fingers over her, and she lifted a hand to his, and pressed him closer, moving her hips into him to feel him in return. "No dream," she said.

He uttered a fierce oath, and this time when he kissed her, she knew there was no turning back, not for either of them. The kiss tasted of blood and fire, of sorrow and anger and loneliness. She arched against him, welcoming it, meeting it, her hands bringing his shirt up so she could touch his back even as his hands pulled away her bra and bared her breasts.

It sounded like wind roaring, like thunder cracking. She was mad with her need of Eli, and when he bent his head to her breast, she cried out and arched into him, her fingers gripping his shoulders.

In that wildness, in that heat and need, she shifted, and pushed at him so she could reach his shirt. He rose to his knees and took off his shirt as Sarah reached for his belt, adroitly managing buckle and buttons to free him, and it came to her that she'd never seen him, not this part of him. She'd always been too shy to look.

But now there was no room, no time, no ease for looking. She pushed his jeans from him as he freed her own buttons and snaps, and she lifted her hips to help him skim her jeans from her body.

And then they were clasped together, flesh to flesh, mouth to mouth, and Sarah tasted the salt of tears on their lips, on their hungry tongues, and even before they joined, they melded, as they always had, him to her, and her to him, and then he grasped her hips, and Sarah reached between their bodies to guide him, and they were one, body to body, soul to soul.

It was so fierce she knew she would be bruised and scratched, that both of them would be, and not only physically. She felt a shoulder bruise, felt the click of teeth and a quick pain. They bumped chins and a knee got trapped, and it didn't matter, none of it mattered as Eli held her close and thrust himself into her, and she met him, feeling whole again. She held him fiercely as he met his release, and clasped his head between her hands and whispered his name, over and over.

Elias. Elias. Elias.

And then she was set free, her soul tangling with his, as she soared into the completeness that she had found only with him. She held him as tightly as she could, her arms and her legs wrapping him close, wanting to somehow make him part of her, so he could never be torn from her again.

He didn't notice it had begun to rain until they had lain together, spent and entwined, for a long time. It began lightly, a few drops over his shoulders, on his hair. It gained strength quickly, wetting his back and thighs, and in his joy, he lifted his face to it, taking it as a blessing.

Sarah laughed, opening her mouth to it, but when he would have moved, she looped a leg around his and would not let him. "You're my umbrella," she said.

He shifted and let the rain fall on her breasts, a cold rain, big drops of it. She tipped back her face, exposing her neck, and opened her mouth again, her eyes closed. As he looked down on her, feeling rain on his shoulders and back and buttocks, a wave of intense emotion washed through him, engulfing and unnameable.

Sarah.

Like a man drinking from a holy well, he bent his head to her throat and sipped the rain. He drank from rain-beaded freckles on her shoulders, and from the swell of a breast. But the rain fell harder, and it was cold.

He lifted his head, feeling water drip from his nose and chin. "Let's get inside the cab."

As if to underscore the urgency, a flash of lightning struck somewhere close by, and a deafening crash of thunder followed much too quickly. Sarah sat up and gathered her clothes in a bundle against her chest, then grabbed the blanket and pulled it over her head. "Hurry!" she cried.

He jumped from the truck, feeling half-dry dust beneath his bare feet, the rain on his head and shoulders, the brush of a wind over his belly and thighs. Impulsively he lifted his face and closed his eyes, and raised his arms to embrace the night and the desert, sending thanks to the forces that had let this night come about. He felt the rain wash over his flesh, and felt it was a baptism, a fresh beginning, and he laughed, opening his mouth as Sarah had done, to bring some rain inside him, too.

"Elias," Sarah said, her voice hushed.

He looked at her, wondering for a fleeting moment if he should feel foolish. Impossible. He was too full for foolishness, and what he saw on her face was a kind of wonder. All the bitter and wary hardness was gone from her features, making her eyes guileless, her skin fresh. Her eyes fell, touching him, all of him, and he saw desire flare her nostrils. "I never looked at you, back then," she said, and slipped from the truck to put her free hand against his belly. "You're so beautiful."

He captured her, swung her into his arms, then bent a little. "Get my clothes."

She snagged the jeans, but the shirt was too far away, and he felt her shiver a little against him. "That's enough."

He carried her to the door, and when she opened it, he put her inside. From her arms, he took his jeans and standing in the rain, put them on, wet and heavy. "*Now* I'm cold," he said. He closed the door and carefully moved around the truck, watching for goatheads and prickly pear. He climbed in his side and started the engine, turning all the heater vents to high. Sarah huddled in the blanket, wrapped in it from head to toe. He slid over and kissed her nose. "Let's go somewhere warm, huh?"

"Okay. My house?"

He shook his head. "Mine. You'll like it there."

A flicker of hesitation. Then, "All right."

A little swell of something painful and sweet filled his belly. "Don't bother to get dressed," he said wickedly.

She laughed. "It hadn't even crossed my mind."

This time, as he drove, she moved in close to him. There seemed no need to speak with words until they reached the gate of Santiago Farms. A light shone from his mother's house, but Eli was glad to see no other vehicles parked in her driveway. He drove by, then past the fields and the plant, and she put her hand on his arm. "Promise you'll bring me out of here before dawn."

He chuckled. "Afraid of the angry hordes?"

"I'd just rather start my day more peacefully." Her grip tightened. "Promise, Eli."

"I promise."

At his house he parked and told her to wait while he came around. "I'll carry you," he said.

"Don't be silly. I can walk."

"There are stickers."

"You don't have *your* shoes on."

"I'm a macho guy, though. You're only a delicate female."

"Move," she said, and pushed him out of her way. When her feet hit the ground, she halted. "Yeow!" she said mildly, and bent to take a sticker out of her foot.

He chuckled and swept her into his arms. Sticking to the flagstones, he carried her to the porch, breathing hard. "You're heavy," he said.

"Hey, you're the macho guy. I'm just a delicate female."

He put her down, putting his hand over his heart as if he was going to have a heart attack. "Yeah, real delicate."

Sarah laughed, then shivered as a wind slammed into the house. "I'm freezing."

"I know just the thing." He took her hand and led her inside, through the living room, down the hall, into the bathroom. Feeling anticipation fill his chest again, he closed the door and turned on the hot water to fill the room with steam.

Then he turned to her and deliberately pushed the blanket from her, and stepped back. Her hair was stuck to her head, and she lifted her chin a little, almost defiantly. "I can't believe I'm here," she said, and took a breath. "I can't believe how much I want you again."

He kissed her, but as steam filled the small room, enveloping and warm, he stripped the heavy denim from his legs and moved in close again, putting his hands on her shoulders and letting their naked bodies brush. ''Let me wash your back.''

But they did not make it that far. Sarah lifted her hands and touched him boldly, and they were making love again with the same fierce, rushed intensity of the first time, cloaked now in steam instead of cold, their mouths and flesh slick and slippery.

Only afterward did they get into the shower and wash each other gently, taking time to see, murmuring in pleasure and surprise and apology for the small marks they had left, bruises they'd made on each other. Sarah made him kneel, and washed his hair, and he returned the favor. When the water ran cold they wrapped themselves in towels and went to his bed, without pausing to turn on the lights, just curling together to make love again, this time slowly, gently, sweetly.

Eli's last thought before he slipped into a dizzy, sated sleep was that she still fit his arms exactly. And what a luxury it was to make love to her in a bed, and go to sleep holding her.

Chapter Eleven

Sarah dreamed she was flying through a sun-drenched sky, her body light as the wind. Below her was the city of Taos, the adobe walls taking the light and reflecting it back, making the town look like Cibola, the mythical city of gold that had drawn the Spanish conquistadors. It was beautiful from here, she thought as she flew, so peaceful.

She became aware that she was not alone, and she looked over to see that Eli, too, was flying with her. He wore no shirt. His shoulders gleamed with copper lights from the sun, and his black hair blew back from his face, showing the high, broad brow. She smiled at him.

He pointed behind him, and there was a young girl, her black hair very long, floating out behind her like streamers. She looked like Teresa, but more like Eli, and she had Sarah's gray eyes. With a swell of happiness, Sarah said, "I've been looking for you! I'm so glad you found us."

Her daughter smiled. "I didn't want to hurt my other mother's feelings, but I wanted to see you."

In her dream, Sarah wanted to say something else, but she was so happy at seeing her daughter that she forgot to concentrate on flying, and she suddenly found herself plummeting toward the earth, crying out Eli's name.

She awakened with a jerk, her arms braced to break her fall. It took a moment to understand that she had been dreaming. She struggled to hold on to the images, but they faded too fast—she couldn't remember what had awakened her. All that lingered was a sense of happiness undercut by loss.

Blinking, she let go of the struggle to reclaim the dream images. But it took several moments longer to understand where she was. In Eli's bed.

With Eli in it.

His windows had no covering, and the first fingers of sunlight were creeping into the room. She looked at him, lying asleep beside her, and her heart gave a wild thud. He sprawled carelessly on his side, his head on one outstretched arm. A sheet covered him to the waist, but she knew he was naked. As she was.

It hurt, looking at him, hurt in a pleasant way, all through her stomach, and hurt in a painful way, like a sword in her chest. In that sleeping face, in that particular arrangement of features, that splay of lashes, that fall of blackest hair over his arm, were contained all the dreams she'd once had.

The night they had spent together now seemed blurred and wild, and yet she could not regret it. This morning her heart felt full for the first time in more years than she could remember. Not satisfied. Not warmed. Overflowing.

"Eli," she whispered, and touched his face.

He stirred and his hand moved, as if he sought something. She caught it and kissed his fingers, saying his name again.

He came awake suddenly, and his dark beautiful eyes fell upon her face. A mix of bewilderment and joy blazed suddenly in his gaze, and he reached for her, pulled her under him and kissed her. "I thought I dreamed it."

He smelled of himself, and of sex, and of shampoo, and Sarah could happily have lain all day right there in his arms, but the need to flee Santiago land was more urgent. "You have to take me home," she said regretfully.

"In a minute," he promised hoarsely, "let me just hold you a minute, to remember this. So if—"

"If?"

"If you don't come back, I will still have this in my heart."

"Oh."

He stroked her face. "It was never us that was the trouble, was it? We always had *this*—" His fingertips brushed her eyebrow, smoothed the line of her cheek. "Our world, apart from them."

She smiled up at him, put her hand on the shelf of his shoulder. "Sarah and Eli's Magic Place."

"Yeah." Soberness filled his eyes. "And it's still there, isn't it?"

Pierced, she could only nod. Then she put her hands on his face, kissed his mouth. "Yes," she managed finally, and closed her eyes. "It's still there. Still here."

He shifted to put his weight on one elbow, and pushed the sheet from her body. Unselfconscious, Sarah allowed it. With one finger he traced the branching, faint scar of her stretch marks, scars she had never minded, because they helped her to remember. He said nothing, but Sarah knew what he was thinking.

"She was almost nine pounds when she was born," Sarah said before she knew she would. It wasn't as hard as she thought to let the image come back. "I went into labor at six o'clock one evening, and didn't have her until almost midnight the next day. She was so big."

Sarah could feel his stillness, and pressed on. "They usually didn't let the girls hold their babies when they were giving them up for adoption, but there was one Sister who disagreed with that. And because it was so late at night, she let me…'' Her voice gave out as the images returned. ''Hold her.''

''If it makes you sad, Sarita, don't.'' His strong hand brushed her hair back. ''I don't have to know right now. Just tell me a little at a time.''

She shook her head, feeling heat behind her eyes. ''It does make me sad,'' she said, and looked up at him, un-ashamed of the tears that welled in her eyes. ''But you have a right to know.''

He nodded slowly, his hand moving on her brow.

''She was red and tiny and squished, from being born. But she had so much hair I could have braided it. And she looked—'' she took his hand ''—exactly like you. Your eyes. Your hair. Your mouth. Even these long limbs. I'm sure she's very tall by now.''

Eli simply moved close and put his face into her neck. ''I'm so sorry.''

''So am I,'' she whispered. ''There has not been a single day since she was born that I didn't think about her. Not one single day.'' At last she turned to him. ''Eli, I did want her. It wasn't you, or us, or anything. I just didn't know what to do.''

''It isn't your fault.''

''That's not true,'' she said. ''It is my fault. I was the one who signed the papers. I'm the one who made the decision. I didn't have to give in, but I did.'' The smallest, meanest kernel of truth worked its way to her lips. ''Some-times I think I did it to get even with my father. Because I knew someday he'd be sorry that he made me do that. And it was the only way I could get even with him.''

''Oh, no, Sarah. No.'' He put both hands around her head. ''It was because you were lost. Because he broke you. Don't blame yourself.''

She closed her eyes. He would never understand. He

would never know what it was like to have a child move inside, feel the tiny feet and the little hands, and then feel it move through you, come into the world. She didn't blame him, but she knew without a doubt that it *was* her fault.

He kissed her ear. Her eyes, her mouth. Tiny butterfly kisses meant to impart comfort. "One day, you will heal, Sarah. One day, you'll forgive yourself."

"Maybe," she said.

An alarm went off, obnoxious beeping, and he jumped up to run across the room and shut it off. "Sorry," he said, turning, comfortable in his nudity.

A pulse of hunger came alive in her belly as she admired him. "Will you come to my house tonight? For supper?"

He paused, then sat on the side of the bed. "Are we going to do this, then?"

"I don't know, Eli," she said as honestly as she could. With one hand she traced the sleek curve of his upper arm. "I have no idea what I'm feeling or what I'll feel next week. Can we just take it one step at a time?"

It wasn't quite the answer he wanted; he bowed his head, away from her. "I'll come." He recovered, gave her a sideways glance. "Promise I won't have to go to the emergency room for food poisoning after?"

Sarah raised her eyebrows. "No promises, but I'll do my best."

He laughed, then patted her bottom. "Get dressed. I'll take you home."

The morning was cool and damp-smelling. Dew clung to the spines of cacti and made beadwork of the loops on yucca and spiderwebs. Sarah paused on Eli's front porch. "This is beautiful, Eli."

He stopped and gazed out over the view with her. "That's why I built here. At night it looks like a thousand stars fell to earth, all the lights glittering in the valley."

"I don't just mean the view," she said. "The land, too.

I've never been here before. I didn't know you had so much." It was hilly, with sharp outcroppings of rock, and an arroyo that would be hidden from any angle other than this. Below, a long tall building stuck up above the low juniper and piñon trees that grew higher on the hill. Spread around it for acres and acres were fields of crops. "I wish I could see the herb fields up close."

"Really? We can stop on the way out."

A press of fear made her shake her head. "I'm too afraid."

Eli laughed. "I'd protect you."

"Another time."

He nodded, and they got into the truck to drive down. Sarah quelled the urge to duck down in the seat as they came to lower sections. There were already workers in the field.

"They're working so early," Sarah commented.

"The flowers of most herbs have to be harvested before the sun gets on them and dries out the oils."

She gazed at the scene, her mind capturing quick shots of the gold-glazed fields and the men bent over the plants. Beyond, behind a sturdy fence, a pair of goats frolicked with some sheep with long, brownish gray wool. A man and a black-and-white dog herded them up a hill. "Are those merinos?" Sarah asked in surprise.

"Yes. The wool was out of fashion for a long time, but it's coming back now. We have a hundred head. That wool brings in a tidy profit." He slowed. "Sure you don't want to stop?"

She met his gaze, smiling to show she meant no offense. "I'm sure. But I wish I had my camera."

"Another day."

At the cottage he didn't turn off the engine. "I have a meeting this morning early," he said. "I have to get home and shower." He touched her face. "I'll see you tonight."

She made her way down the path to her cottage, humming happily under her breath. In the courtyard was the big stray tom, waiting patiently, his tail switching. "Good morning," she said to him, and he meowed plaintively, rising to rub against her leg. "Are you hungry?"

He meowed again and trotted over to the door with her, hopefully, she thought. It made her sad—obviously he had once belonged to someone and had been abandoned to make his own way as well as he could. Sarah glanced over her shoulder. "Okay," she said, "you can come in, but just this once."

She found a can of tuna, which she opened and put on a dish for him, along with a bowl of water. "Don't get used to it, okay? The next people who come here might not care about stray cats." The thought of leaving him to that fate troubled her. She wondered if she might be able to find a home for him before she left.

It wasn't until she was untying her shoes that she realized that she did still expect to leave Taos. Expected to go back to the career she'd built on the East Coast, back to her sublet apartment and her friends and the whirl of travel. A tennis shoe hit the wooden floor with a heavy thud. Was that what she still wanted?

She didn't know—and what was more, this morning she didn't care. This morning she wanted only to be in this moment, with a stray cat keeping her company, and the whole day ahead of her to spend as she pleased. She wanted to revel in the well-loved glow that enveloped her, and be free to enjoy the little sensual shocks of memory that pulsed through her. She pulled off her blouse and breathed in the scent of Eli that remained on the fabric. She stood to un-button her jeans and felt a tiny pull of muscles along her sides. In the bathroom she reached for the shower faucet and thought of her last shower, and Eli washing her hair.

Turning to take a scrunchie from the drawer to pull up her hair, she caught sight of herself in the mirror, and paused to see her body as he might have. It was only then that she saw the little bruises and scratches, the swollen look of her mouth, the red mark on her shoulder, one very low on her breast. Her clothes would hide them. There was another on her neck below her ear.

Her hair would cover it, she thought, but she leaned forward, touching the mark, remembering with a deep sense of pleasure the moment it had been made. Her skin had always shown bruises like this, and when they were teenagers, she'd made a rule he couldn't even kiss her neck. But she loved it, and he knew that, so he grew adept at pleasing her, leaving the marks where they would not show. When they were in school, or eating lunch, he'd sweep her hair aside and kiss the marks, making her remember all over again what they'd been doing.

Steam obscured the mirror and Sarah straightened, realizing that she was aroused all over again. She leaned against the door, closing her eyes, letting all of it, the rain and his mouth and their joinings, swell up in her like pure pleasure. Pure joy.

With effort, she shook off the drifting haze of sensuality and adjusted the water, chuckling when she realized she'd never had to resort to cold showers before. Only Eli made her feel this way. Only Eli.

As she stepped under the spray, gasping at the cold, a fist of terror punched through the sensual glow. Fear that she was in over her head, fear that this was too much, fear that one or the other of them would be hurt. Fear that—

With the control learned over years of denial, Sarah simply pushed the thoughts away. She didn't have to think about the fear today. Today she would simply live in the moment.

After she'd dressed and eaten, Sarah loaded a camera bag with film, her favorite old Minolta and two lenses, and wandered out into the world. The golden vision of Eli's land this morning, the peaceful, quiet images, had roused a creative fire in her, and with a sense of anticipation she joined the flow of tourists, letting her feet take her wherever they would.

And the world rewarded her with beautiful and poignant and earthy images: two old Hispanic men sitting in the shade of the plaza, drinking coffee; a tiny girl in a blue dress, trying to catch a pigeon; two elderly tourists arguing over a map. Up the road a way, a Native American man in obviously fancy dance dress rushed out of a bead shop, tiny brown bag in hand, and she lifted the camera, amused that someone would have to make an emergency bead stop. Through the lens she saw he had a giant safety pin in his mouth. He stopped by his truck and scrambled in the bag. Seeing Sarah, he took the pin out of his mouth and mugged for the camera, spreading his lovely arms to show his costume, and Sarah laughed, pleased by his beauty. He called out his name to her, and she lifted a hand in thanks. Obviously he'd been a subject before.

She wandered farther afield, down a side street, and shot the turquoise doorways and windows of very old adobe houses, remembering the color kept out evil spirits. On a back road bordering a field she shot wildflowers and single trees, and landscape photos suitable for postcards. That was always a hard trick—taking a wide-view landscape that meant anything at all—but she did her best, trying to capture the layers of color, the promise of heat, the look of sunlight shimmering over an acequia.

Kneeling in the dirt on a barely used track to shoot a stand of cattails in the acequia, she found herself remembering what Eli had said the night before—that she needed to find a way to put her art back into her life. Her fashion work required expertise and creativity, but it was very structured.

Her youthful dreams had never centered around commercial photography of any kind, although she'd known she might have to do calendar or postcard work to support herself. As a girl, she'd dreamed of following the tradition of art in the valley. This morning had given her back small, lost pieces of herself, had made her feel whole and well and—

Happy. She smiled in surprise at that thought, and wandered back to her cottage, sunburned and hungry. She let the cat out and scrounged for something for lunch in the bare cupboards. If she were to cook for Eli this evening, she'd have to get to the market.

Cook for Eli. She chuckled, wondering if he'd mind cold cereal, and then more seriously wondered what she could make. She was pretty handy with various salads, but suspected he'd want something more substantial.

The phone rang, and Sarah picked it up distractedly.

"Ms. Greenwood?" Teresa said.

"Yes, Teresa. Did you get the tea?"

"That's why I'm calling." She made a tsking sound. "I went there yesterday and my *bisabuela* wouldn't give it to me. She said she'd make it, but you have to come get it."

"Me? Did she say why?"

"She said she has to tell you how to give him the medicine. That's the only way you can have it, if you come get it yourself."

"Oh." Sarah thought of the drive down the mountain this morning, trying to remember if she'd seen an old woman in the fields. "I wonder if—" She broke off. "Never mind. Did she say when?"

"She said you should come at three this afternoon. I don't know why she picked then, though. Everybody is around at that time."

To punish her, Sarah thought. If she wanted the tea badly enough, she had to brave the entire Santiago clan to get it. She closed her eyes, wondering if she had enough courage. "Thanks for trying, Teresa. I don't know if I can do it or not. We'll see."

"Okay. I just wanted to tell you."

"See you tomorrow. We should be able to finish up, and start choosing which photos you want in your portfolio this weekend. Are you up for that?"

"I'm s-o-o up for it."

"Good. See you then."

It was only as she hung up the phone that she let the full import of the conversation sink in. It felt like a challenge, a test. Did she have the courage?

The girl she'd been would never have been able to do it. Sarah doubted she could have done it even as recently as yesterday. Today she picked up the phone and called her mother. "Can I borrow your car for a little while this afternoon?"

Mabel sounded peevish and tired. "I suppose so. Are you planning to come over for supper?"

A twinge of guilt touched her as she thought of her plans with Eli and how her parents would react if they knew why she wouldn't be eating with them. "I can't, not tonight. But I only have a very short errand to run, and I'll visit for a while then, okay? Do you need anything?"

"Well, I wouldn't mind if you wanted to go to the grocery store for me while you're out."

"No problem. Make a list."

"And maybe you could pick up some of that ice cream your dad likes so much."

"All right." The twinge of guilt grew a little more insistent. "Are you okay, Mom?"

"Oh, I'm fine. Just tired of this hot weather. You'd think September would be a little cooler."

Sarah made a mental note to pick up a six-pack of beer for her mother. It was her secret vice, one she didn't think she ought to indulge, but loved anyway. Garth couldn't drink because of his medications, but Mabel liked to take a beer into the backyard just before bed. She said it helped her unwind, and never gave her a hangover the way the sleeping pills did.

"I'll be over in a few minutes, Mom."

Eli had trouble concentrating at his meeting. For one thing, the weather was extremely hot. At eleven, he heard on the radio the temperature was ninety-two, and it felt it. It was muggy from the heavy rain the night before, and the combination of humidity and blazing sun made tempers short.

For another, he'd not had much sleep the night before, and he couldn't stop yawning. He considered going up to his house for a short siesta, but thought instead of his mother's cool basement. An hour in the dark, cool rooms, and he'd be a new man. Especially if she had some tamales left from the batch she'd made for a birthday party the week before.

He found her in her sewing room, working on a quilt for one of the cousins who was expecting a baby. "Got any tamales left, Ma?" he asked.

She answered in Spanish. "There's some in the big freezer. Heat me up a couple, too, please." She took pins out of the fabric, her glasses sliding down on her nose. "Teresa made some sun tea. Maybe look on the back porch."

He found the tea and heated a pile of tamales in the microwave. In his dull state, he burned his fingers taking the husks from one of them, and dropped it with a splat on the floor. Definitely time for a nap.

He took the plate to his mother, and fixed another for himself. Two of his brothers and one sister came in as he was heading downstairs. Miguel carried a huge bag of take-out hamburgers. "Hey, I didn't know there was tamales."

"There aren't anymore." He left them to gather around the kitchen table, and went downstairs. Because her house was close to the plant and the siblings who worked there often went to her house for lunch, many of the others also stopped by at lunch. Eli hoped he'd have the basement to himself. He turned on the television to watch a game show as he ate, then stretched out on the couch and fell into a deep sleep.

He wasn't sure what wakened him, but it was sudden. Blinking, he looked at his watch. Almost three. He'd slept nearly two hours. Overhead, dismayed voices rose and fell, not quite an argument, and he wondered what was going on. He collected the remains of his lunch and went upstairs.

Miguel turned from the window, a bitter look on his mouth. "She's driving her father's car, right in here, as bold as can be."

"What? Who is?"

Teresa materialized at his side. In a quiet voice she said, "It's Sarah. She asked me to get a tea for her father from Great-Grandma Octavia."

Still befuddled from his nap, Eli shook his head. "I don't get it."

"Sarah," she said, "is outside."

Suddenly it penetrated. He bolted for the door and nearly ran into his mother, who stood on the steps with her arms crossed, her chin lifted in a haughty expression as Sarah stepped out of a late-model Buick to speak to a field hand. Asking directions, obviously.

"What is she doing here, Elias?"

His heart felt like a rock in his chest. "I don't know," he said harshly, and walked toward the car.

"Sarah!"

She turned, putting a hand over her eyes to shade them from the sun. That same sunlight struck the top of his head with fierce late-afternoon weight as he walked toward her. The hesitant welcome on her mouth faded as he approached.

"You could come so your father could have medicine," he said, his pride smarting, "but you couldn't stay for me earlier, so I could share the morning with you."

"Eli, don't. Please." She glanced over her shoulder.

"I'm so nervous my tongue is sticking to the roof of my mouth. But I had to come. She would only give it to me personally."

"You should have asked me, Sarah. I would have got medicine for your father. A few ounces of hemlock should do it."

All expression bled from her face and Eli found himself looking at a stranger. "Excuse me," she said. "I have an appointment." She climbed into her car.

For one moment Eli considered just letting her go, but his anger was too wild, his sense of betrayal too deep. He rushed to the side of the car and put his hand on the hood, bending to look at her through the window. "I can't believe you," he said. "I can't believe you still put him ahead of your own happiness."

She stared out the windshield, her face stony. Around her mouth was a thin white line. "Let me go, Eli."

On her shoulder was a love bruise, edging out from the neckline of her dress, and the sight of it was like a bucket of water over his raging emotions. He reached in through the window to touch her, but she flinched away.

Slowly he straightened, took his hand off the car, feeling mingled regret and panic and fury. "Sarah—"

"Don't bother to come to supper," she said, and threw the car in gear.

Watching the car pull away, he swore, a feeling of despair welling in him. They were doomed. Doomed to repeat all of it, unless one or the other of them could break the cycle. He seemed unable, and Sarah seemed unwilling.

He slowly became aware of the eyes watching him. From the fields, from the porch of his mother's house. Probably from the offices of the plant, as well. With as much dignity as he could muster, he turned and moved toward the plant, refusing to meet anyone's gaze.

Safely behind his closed office door, he allowed himself

to put his head in his hands, wondering how a few moments could change everything so drastically. Again.

It was her father. Always her father. His dark emotions metastasized into hate. Hate that was black and cold and hard, hate focused upon one man, the man who had tried to steal his life, and, given the chance, would steal it again.

And as it always had, the coldness steadied him, made him strong. To reinforce it, he named the sins Garth Greenwood had committed against him. He called forth the indignity of his arrest, and the weeks in jail. He thought of Sarah, sent into exile and bullied into giving up their child for adoption. He thought of the baby. The baby that Sarah still carried in her heart, an open wound that would never heal.

And he thought of the years that had been stolen from him. He could not get them back, but he vowed this time he would not lose the war with Garth. This time, Eli was stronger.

This time, Eli would be the victor, and Sarah his prize.

Chapter Twelve

Sarah followed the directions the man had given her, up a road that was little more than a dirt track. It gave her time to calm her racing heart, shove Eli and her nervousness and everything else out of her head. She found the old woman's cottage easily enough. By the size of the ancient cottonwoods towering over the small Territorial adobe, Sarah thought it must sit over an underground spring. The window and door frames were painted traditional turquoise, and the walls had been freshly mudded, probably during the past spring. Sarah could almost make out the handprints of the woman's daughters and granddaughters in the smooth adobe finish—or maybe her sons and grandsons. Chores were not always divided by gender lines these days, after all.

The old woman herself stood between rows of an impressive vegetable garden. At her knees were tomato plants with ripening fruit the size of baseballs, and behind her the corn had tassled, but still hung in soft, pale green hanks.

Impulsively, Sarah grabbed the camera at her side and got out of the car. She leaned on the hood and focused carefully, shooting a quick series of the woman in her garden, feeling she should ask permission, yet feeling it was urgently important that she shoot *this* photo, right now.

Mrs. Santiago looked up as Sarah shot the last picture, and by her smile Sarah could see that the camera alarmed her not at all. Still, as Sarah approached, she called out, "I hope you don't mind that I took your picture. You and your garden are a happy sight."

"No." She waved a hand, coming out of the garden to greet her. She was well past eighty, but Sarah saw only a hint of stiffness in her movements. She was small, with white hair pulled back into a bun at the nape of her neck. Her thin body was covered with a purple-and-white-print housedress. On her feet were rubber plastic thongs that matched the purple in her dress and were dotted with glitter of the sort young girls wore with their shorts.

"You must be Sarah," the old woman said. "So long I have heard your name, and I have never seen you."

"Same here, Mrs. Santiago. I'm glad to finally meet you."

She waved a hand. "Call me Octavia." Her dark eyes glittered. "Or *bisabuela,* like everybody else."

Sarah nodded. Octavia she could manage. *Bisabuela* seemed a little scary, for no reason she could pinpoint.

"Let's go inside," Octavia said. "I have made iced tea for us to drink while we talk."

Sarah waited respectfully for the woman to make her slow but steady way across the yard, then walked behind her to the steps, where Octavia paused. "Come, Sarah, give me your hand. My knee, she ain't what she used to be."

Sarah offered her elbow and Octavia leaned on her. She smelled of sunlight and sage, a scent that reminded Sarah acutely of Eli, and she scowled.

Octavia settled in an overstuffed blue chair and pointed

to an opening between the kitchen and living room, where a blue glass pitcher of tea waited. "Bring that here. Sit on the couch."

It was surprisingly cool within the thick walls, even without a swamp cooler. Sarah fetched the tea and glasses, and poured for each of them before she settled on the couch as she'd been commanded.

"So, tell me," Octavia said. "Your papa is pretty sick, eh?"

"Yes. Nothing is really helping."

"I know." She took her time sipping tea. "It's in his heart, you know?"

Sarah nodded. "Yes. His asthma has put a strain on his heart. He had a heart attack three months ago."

"No, no. Inside." She pointed to her chest. "His soul."

"Oh." Sarah smiled at the misunderstanding. "I see."

"You been seeing my grandson again, yeah?"

Sarah took a breath, opened her mouth to deny it, then thought better of it. The scene in the yard below rushed back and a physical pain went through her chest. "We have been, but I think there's too much in the past for us to overcome."

Octavia folded her hands in her lap. "This war has gone on too long."

Sarah nodded wearily. "Tell me about it."

"You can stop it, Sarita."

The endearment wounded, but also made her want to please. "Me? No, I tried." She bowed her head. "I failed."

"No, not yet." She reached into a bag at her feet and took out a baggie filled with herbs and held it up in the air. "This tea is what I made for your papa. It will help him if he drinks it every day." She didn't hand it over. "But you must do one thing—you must tell him where it came from."

"He won't drink it if I do."

"Let him have the first cup without telling him. Let him see it makes him feel better. Then tell him."

Sarah frowned. "I don't understand. Why?"

Octavia grew serious. Her gaze shifted, not to any external view, but one within. "When I was fourteen, my brother fought a Greenwood boy. It was a terrible, foolish fight," she said. "My brother was a—" she seemed to struggle for the word "—I think you say 'hothead.' He had to have his knife with him all the time. I was there, you know. The Greenwood boy only said hello to me, and my brother started a fight, and he ruined that boy's face. That was your grandfather."

"I've heard the story," Sarah said quietly. She'd heard all of them at one time or another.

"Two weeks later they found my brother dead in a ditch, his head smashed." Octavia looked at her, shook her head. "So foolish. All of it.

"When your papa put Elias in jail, I dreamed that he got out and killed your father. You would not have known your love in those days, Sarah. He was like a bonfire, burning hot, eating everything up in front of him. He was mad with grief."

At the terrible image of her father's blood on Eli's hands, all the air left Sarah. "But he didn't, thank God."

"I put a charm on him, but he has self-control, our Elias. He chose to go another way—and because he did not become violent, as all his people and your people did before him, the three of you have a chance to end it now."

Frustration welled in Sarah's throat. "I've tried!" she burst out. "Don't you think I tried? They always put me in the middle. They're still doing it."

"The middle is a good place to see both sides, eh?"

Sarah stared at her, gaping at the simplicity and clarity of the statement.

Octavia pressed the bag of herbs into her hand. "You

are stronger now. You know what must be done. Only you can make them take the steps they must.''

Tears of fear and frustration and loss and anger rose in her eyes. Furious with herself, Sarah brushed them away. "I don't think I can do this," she said. Her voice was unsteady. "I can't face it all again."

Octavia said nothing for a moment, then she got up and moved to a bureau against the far wall and brought back a very old miniature. She looked at it for a long moment. "This belonged to my mother, and her mother and her grandmother. Look at it, Sarita."

Sarah's hand shook as she reached for the small painting. It showed a young man in a vest trimmed with gold, a twinkle in his beautiful eyes. Eli's eyes. And his mouth, and his clean high cheekbones. "Who is it?"

"That was the Santiago boy who was hanged. Manuel Santiago." She paused. "I want you to have it."

Suddenly Sarah felt panicky. She shoved it back at Octavia. "I can't."

"Yes, you can." Octavia bent and closed Sarah's hands around the miniature. "Let him speak to you. Let the past tell itself to you and give you courage."

"I have to go," Sarah said shakily.

Octavia released her, and Sarah stood up jerkily, her vision blurred with tears. She'd cried more in the past two weeks than she had in a decade, she thought wildly. It was driving her crazy. Half-blind, she grabbed her purse and tucked the bag of herbs and the miniature inside. "Thank you," she said.

Octavia followed her to the door. "Heal us, Sarah," she said quietly.

Sarah bolted. She drove back down the hill and past the plant without seeing a single person, and only realized when she drove through the gates that she was holding her breath.

The market was on the way back to her parents' house.

Sarah pulled in and turned off the car, her emotions a tangle. Her heart pounded and sweat broke over her brow and against her palms. Even her stomach rebelled with a nauseous rush. Her hands were shaking.

She put her head down against the steering wheel and took long, slow, deep breaths, trying not to think about anything. She pictured the garden of cosmos outside her door at the cottage, their pink and white loveliness after the rain, and breathed in. Only the flowers. Pink and white.

And to a degree, she was successful. The vision of flowers built a wall between her and the turbulent images that threatened to overwhelm her: Eli, so angry at her today, and Octavia putting the miniature in her hand, and last night...

As if lying in wait for a vulnerable moment, her dream suddenly came back to her, her dream of flying with Elias and her daughter over the town of Taos. She remembered her pleasure at the freedom of flying with Eli, and the startled joy she had felt at seeing her daughter, almost twelve and beautiful.

But the moment she had really focused on that girl, Sarah had been unable to concentrate on anything else, and plummeted toward earth.

Shakily she lifted her head and rolled down the window to let in some air. It did not help much. Waves of nauseous terror washed over her and she didn't trust herself to be able to get across the parking lot and inside. She closed her eyes and again breathed deeply, in and out, in and out.

The symbolism of her dream was simple enough to decipher: she'd managed to fly with Eli—make love with him last night—only because they had not faced the past. And Sarah was afraid that if she did, if she looked back to make peace with her daughter, she would lose everything.

A knock on the hood of the car startled her. She opened her eyes to see an older Indian man bending down to look at her in concern. "Hey, lady, you okay?"

Sarah straightened. "Yes. Thank you."

"The heat's bad today. You don't want to be sitting in a car like that if you're not feeling good."

She realized he was right. It was probably the heat that was bothering her. She wasn't used to the intensity of the high desert sun. "You're right. Thank you."

He dug in his bag and took out a can of soda. "It's cold. Make you feel better."

"Thank you," Sarah said for the third time, and began to feel a little foolish. She accepted the soda and he shuffled off.

She opened it and drank a long, cold swallow, and it felt so good, she put the cold can against her face. Immediately she started to feel better.

Just the heat, she thought, feeling the panic ebb away. The heat and too many ghosts. She'd do her mother's little bit of shopping, then go home and turn on the swamp cooler and sleep for a few hours.

By the time she carried groceries into her mother's living room, Sarah was feeling much better. She didn't know if it was the cool of the store or the cold drink, or maybe just the sugar, but the strange weakness had passed.

"Hi, Dad," she said, pausing to look over his shoulder. "What are you watching?"

"'Dragnet.'" He punched the mute button. "I can change it if you want to watch a movie or something."

"No, go ahead. I'm going to put these groceries away."

Mabel came out, drying her hands on her apron. "You're an angel," she said, taking one of the bags. "Did you remember the celery? I thought I'd make some with cheese and onions, the way you like. I know you can't stay to dinner, but we can have a little snack, can't we?"

"Sure, Mom." She put her load on the counter and started putting things away.

"Your dad has some movies. Walked to the video store

all by himself to get them.'' Her voice dropped. ''It would thrill him if you'd sit down and watch one with him. I suspect he picked some of them with you in mind.''

Sarah glanced over her shoulder at the stack of videos on the television. ''You know, Mom, my plans fell through. If you have enough, I'd like to stay for supper. Maybe we can all sit down and watch a video together.''

Her mother looked up with wary hope. ''Really?''

All at once Sarah realized how careful they both were with her, as if she were some slightly dangerous forest creature that might bolt at any moment. Everything they did seemed calculated to placate and please her—and that was wrong.

For the first time, she realized how selfish and cruel she had been to her parents, dangling the one thing they wanted right in front of them—herself—threatening them with a precipitous withdrawal at any moment. It did not negate their crime against her, but she'd committed her own sins. ''Really,'' she said firmly. ''I can't think of anything I'd rather do.''

They set up old aluminum TV trays that had been around as long as Sarah could remember. Mabel pulled the heavy drapes against the sunlight, and they all three came to a consensus on *The Last of the Mohicans,* which had something for all of them—adventure for Garth the ex-cop, historical drama for Mabel and romance for Sarah. She'd seen it several times already, but didn't say so. Eric Schweig as Uncas would be no hardship to watch even after a hundred viewings.

A fact she also did not share with her parents.

In the dark room, with the swamp cooler roaring softly in the background, they ate stuffed celery and Waldorf salad and cold cuts, with toffee ice cream for dessert. Feeling satisfied and renewed when the movie went off, Sarah had the courage to reach into her purse for the plastic bag of herbs. ''Dad,'' she said. ''I know you aren't a fan of alternative medicine, but I took the liberty of talking to an herbalist for you today.''

"You went to all that trouble for your old man, huh?"

Sarah grinned, thinking ironically of just how much trouble she'd gone to. "Yep. You're stubborn, but I wouldn't mind keeping you around for a while."

Mabel patted her leg and picked up some dishes to take to the kitchen.

"She gave me this tea," Sarah said, holding it out for him to look at. "She said if you drink it once a day, it will make you feel better."

He lifted his glasses to the top of his head and took the bag. "Looks like grass."

"Grass you smoke or grass you mow?" Sarah teased.

He guffawed. "Good one. Both. What is it?"

Sarah lifted a shoulder. "I didn't ask. Mom might be able to tell by looking, but I sure can't."

"Tell what?" Mabel asked.

"What the herbs in this tea are."

"Let me see." Mabel took the bag. "Looks like mostly yarrow and some kind of mint." She opened the bag and sniffed. "Not peppermint or spearmint, though. Hummph." She gave it back to Sarah. "Try it, Garth. If you don't like the way it makes you feel, quit."

"All right." He shrugged. "I'll drink a cup."

Sarah went to the kitchen, feeling faintly nauseous again as she considered her upcoming betrayal of his trust.

Maybe she just wouldn't tell him. She'd let him drink it, see if it helped, and go from there. It seemed the ultimate cruelty to trade on the ease between them tonight.

But wasn't it a false ease? If she marched in there and told her father she'd slept in Eli's bed last night, he'd be furious. And if a grown woman had to lie to her father, what kind of relationship did they really have?

Standing there in her mother's kitchen, Sarah realized that in order to heal the past, they first had to clean the wounds and let them heal properly. Octavia's words came back to her. *The middle is a good place to see both sides.*

She made the tea, tasting a little to see what it was like. To her surprise, it was faintly sweet, with a pleasant, interwoven taste of summer.

Her father liked it, too. "Hey, this is pretty good," he exclaimed.

Sitting on the couch with some darning in her lap Mabel asked with mild curiosity, "Where did you get it?"

Sarah took a deep breath. She had not expected to reveal the source yet, but something told her not to lie. She was tired of lying, of sneaking around, of pretending to be so many things she wasn't. She'd pretended so long, she'd almost lost herself entirely. Letting go of the breath, she said calmly, "Octavia Santiago made it."

Garth, who had taken a swallow, spit the remaining tea back in the cup and slammed the rest of it on the table, spilling tea everywhere. "How dare you!" he roared.

"Sarah!" Mabel cried. "How could you?"

Surprised at the lack of agitation she felt, Sarah lifted a shoulder. "She's the obvious choice. Where do you think all those recipes for Santiago Teas came from? She's been doing this for more than sixty years."

Garth turned red. "You've been whoring around with him again, haven't you?"

"Garth!" Mabel said sharply.

Stung, Sarah narrowed her eyes. "I'm a grown woman, and my personal life is no longer any of your concern."

"I knew it." His color darkened to a brick red. "You haven't changed a bit. Still sneaking around behind my back."

Sarah jumped up. "Sneaking around? I'm thirty years old! I don't need your permission or your approval for anything I do."

Mabel wrung her hands. "Stop it, you two. This minute!"

"I saw those pictures in the paper and I believed you when you said it was nothing! You made a fool of me!" He shifted and took a breath, his hand automatically going for his inhaler.

With alarm, Sarah saw that he was on the verge of an asthma attack and she leaned forward to put her hand on his shoulder. "Dad, calm down. I'm sorry I tricked you, okay? I just wanted you to try—"

He pushed her hand away. "Get out of here. I don't want to talk to you anymore. You betrayed me." He used his inhaler, his blue eyes shooting fire.

"*I* betrayed *you?*" Sarah asked in a hot, steady voice. "I'm not the one who tore the love of your life out of your arms. I'm not the one who sent his daughter away to bear her child alone, without support of any kind. I'm not the one who badgered that child until she gave in and let her baby go!" Her hands shook with the force of her long-denied fury. "I didn't betray anyone except my daughter."

"Stop it!" Mabel said, lifting a hand.

"If you hadn't been lying and sneaking around, you never would have been pregnant in the first place!"

Mabel stood up and put herself between them, a hand on Sarah's chest. The action was so out of character, both Garth and Sarah stopped in sheer surprise. "Stop it!" she cried, and stamped her foot for emphasis. "I will not have this in my house again, do you understand? A more stubborn pair of mules I have never met, and you made my life miserable for years."

Sarah stared at her mother, and words rose to her lips, but did not fall: *Where were you when I needed you?*

"Garth, apologize for that 'whoring' remark." Mabel gave him a hard look. "Now."

His breathing came hard, but he didn't give in. He turned his face away.

Sarah realized that with her mother's intervention, she'd been hoping there would be a different outcome to this old scene, and it hurt her when her father would not give an inch. "Fine, Dad," she said. "You stew here in your own temper. I couldn't get away from you then, but I can now."

"How can you let him win like this?" Garth growled suddenly. "Make a fool of me? That's all he wants, you know. To use you to get at me."

"That's what you always said, Daddy! That he was using me. But he was going to marry me! Don't you understand? You stole my husband and my baby because you're too damned stubborn to admit you're wrong!"

"You'll...see!" His breathing grew so labored he couldn't say any more.

"Go, Sarah," Mabel said. "I'll call you later."

She didn't need a second nudging. She stormed out of the house and down the hill toward her cottage, her heart racing, her head pounding. Self-righteous anger gave way to self-pity, then crumbled to depression by the time she reached her cottage. She sank onto the porch without bothering to go inside.

She stared at the mountains, looking serene and eternal and protective as they rose above the city, and imagined they had looked the same when the whole thing began, so many years before, when Manuel Santiago had raped Emily Greenwood and been hanged in the square.

Remembering the miniature Octavia had given her, Sarah reached into her purse and took it out, looking at the face that was so much like Eli's. "Why did you rape her?" she asked the picture.

Times had been different then, with the Anglos coming in after the war, but the Santiagos had been wealthy and well-thought-of. He would have had his pick of young women to take as his wife—why risk so much for an act of violence that was sure to be discovered? And even if he'd been intent on rape, why the daughter of a wealthy Anglo neighbor? Why rape the one person who would almost certainly doom him, and had?

She sighed and let her hand drop. That line of thinking assumed rape was a rational crime, and it was not. Maybe he'd intended to punish the Anglos by defiling one of their daughters. Maybe he'd seen it as an act of war, and didn't mind dying. Maybe there had been fighting between the families already, over land or water or customs, and the rape had been a payback for some real or imagined slight. Unfortunately, rape had often been a method of retaliation in history.

It made her lonely to think of that poor young girl, disgraced and despairing. Emily had been so ashamed of her public defilement that she'd refused to go to the hanging. When her family had returned, they'd found her dead in the barn, hanged by her own hand.

Stop it, she said to herself. Thinking about the past only made her feel worse. "Here, kitty, kitty," she called. But the cat did not come.

What a day. Somehow she'd managed to alienate Eli by trying to care for her father, and alienate her father by her connection to Eli.

Nothing had changed in more than a decade. They still put her in the middle, neither willing to budge. And who had paid?

With a cry of fury she flung a rock across the courtyard. "Men!" she cried, and buried her face in her arms, pulsing with emotions she'd managed to keep safely behind walls for years. Now she ached all over with them, and as she'd always feared, into the wide-open, unprotected space of her heart came her daughter.

It had been coming for days. She'd felt it, the long-denied grief and anger and guilt, pushing at her walls every time she looked at Eli, every time her father nudged the wound. The reckoning had been dangerously close the night Eli first kissed her, but even then, she had not allowed herself to articulate her feelings.

Now there was no denying it and she simply gave in.

She let the images she'd shared with Eli this morning come back: her beautiful baby daughter with thick black hair. Her tiny nose and fingers, her rosebud of a mouth. She embraced a tactile memory of the feeling of that child against her arm and breast, tiny and trusting. She remembered acutely the warm tones of her baby's flesh against her own white arm.

The nurse had come and taken her, and Sarah had held on, resisting, trying to find the courage and the energy to say no, and defy all of them. But in the end she had not found the nerve.

Twelve years after the fact, she finally let herself acknowledge her guilt and her sorrow, and she cried in release. "I'm sorry," she whispered. And knew she would never forgive herself.

Chapter Thirteen

She sat there a long time, utterly winded and empty after the emotional storm. Dusk gathered at the top of the sky and spread downward, bleeding the color from the mountains and the trees. Far away she heard drums begin, the nightly summer tourist ritual at a motel.

The cat finally appeared, slipping between the slats of the fence and plaintively meowing as he came toward her. He leapt easily into her lap and flopped down, flipping his tail as if to ask her assistance in removing the burrs that had lodged there in his morning's travels. She obliged him, happier to have his company than she would have imagined. He purred as she plucked out the stickers, lifted his head to hers when she bent down to cuddle, and she found her heart easing with his unconditional love.

She smiled at that. Unconditional had been pretty rare in her life, after all.

As if on cue, the gate clicked and Sarah looked up to see Eli, bathed in the soft purples of the gathering twilight.

And as always, he was beautiful in her eyes, tall and straight, with pride on his brow and in the set of his broad shoulders. For a fleeting moment she remembered her deep sense of peace and happiness this morning and wished to have it back again. It made her feel even wearier.

"What do you want, Eli?" she asked, and heard the exhaustion in her voice.

"I don't know." He crossed the bricked courtyard and sat beside her, silent for a long time. She leaned sideways against the post, stroking the cat, too weary to summon a challenge or a comment of any kind.

Finally he said, "I'm sorry, Sarah, for being cruel this afternoon."

"Accepted."

"I was jealous."

She nodded.

Silence fell again, but there was no tenseness in it. Eli shifted to lean on the wall, his long legs stretched out in front of him. He gazed at the mountains, and she heard him sigh. "You turned my life upside down, coming back," he said.

"Mine, too." She remembered the miniature and passed it over to him. "Your grandmother gave me this today."

"Who is it?"

She told him.

He looked at her intently. "And she gave it to you? Did she say why?"

"No."

As if he'd only just really seen her, his gaze sharpened. "Have you been crying, Sarah?"

She looked at the sky, seeing a few stars begin to wink on. "Yes."

"Ah, I'm sorry."

"Not over you," she said, and didn't realize how cold it sounded until the words were out. "The baby," she added, hoping he would understand the shorthand.

He stood, then knelt beside her. "You're so tired, Sarita," he said. "And some of that is my fault." As if she were a child, he picked her up, cat and all. "You need to go to bed."

She considered protesting, but his arms offered the support she needed, and his shoulder beneath her head sucked all protest from her throat. She sighed, holding on to the unprotesting cat, letting Eli carry her into her bedroom. Without turning on a light, he put her on the bed and gently took off her shoes. The cat, purring loudly at the unexpected comfort of a bed, kneaded a place near her hip, and curled up. Exhausted, Sarah closed her eyes.

She felt the bed give under Eli's weight, felt the quilt come up over her shoulders, and the warmth of his body surrounding her, but that was all she registered before sleep rose and claimed her.

Eli did not sleep. He lay beside Sarah in her bed, simply holding her as she slept. Cradling her in his arms, with her hair against his neck, Eli was swept with waves of deepest gratitude, deepest love. He felt no urgency to make her naked and take her in a sexual way. It was just as powerful in its way to simply hold her, smelling her hair and feeling the weight of her arm across his belly.

She had confessed her daydreams of cooking for him, the symbol to her of the life they would make together. Eli's fantasies had run to this kind of moment, lying in the dark in a warm and comfortable place, with Sarah in his arms. It had seemed such a simple dream in those days—not that he'd underestimated family opposition to the match—and it was, as dreams went, very small. His love, in his arms at night, for the rest of his life. With so much wrong, so much greed in the world, how could the heavens have denied such a simple, clean, pure wish? To be a husband. A father. Make a family and live peacefully.

Yet it had been denied him. Denied them both. In the quiet, he had to wonder what good had come of it.

But he knew. The business had come from that denial, a business that had made his family wealthy again, as they had not been in a hundred years—and it had benefited not only his own family; sixty-two people were employed permanently, with another thirty seasonally. And he did not think of it often, but he knew, somewhere in the back of his brain, that it was good for his *people* when an ordinary man made a success of things. He liked to think of some young boy, somewhere in the world, seeing an Hispanic name on a product and realizing that, he, too, could have a big dream.

But what a price he had paid!

He fell asleep finally, and stirred awake only as wrens and sparrows started their morning hymns in the chamiso and juniper outside. It was their song that roused him, insistently drawing him from a pleasurable dream he didn't quite want to release. More slowly, he became aware of the sound of a purr close to his ear, a deeply satisfied sound—and felt the soft brush of fur against his ear.

And then he realized what pleasantness he'd been unwilling to leave behind, for his hand cradled the luscious heaviness of a breast. And her hand was under his shirt, moving slowly against the skin of his belly.

This was part of that lost dream. Awakening to Sarah in his arms, in a silent room with the first fingers of light breaking the night. He did not open his eyes to see if she was awake or asleep, but luxuriously stroked the sweet curve, moved his thumb against that nipple that came to life at his touch. She stirred a little, moving closer, her hand moving sensually over his hip, down his thigh, sliding forward to brush his member, then up to his stomach beneath his shirt.

He unbuttoned her blouse, finding her bare beneath it, bare and plump and beautiful. He groaned and bent over the ripe offering, opening his mouth to suckle the aroused tip, feeling her grow more aroused. A soft sound of pleasure came from her throat, and her hands moved on him boldly, finding his buttons and zipper, opening them, her fingers teasing inside until he was free.

He made a strangled sound as she touched him. They shimmied out of the rest of their clothes and slid together, pressing naked chest to naked breasts, clasping each other close. He stroked her back and kissed her neck, her chin, her shoulders, weaving their legs together. She arched against him, drawing her hands down his back, over his buttocks and thighs, and back again. They touched at every possible point, entwined and rubbing, until at last they moved as one, to join in a single, piercing thrust. He caught his breath as he felt her close around him, and kept his hands still on her shoulder blades, reveling in the feeling of her so close, so intimate.

When she would have moved, he tightened his grip. "Wait," he whispered. With iron control, he kept his hips still, and brushed her breasts with his hands, put his lips to her sensitive throat, trailed a hand down to stroke her thigh. She shuddered, gripping him.

"Sarita," he whispered. "Look at me."

Her eyes opened, and the blazing expression there nearly tumbled him over the edge, but he took a breath and pulled her even closer, holding his hands against her lower back. "This is who we are," he whispered. "Right here. Right now. Us."

She held his gaze for a long moment, and then he began to move. She moved with him, and they met in a slow, long, rocking heat, slow as he could bear, fully aware of what they did.

She lost control before he did, and the shattering convulsive movements of her body evoked an explosion from his own. They lay together in silence for a long time, letting the heat fade to embers.

At last Sarah turned in his arms and put her hand on his face. "Elias de Jesus Salimento Santiago," she said with a faint smile. "I love your name."

"I love the way you say it."

With her fingers, she traced the line of his cheekbone, his jaw. "I love your face, too." Her eyes were wide and sober.

He smiled. "You sound like a satisfied woman to me."

She only gazed at him, very seriously. She opened her mouth, looked away, then said in carefully measured tones, "I love you, Eli. I don't think I've ever stopped."

A burst of almost painful happiness spread through his chest, so fierce he had to bury his face in her neck to hide the sudden rush of tears in his eyes. He pulled her tight, breathing in the scent of her, the preciousness of her body against his own. "And I," he whispered against her ear, "love you. It's a miracle we have had a second chance."

"Or fate."

He shifted, propping himself up on one elbow. He twined his other hand with hers. "I keep thinking of the proverb. *'La ausencia para el amores lo que aire pal fuego,'*" he quoted softly. "*'Si es chica se apaga luego, sue es grande mejor.'*"

"Always trying to dazzle me with Spanish," she said with a grin. "Translation, please?"

"'Absence is to love what air is to fire. If it is small, it soon goes out. If it is great, it burns stronger.'"

A sudden moisture glazed her eyes. "That's beautiful."

He remembered suddenly that it was a workday, and looked at the clock. "I have an employee meeting in two hours," he said regretfully. "I am going to have to go get ready for it."

Her fingers tightened around his. "Wait, Eli. I have to say something before you go."

A frisson of warning passed over his nerves. "What?"

"Yesterday I had plenty of time to think about all of this. The past, both our own and the distant past."

"I'm sorry I got angry with you," he began.

"That wasn't it. Well, it was part of it." She took a breath. "I went to see my father last night, and I took him the tea your grandmother made for him. He practically spit it out when he found out who it was from." The memory obviously amused her.

A thread of annoyance wound through him. "Why is that funny?"

Sarah gave him a quick glance. "Because it's so melodramatic. All of this is pure melodrama. The Hatfields and the McCoys, Romeo and Juliet. It's ridiculous."

"How can you say that?" He pulled away from her, wounded and angry. "That 'melodrama,' as you call it, nearly ruined our lives. We lost our child, we lost all those years."

She raised her eyebrows. "We lost our child. That's a tragedy I know I will never forget, and I'm sure you won't, either. But did we really lose the years?" She touched his chest. "I always wanted to see the world. Now I have. You wanted to be wealthy, to restore your family's standing in the world, and you've done that." She took a breath. "Maybe it's time for all of us to just forgive and forget. Move on."

"No!" He pulled away from her, struggling to articulate the fury her words roused in him. He sat up. "No. I will never forgive your father for what he took from me."

She sat up, too, and he saw that it wasn't hurt in her eyes this time. It was anger, as clear and pure as his own. "You won't even try!"

He stood up, taking his clothes from the floor and using them as a shield over his nakedness. Pride, cold and still, made his chin lift. "Don't ask me for the one thing I can't give, Sarah."

She shook her head, resigned. "I should have known."

She pulled the sheets up around her. "You're as stubborn as he is."

"So be it," he said. He took his clothes into the living room and dressed, and without bothering to say goodbye, he left her, holding his pride close. He would never forgive her father. He would never let the old man win.

Sarah was not surprised by the vehemence of Eli's refusal to consider a truce with her father. When she recovered from her own sense of pique, she even understood. Standing in the middle, she could see both sides.

It would have been nice if she could have made suggestions and everyone just simply gave in to please her. Healed the war, signed a truce, got on with everything. Standing in the shower, she grinned at the absurdity of that wish.

Yeah, right. When pigs could fly. If all this was easy to solve, someone would have done it long ago.

In an oddly buoyant mood, she fed the cat and then went out to cut some of the cosmos to put in a vase. Remembering that Teresa would be coming later to go over the prints generated from the photo sessions, she realized she had still not developed the photos the girl had shot the day they all picnicked together. She also remembered the undeveloped rolls she'd shot yesterday, and to her relief, she felt a little rush of excitement at the idea of working with that material, at seeing what she'd captured.

She turned the darkroom radio to a classical music station and hummed along with Haydn and Brahms as she worked, the light, pleasant music suiting her peaceful mood. Her thoughts wandered aimlessly and she didn't try to rein them in or analyze them. It occurred to her that something interesting was brewing, something that was about to be born from the events of the past two days. It was a feeling she'd forgotten, one that had been lost in the emotional violence of her eighteenth year. She'd sometimes felt it, working in some gloriously beautiful location, a creative rush that felt like colors in her head, but never quite like this, so full-bodied and rich.

She made a contact of Teresa's negatives, thinking vaguely of the portrait Octavia had given her of Manuel Santiago. Vaguely she wondered if there was a daguerreotype of the Greenwood girl. Maybe. A lot of the early photographers had loved the West, especially Indians. She couldn't remember if she'd ever seen a daguerreotype of the pueblo—but there might be one. Emily's parents had been wealthy; perhaps they would have indulged in something like that. Sarah made a mental note to check at the library.

Teresa's photos surprised her. There were a predictable number of just-out-of-focus shots, and some off center or oddly composed. But there was a handful of photos that were excellent, including one shot of a doorway at the end of a hallway at the Martinez Hacienda that showed a promising sensitivity to light and shadow.

But it was her shots of Sarah and Eli that were most telling. Excited, Sarah printed an entire series of eight-by-tens. Over and over, the girl had caught the play of light and emotion on their faces. A coy glance, a surprised burst of laughter. One showed Sarah gazing off to something out of sight, and everything about her face—her mouth, her eyes, her hand lifting to brush blinding hair from her vision—expressed a wistful, aching yearning that was nearly painful to behold.

It took a very observant eye to catch such a piercing expression, to shoot the photo at the exact instant that all the elements fell together. And although Sarah suspected Teresa had been deliberately waiting for such moments in order to tell a story with a photo, it showed a rare eye.

She loved the picture on a personal level, and that amazed her, as well. Three days ago she would have been appalled to have seen such an expression on her face. Would have been terrified to admit she still felt those things for anything or anyone. Emotional distance had given her the only peace or safety she'd found these past twelve years.

Yesterday she had realized distance was impossible. It was also a lie. By nature she was a passionate person, one in love with a man, but also with the beauty of a morning sky. And it wasn't only love she felt strongly. She'd felt hate and sorrow and grief in such powerful portions she had believed herself doomed.

She clipped the picture to the line to dry, and started on her own work. As the varied images emerged, artistic and colorful and poignant, an idea began to grow in her mind.

Like a mystical wise woman in a fairy tale, Octavia had laid upon Sarah an almost impossible task. And like any heroine, Sarah had first protested that she could not possibly carry it out.

And perhaps she could not. Perhaps her quest was doomed, and none of them would find happiness. Perhaps another heroine, in a future time, would have to finish it.

One thing Sarah knew for sure: Octavia was right. Only Sarah herself had a prayer of bringing this long war to an end. Only she knew the main generals well enough. As insane as it seemed, her heart sang with the possibility that she might pull it off.

In the red-lighted room, she closed her eyes and prayed at random to the spirits of the past and to the generations still waiting in heaven for their turn. "Help me. Make me wise. Make me strong."

She made a quick lunch of soup and peanut butter crackers, sharing the leavings with the cat. "I guess you belong to me now, don't you?" she said to him. "What should I name you? You're not exactly a Fluffy or Tinker Bell type."

He regarded her steadily from big green eyes. Licked his lips as he eyed the cracker in her hand. She chuckled. "I never knew cats liked peanut butter. Or do you just like anything you can get?"

She put the cracker on the floor, peanut butter side up so he could lick it off, and petted his big head. "That's probably it. You've been hungry so long, you'll settle for anything."

With delicate laps, he made short work of the peanut butter. Sarah considered the problem of his name, but nothing came to her immediately.

When the phone rang, she got up to answer it, expecting Teresa. It was her father. "Sarah," he said gruffly. "I'm sorry I yelled at you last night."

She blinked. "You are?"

"Sometimes acting a certain way just gets to be a habit. Not a good habit, either. I just got going and couldn't stop." He cleared his throat. "Can we forget it?"

"I can. Apology accepted." She swung the phone cord in an arch, weighing her options, wondering if she dared. She did. "Will you try the tea anyway?"

He said nothing and Sarah could feel the resistance from him.

"Please, Dad? Just try it for a few days and see if it works. If it doesn't, nothing is lost. If it does, maybe you'll end up feeling a lot better."

"Well, how about if we make a deal?"

"What kind of deal?"

"You come over and get your mother off my neck. She hasn't spoken three words to me since last night."

Sarah thought of her idea and demurred. "I can't come till tomorrow afternoon, but why don't you put her on the phone, and I'll see what I can do."

"Deal. How much am I supposed to drink?"

"A tablespoon steeped in a cup of hot water every day."

"Can I put sugar in it?"

Sarah chuckled. "Sure."

"Here's your mother."

"Sarah?" Her mother sounded tired and querulous. "You don't have to do anything against your conscience on my account."

"He said he'll drink the tea, Mom. He met me more than halfway. I got over it."

"Oh, good."

"You need anything, Mom? Groceries or something?"

"No. The housekeeper comes in today, thanks to you." She sighed. "I'm just tired of the heat. I'll feel better when it's fall."

"I understand. Not long now."

They hung up, and Sarah stood by the phone for a long moment, a surge of optimism rising in her chest. If her father would come this far, maybe it wouldn't be as hard as she'd anticipated to find some common ground between him and Eli.

Maybe. All she could do was try.

Chapter Fourteen

There were few people about in the library on such a hot, sunny day. Sarah approached the reference librarian behind her desk and told her what she wanted.

"Hmm," the woman said. She was a small, pretty black woman with her hair cut close to her head; her name tag read Glenna O'Neal. She pushed back from the desk and waved for Sarah to follow her. "That stuff is buried in the back. Some of it is on microfiche, but we have some bound copies of the newspaper all the way back to the first issue. Which would you prefer?"

"The bound copies, I think." They would feel more immediate.

The woman led her to a row of dusty, tall volumes. "Here they are. Do you know the year?"

"Yes, it was 1859." No Greenwood child—or Santiago, either, for that matter—could fail to have memorized that information.

"Here we go, then." She tugged the volume out and set it on a nearby table. "Are you writing a novel?"

"I probably could, but no. I'm Sarah Greenwood. My family has been at war with the Santiago family for more than a century over this and I decided I was tired of the legends and want to get the facts."

Glenna O'Neal's face brightened. "That's why you look familiar! I saw your picture in the paper last week."

"Yes."

"Are you really Juliet?"

"I hope not," Sarah said with a laugh. "She killed herself."

The woman laughed with her. "I guess you're right. If you need anything else, let me know."

"I will."

With a sense of excitement, Sarah opened the book and started leafing through the newspapers, crackling and brown. She found herself drifting, stopping to read an article here, another there. The world in which Emily Greenwood had lived was very different from the one Sarah had been born into. There were reports of "red Indian savages" attacking settlements in faraway places, and reports of the railroad being built. She read ads for patent medicines and herbal lozenges.

Bemused and seduced by the world of the past, she was startled when she turned the page to a paper dated September 1859, and saw a bold headline: Santiago Man Accused of Rape.

For one long second Sarah felt a powerful, intense sensation of déjà vu. It made her so dizzy she had to close her eyes and take several long deep breaths. When the feeling passed, she read the article. Told in nearly histrionic language, it detailed the story Sarah had heard over and over again, all of her life. From her grandparents and her father, and on the lips of sympathizers. Emily Greenwood had been brutally set upon and raped by Manuel Santiago. Emily's brothers had dragged the man to the town square and demanded justice for their sister's honor. She'd been ruined and violated, and they would have justice.

As she read the familiar details, Sarah was transported to the Taos of those days. She imagined the square, smelling of dust and wind and sage, the cottonwoods glittering, the smell of horse and dung. In her mind's eye she saw Manuel Santiago, probably barely standing from the beating Emily's brothers had delivered. She wondered if he had protested his innocence. The story did not say.

The next paper, a week older, told the rest of the story. Santiago had been hanged. The same day, disgraced and humiliated, Emily Greenwood had been found in the barn, hanging from the hayloft. The family was despairing. In the last paragraph of the article there was a horrifying comment from one of the brothers. "Like any decent woman, she didn't want to bring that mixed-race bastard into the world. At least this way, she'll have some peace."

Sarah felt the world rock a little. She slumped back in her chair, staring sightlessly at the shelves.

Emily had been pregnant?

But how could they have known that, in the days before pregnancy tests, only a week after the rape?

Feeling winded, she stood up and carried the pages to the copy machine. Her heart and her thoughts seemed to move into a thready chaos—how had they known?

The only answer was that Emily Greenwood had been a lot more than a week pregnant. At the very least, she had missed a period or two—but why would she have shared that information if she planned to kill herself anyway?

Taking the copies from the tray, Sarah carried the book back to its place, trying to fit this bit of information into what she already knew.

She frowned, looking at the quote again. Maybe Emily's brother had only meant they were afraid she *might* be pregnant. No. The reference seemed to refer to a specific child—"*that* mixed-race bastard."

On the way out, she stopped at the desk. "Thank you, Ms. O'Neal."

"Did you find what you wanted?"

Sarah didn't know how to answer. "Maybe," she said. "I'm still missing some information. Is there a historian in town who might have specialized in Taos history? Someone who might know more?"

A decisive nod. "You should talk to Deborah Lucero." She pulled a Rolodex over and flipped through the cards, then copied the phone number down on a card she handed over to Sarah. "Good luck on not being Juliet," she said with a grin.

"Thanks."

The walk back to her cottage was brutally hot. By the time Sarah entered her swamp-cooled rooms, she was exhausted, and she fell onto the couch to rest for a few minutes before she called the historian.

Her mind whirled with images: the dusty square of 1859, the brothers dragging the Santiago boy to the sheriff. Manuel's face, bloody and bruised, which melded into Eli's face. A girl's slim body, hanging in the barn. A bright blue sky over the mountains.

She fell into a doze and dreamed of a gilded blue-and-gold world. As she walked through a grove of cottonwoods, she realized she could hear the Rio Grande, rushing through the canyon. Every leaf, every blade of grass, the thickly patterned tree trunks, all were edged with gold, like a fancy book she'd seen in a museum once, before they moved to Taos.

As if made from the light itself, a man walked out of the sunlight into the shadows, and Sarah's heart leapt so painfully she raised her hand to her chest, as if to hold it in place. The man was tall and slim, his hair long and caught back from his face in a leather thong. She rushed toward him, and when he caught sight of her, he ran to greet her, his face wreathed in a smile of joy.

They kissed, clumsily at first in their haste, then with more hunger and skill. And amid the gold-edged grasses, beneath the blue, blue Taos sky, they made love, flesh to flesh, alone in a secret world that belonged only to them.

Sarah jolted awake when the cat jumped onto her belly. Blinking at the odd dream, she glanced at the clock. She'd been asleep for only twenty minutes, but it had refreshed her. Teresa would be here any minute.

But she didn't move right away. Instead, she stroked the cat on her belly and wondered sleepily what if? What if the dream was more true than the legend? What if there had been no rape, only a forbidden love that ended in a classic Romeo-and-Juliet ending?

Pulling from her pocket the card Glenna O'Neal had given her, Sarah dialed the number. A woman answered in Spanish, which disoriented her for a moment. "Mrs. Lucero?"

"Yes. Can I help you?"

Sarah took a breath. "I was hoping I might be able to visit with you, Mrs. Lucero. The librarian told me you might be the only one with the information I'm looking for." She outlined her need.

"Sarah Greenwood?" the woman repeated.

"Yes."

"You may not like what I have found," she warned. "But if you want truth, I will be happy to give it to you."

Sarah took a breath. "I'm tired of the legends and the lies. I'd really like the truth."

"Come tonight, seven o'clock."

Teresa and Eli showed up a few minutes later. Eli was polite and distant, his expression cool. Sarah sighed as he took a magazine to a shady place on the porch and sat down, as impersonally as if he were at a dentist's office.

"Don't you want to see the pictures?" Sarah asked.

"No, thank you."

She rolled her eyes and waved Teresa into the cottage ahead of her, waiting until the girl was out of earshot to say, "You know, Eli, it doesn't have to be like this."

"No." His mouth was tight. "But you have made your choice."

"Why does it have to be a choice, Eli?"

His expression did not change, and he gave every appearance of ignoring her as he turned the pages of the magazine. She narrowed her eyes, feeling a surprising urge to slap him, to literally knock some sense into him. "I don't know you when you are like this," she said at last.

He raised his eyes. They were nearly black, luminous with powerful emotions. "You never saw this side of me, because it was formed by hatred and loss."

Sarah shook her head. This would lead nowhere except to an argument. "Suit yourself," she said, and went inside.

She and Teresa settled at the kitchen table and began to go through the shots of Teresa, deciding which to keep for the portfolio and which to set aside. In the end, the assembled photos in the keeper pile were a wide variation of poses and styles, from glamour queen to ingenue.

"I'll get these mounted and put in a book for you," Sarah said, making a neat pile. "Then we'll go on to the next step."

"Which is?"

"A trip to Albuquerque and Santa Fe, to see if we can find an agency willing to take you on. Your mother will have to go, and she needs to understand what's involved. Will she sit down and talk with me about it?"

Teresa looked down and shrugged. "Maybe. Maybe not. You could call her," she added hopefully.

Sarah decided this might very well be another stitch in the weaving of their families. "I'll do that.

"Now," she said, pulling the other stack of photos over, "I want to talk about something else, and I want you to really think about what I have to say before you object, okay?''

Teresa frowned suspiciously. "Why do I get the feeling I'm not going to like this?"

"You might like it a lot. I don't know." She took the best of Teresa's shots from the top and spread them out before her. "These photos are amazingly good, Teresa. Have you ever worked with a camera before?"

"No, not really. Just one of those little things for vacations, you know. My teacher had one of my pictures from the Grand Canyon blown up to put in the yearbook, though."

"I'm not surprised." She pointed to the arched doorway at the Hacienda. "This is the one I noticed first. It shows a terrific eye for balance and light."

Teresa looked at it critically. "I saw it better through the camera," she said. "It doesn't look as good there. I should have got closer, maybe."

Sarah smiled, hearing the criticism of a natural. "That might have helped," she agreed mildly. She pulled out the series of Eli and Sarah, some separate, some together. She pointed out the one of Sarah, looking so obviously full of yearning, and another of Sarah and Eli together. "These two are..." She halted, wishing for some brand-new adjective to express fantastic, so Teresa would know she meant it. "They're just unbelievably good, Teresa. This one—" She pointed to Eli and Sarah together. The angle of Eli's head, the curve of his neck, the way his eyes focused on her lips, all spoke volumes of desire. Sarah's posture was more hesitant. With her hand, she brushed her hair away from the side of her face and neck that faced Eli, as if to reveal herself to him, and though her gaze was on his face, the angling away of her body, the slight turning of her shoulder showed her reluctance. "What do you see?"

Teresa grinned wickedly. "Girl, he wanted to kiss you bad. And you kind of wanted it, but weren't too sure." She lifted a wicked eyebrow. "I waited and waited until it was just right, and then—bam—there it was."

Sarah wanted to chortle aloud. She had not believed, looking at the pictures, that Teresa's shots had been accidental, but to hear she'd been waiting for the shot, that she had seen it when it appeared, was exactly what she had hoped. "Honey, you could be a model. You have the kind of face a camera loves, and you're a natural in front of it." She paused.

"But?"

Sarah tapped the photos. "But I have never seen such raw talent for photography. I think you're so good in front of the camera because you understand so well what makes a good picture, because of that inner eye."

"Really?" She pulled the pictures over, bent her head over them. "You're not just saying that to talk me out of being a model?"

"Modeling is a perfectly respectable career," Sarah said. "And you might love it for a long time, but sooner or later—"

"You get too old," Teresa interjected.

"Yes. I'd never presume to know what's best for anyone when it comes to picking a career. Only you can know that." She smiled. "But I've been a photographer for twenty years. I've poured everything I have, everything I am, into understanding it. I love it. It makes me whole. I'm also very, very good, Teresa." She paused for emphasis. "And your gift is so much bigger than mine that I even felt a twinge of envy when I looked at these pictures."

"Oh, wow." She leaned back.

"Don't decide anything right now," Sarah said, gathering the pictures. "I'll get your portfolio together, and I'll also call your mother. You can at least try the world of modeling on a local level until you graduate." In a sudden fit of inspiration, she hopped up and got her camera bag, which sat by the counter. From within, she took the old, beloved Minolta. "I've had this camera for fifteen years. It's not fancy. It doesn't have any automatic settings. You have to focus. You have to learn how to figure out depth of field and light and balance in your head with f-stops. But I want you to have it."

"Oh, I can't," she said. "You've already done so much."

"I can. Take it. Learn to live with it. Give it a chance and give your heart a chance to decide what it loves most. Can you do that for me?"

Teresa hesitated. Accepting the camera, she nodded. "I'll try."

"That's all anyone can ask, sweetie. And now, you can do something for me."

"Name it," Teresa said.

"It's not as much as you think," she said. "I just want this photo, and your permission to put it in a show I'm putting together."

"You and Eli?"

Sarah nodded. "It's important. I can't tell you right now what I'm doing, but your name will be on it. Is that okay?"

"Yes," Teresa said. Abruptly, she stood up and hugged Sarah tightly. "Meeting you is one of the best things that ever happened to me," she said emotionally.

Sarah closed her eyes and breathed in the scent of shampoo and the sweetness of Teresa's flesh. "Me, too," she said. She patted her back. "Now, go take your grouchy uncle home."

"Wait till I tell him!" She flowed out, practically floating.

Pleased, Sarah didn't move for a moment, filled with a kind of satisfaction that came from being able to help a young person. She bent over the photos again and spread out some of her own, narrowing her eyes as she shuffled them, setting them side by side, seeing how they balanced in relation to each other.

Eli's voice startled her. "Sarah."

She turned, bracing for his anger. He'd halted by the door, and the light coming in behind him haloed his dark, dark hair. Sarah found herself remembering the day he'd come to her in the rain, and she'd wept in his arms at the beloved, familiar, much-mourned taste of him. The memory prompted her to keep her voice gentle. "Let's not fight, Eli."

"No." His mouth was tense. "I wanted to tell you I'm sorry. I should not have left this morning the way I did."

"I understood."

"Did you, Sarah?" His voice was weary. "Can you understand what that was like for me, when I went to jail, and then came out to find you gone? All I've had to comfort me all these years is my hatred." He paused and she could feel his anger, but even larger, his confusion, his sense of despair. His voice was rough when he finally spoke. "I'm not sure I can let it go, Sarita. That's as honest as I can be."

An ache touched her. "And I'm being as honest as I can be when I say I will not live in the middle of this war. I can't."

They stared at each other across the room, separated, as they never had been, by the genuine conflicts of adults, not the powerless melodramas of youth.

At last he said, "It does not mean my love for you is less."

She closed her eyes. "Nor mine," she said. When she opened them again, he was gone.

Deborah Lucero lived in a gleaming ranch-style house set back in a thicket of cottonwoods, the back of her property abutting the creek that ran through town. The woman who opened the door was small and neat, with a sleek page-boy around her delicate face. She was no more than forty, and Sarah was surprised. She'd expected someone older.

"Come in," she said with a friendly smile. "I had hoped we could sit on the patio, but the wind is blowing in, and my papers would be scattered over the whole yard." She led Sarah into a room lined with bookshelves and file cabinets. Two book covers were framed on the walls, one about Hispanic legends in the Southwest, another about women in the Spanish colonial period. Notes and file cards and piles of resource material were piled around the computer on a wide desk. Sarah gestured at it with a smile. "Is that book number three?"

"Yes. I'm gathering the legends of lovers in the area, from the earliest period to now. Which is how I know so much about your family history." She settled on a low, long sofa and gestured for Sarah to join her.

"Sounds like a fascinating book."

"I think so. I don't make much money on books like this, of course, but they stay in print a long time, and I like to think I'm adding something to Hispanic history." She slid a bulging file toward Sarah. "This is what I've collected on your family's story. It may not be what you think it is."

"I read the newspaper articles today," Sarah said, and took a breath, bracing herself. "Was Emily pregnant?"

Deborah nodded sadly. "She was. Nearly five months along, by the accounts some of her neighbors gave."

"Then it wasn't rape."

"No. This story has bothered me ever since I could remember. I saw a copy of a miniature of Manuel Santiago when I was sixteen or seventeen, and his face has stayed with me all these years. It never felt right, you know?"

From her purse, Sarah took the wrapped miniature. "This one?"

Deborah made a soft sound. "Yes." She held it in her palm as if it were a precious ruby. "Yes," she said again more quietly. "His eyes are full of mischief, but there is no meanness. You see cruelty on the mouths of a lot of those men—they were patriarchal to a fault, and arrogant...." She shook her head. "Not this one."

"Elias Santiago looks just like him."

"So I have seen." She opened the file. "I wonder if you have seen this." She put in Sarah's hands a grainy photocopy of an old photo. "That's Emily."

The winded, dizzy sense of déjà vu returned so fiercely that Sarah's hands shook as she stared at the picture of a very young woman, no more than sixteen or seventeen, dressed in a Victorian gown. Her light hair was swept away from her face, and she wore the hideous bangs of the period, but there was no mistaking that the image was Sarah's face. Her nose. Her mouth. Her high forehead.

"I had never seen you before the picture ran in the paper last week," Deborah said quietly, "but it gave me chills. How much each of you resembles these two."

Sarah took a long breath, trying to rein in the odd, unsettling emotion. "I haven't seen this before, either. I went to the library looking for one after Octavia gave me the miniature of Eli—I mean Manuel." She swallowed. "I'm not sure why I wanted to find it, but now I know."

Unexpectedly, tears welled in her eyes. "All this tragedy...all those fights, all those deaths on both sides...." Tears fell hot down her cheeks at the waste of it. "And it was all a lie from the beginning."

The woman covered Sarah's hand. "Yes, it was. Manuel Santiago petitioned Emily's father for marriage three months before the hanging. Greenwood threw him out and threatened legal action if he came near his daughter again." She paused, as if weighing her next words, then seemed to make a decision. "I hope you don't mind me talking about your ancestors in a frank way."

"No."

"He was an avowed racist. Hated Indians and Mexicans and the blacks who were drifting in, a few at a time. He was furious with Emily."

"How did you find this information?"

Deborah pointed to the file. "There are letters from Emily to a friend of hers in Philadelphia. I found them at the University of Pennsylvania archives when I did some background research into Emily's family."

Sarah opened the file with a hand that shook, and took out the photocopied letters. Long, youthful, exuberant, they told of a dashing young man and Emily's hopes for the future. "I'd like to read these some time," she said finally. "Would you mind if I make some copies?"

"Take those. I have copies." She smiled. "I once left a folder on a bus. Now I make three copies of everything and put them in different places."

"Thank you." Sarah rose. "I won't keep you, but you've been very helpful."

"Let me know how it turns out, huh?"

Sarah nodded. "I will."

Chapter Fifteen

Sarah worked in a fever all night, matting photographs and newspaper articles and even one of the letters from Emily. She had gone by her mother's house before coming home, and she dug through the photographs she'd taken from Mabel's cedar chest, to find the most illustrative ones for her purposes.

At dawn she dragged herself to the couch and fell asleep for a couple of hours, but the work fever was in her. She called Deborah to tell her what she planned, and asked her permission, which Deborah freely gave. She made a second call to her friend Joanna to ask where she might get display space immediately. "It doesn't have to be much," Sarah said. "And I only need it for a week or so."

Joanna promised to call her friends in the art community and see what she could arrange.

After a hasty shower and a breakfast of a stale bagel, Sarah was at the library. Glenna, evidently pleased to have a project to amuse herself with, helped Sarah copy old photographs, newspaper reports from various times through the years. Sarah stopped on the way back to pick up some more supplies, and ate a fast-food lunch. When she got in, there was a message from Joanna about the gallery space.

By two, she could see she was nearly finished, and she called her father. "Dad, I have something really important to show you, and something I need to tell you. Do you think you can give me…say, two hours, without any objections to anything I say or do?"

"What's this about, Sarah?"

"It's about everything, Dad. But mainly it's about us. Two hours. Can you do that?"

A brief pause. Then, "Sure, honey. I can give you a whole day if you want it."

"The big thing is not getting angry, Dad."

He chuckled. "You want me to take a tranquilizer?"

She let him hear her laughing at his joke. "Well, maybe that's going too far."

"I'll listen, Sarah. I promise."

Emotions, rushing too close to the surface, threatened to send her into another weeping fit. She swallowed. "I want you to meet me at The Blue Cock tomorrow evening at seven-thirty. Bring Mom. She needs to see this, too."

"We can't see you today?"

"Sorry, I'm working," she said.

"Working, huh? That's great."

She hung up the phone. One down, one to go. She leaned back in her chair for a moment, suddenly feeling the long hours rush over her. Her neck ached and her eyes were grainy, and she was afraid she'd lose it if she heard Eli's voice.

So much was riding on the next twenty-four hours! All at once she wasn't sure if she could bear to lose him again. With a sigh, she put her face in her hands, and, as if waiting for the darkness of her eyelids to unreel, a filmstrip of images rolled over her imagination. Eli in his truck that first day she came home, looking severe and angry and hungry; the day he'd come to ask her if she'd shoot Teresa's portfolio, when he'd been so delectably sexy she'd wanted to invite him inside to her bed no matter how many bad years lay between them.

She thought of his hand, light as a butterfly, on her spine as she bent over the flowers, and of his pride over his land—pride she had never truly acknowledged, she realized with a pang of regret.

And more—she remembered him standing naked and free in the night, his face and arms uplifted to the blessing of rain in the desert, accepting it with joy and pure abandonment.

But most of all, she thought of the way it felt to sleep next to him, in a bed, all night long. His hips, warm and bare, against her side. The smell of his skin in her nose when she awakened. How right it felt to wake up to him and eat a meal with him, and talk of little things.

All those years of wandering, and she had come full circle. She loved Elias Santiago. She wanted to marry him, to live next to him, and carry the children they made inside her body. She wanted long days of ordinariness, with babies sleeping against her breast, and teenagers who drove them both crazy. She wanted to breathe her last breath in his arms, or hold him as he breathed his last.

"Please let it work," she whispered to any sympathetic spirits who might be listening. She picked up the phone and dialed Eli's number. When his answering machine picked up, she was almost palpably relieved. She left a message telling him almost exactly the same thing she'd told her father—that she needed to show him something—but she asked Eli to come a half hour later. "Eli," she said at the end, "please just give this a chance."

She hung up and stared at the phone for a minute, then called back again to leave a postscript, but to her dismay, he answered this time.

For a moment she was speechless. "Did you hear my message yet?" she asked.

"Yes. I was trying to get the door open. Did you forget something?"

Sarah took a breath. "Um…well, I was going to leave another message."

"Yeah?" His voice grew intimate and she thought she could hear the smile in it. "What was it?"

She closed her eyes, liking the feeling of his voice in her ear. "I don't think I can say it to you," she said at last.

"Must be good. Should I hang up and let you say it to my machine?"

"I'd know you were listening."

She heard a clink of keys on a table in the background, and imagined him kicking off his shoes, going to the fridge for a glass of tea. "I could go get in the shower. Although—" his voice turned liquid, seductive "—it would be better if you came over here and took it with me."

Her body liked that idea, she noticed with amusement. "I'm working."

"Are you?" He sighed with pleasure, as if he'd just sat down after a long day. "I'm not working anymore. I could come rub your back."

Sarah chuckled. "I'm sure I'd get tons of work done." Relaxing a little, she tucked the phone between her shoulder and her ear, and went to the kitchen to pour a glass of milk. "I seem to have this slight hormone problem when you show up."

His laugh was as rich as a cello. "Hormones, huh? I would have called it something else."

"What?"

He was quiet for a moment. "Love," he said. "I would call it love."

"That's what I called to put on your machine," she said before she could censor herself.

"That you would call it love?"

"That I love you, Eli."

"I know," he said roughly. "It hasn't changed, that love between us."

"No."

Another clink in the background, maybe a pan. "I want you to sleep next to me tonight," he said roughly. "I want to hold you."

"Is that all?" she teased.

"No. Do you want me to tell you what I want to do?"

"Yes." The word was barely a whisper.

"I would like to kiss your neck, right under your ear, that place that makes you sigh. I'd like to kiss it and then put my tongue on it, while I put my hand around your breast."

A wave of erotic longing burst in her, and she sat down on the floor, her back against the wall. "I changed my mind," she said, surprised at how breathless her voice sounded. "Don't tell me. I don't think I can stand it."

"I deliver," he said. "Thirty minutes or less. Let me come over."

It was desperately tempting. It might be her last chance ever. "I can't." She sighed. "I really have to finish this work."

"So what is this big project? What are we doing tomorrow night that's so important?"

Dread dropped like a rock in her belly. "You'll have to just wait and see." She weighed her words carefully. "It's really important, Eli, that you give me one hour, without judgment. Can you?"

"Sarah, I swear I'll do my best."

"Okay. That's all anyone can ask." She fell silent for a moment, listening to him breathe, and she was suddenly transported back to a time when they had spent hours on the phone, sometimes talking, sometimes not. She grinned. "Do you remember when we used to watch TV together over the phone?"

His laugh was warm and surprised. "'Miami Vice.' I haven't thought about that in a long time. I wanted to be Crockett in the worst way."

"I just wanted Crockett," Sarah said with a throaty chuckle.

"I wanted the girl in the little bikini in the beginning."

"Ah, and here I thought it was the fast cars and gun battles you were watching." Her rear end started to ache, so she stood up to heat water for tea. "And the fashion dictates—remember when you didn't wear socks for a whole month?"

"No fair," he said, laughing. "Bring up my sockless era and I'll talk about your henna era."

"I still have no idea what possessed me to go red." In the background she heard a sound like meat frying. "What are you cooking?"

"Steak. It's a really juicy T-bone, too. I've got thin little onions, and a little garlic that I rubbed in the pan—" a rattle while he put the phone under his chin "—fresh ground pepper."

Sarah's stomach growled and she laughed. "My stomach is growling, you rat. All I have in my cupboards is a box of instant oatmeal and a dried-up tortilla."

"*Pobrecita.* You know I'd share this one with you if you came over. Now I'm putting a giant red potato in the microwave, and I have sour cream and fresh chives from my own little garden to put on it."

"You have a cold, cold heart, Elias Santiago."

"No, it's warm. Very warm. Hot, even." A sound in the background. "Hang on a minute, okay?"

"Sure."

"It'll sound like I'm hanging up, but I'm not."

She smiled. "I'm familiar with call waiting, Eli."

"Touché."

The line went blank, and Sarah dug hopefully through the lower cupboards and the bottom drawer of the fridge, looking for anything remotely edible. "This is getting ridiculous," she said. "Gotta grow up someday, Sarah, and buy groceries like a real person." Tucked into a corner of the bottom drawer she discovered a container of tuna salad. She almost put it on the heel of bread left in the bag, but remembered the cat, who was curled on her bed as if he lived here.

Which she supposed he did. The Cat Who Needed A Name.

Eli came back on the line. "Are you there?"

"Still here." She discovered a half bag of raisins, hiding behind the peanut butter, and gave a little cry. "All right. I found some food."

"Bet it isn't a T-bone."

"Well, not exactly."

"I just turned this one over. Oh, it's beautiful…and you should smell it, Sarita. Onions, that grilled steak scent, the garlic."

"Not going to work, Eli." She dropped raisins into her mouth. "I now have food to fortify me."

Eli loved talking to her on the phone like this for the same reasons he had as a youth. It was intimate without being overwhelming. He was not distracted by the physical details of her body or mouth, or the constant need to put his hands on her. It freed them to ramble, explore, share anything and everything. The conversation rose and fell simply, sometimes slipping into an easy silence for minutes at a time, minutes he felt no need to fill up, minutes neither of them seemed to think signaled an end to the conversation, because it didn't. They dipped into the past, remembering things only the two of them had ever known about each other, about their private times. They'd had very few public times, after all. They wound around his business dealings for the day, slid into Teresa and her dual gifts, then into more general subjects, then drifted back to Taos or their shared history, or the unshared history they felt moved to share.

He ate his steak and his potato, trying to be polite. Years ago they'd shared not only television, but the snacks that went with it, and he'd perfected a technique of eating without noise.

When he heard the doorbell ring, he grinned. "I'll wait," he said.

"It's weird not having a remote phone now. I'm not used to being trapped in one spot. Hang on." The clatter of the phone as she set it down.

He listened carefully, hearing only murmurs, then the sound of her feet as she came back. "Eli, you are the king of all men. The emperor of the world. The god of my stomach."

He had called for a burrito to be delivered to her from a restaurant she'd always loved. "I couldn't let you starve."

"Oh, it's beautiful! Just the way it's always been."

"So eat it."

"Don't rush me. It's worth savoring, okay?" The sound of a silverware drawer. "You know what I missed while I was gone?"

"Tell me."

"Beans the way they're made here. Most everywhere, the beans are so squished up, you know, there's not even one recognizable pinto in the whole pile. They're like mashed potatoes. And I ate them, but it's not like here." A pause. "Mmm."

The sound was almost sexual in its enjoyment, and Eli shifted his shoulders a little, trying to keep his mind clear.

"Eli, really, thank you. Is that what you did when you put me on hold? Ordered takeout for me?"

"Yeah, but I was mainly hoping it would make you grateful enough to come over here and illustrate your gratitude."

"What, you want me to draw on you?"

He laughed. "Depends on what you're drawing with."

"You are really on tonight," she said.

He sobered. "Not just tonight. You're all I think about, all day. All night." He paused. "Flowers smell like you."

"Eli, please quit it!"

"Are you weakening?"

She sighed. "It's always been wonderful when we only had to worry about each other. But we have to let the outside world in."

He winced at the way that felt like a slammed door. A well of frustration rose in him, and not only over her challenge to him to put down his hatred and take up forgiveness. The very idea made him feel faintly panicky.

But there was more, too—his mother and brothers, his family and the past. So many roadblocks. "Let's not talk about that."

"It's a deal." She chuckled. "We've already been on the phone for more than an hour. Aren't you talked out yet?"

"Are you?"

A slight, small hesitation. "No," she said in a husky voice.

"Then don't hang up. Eat your burrito and do your work and I'll just stay on the phone with you all night."

She laughed. "My ear might not hold up."

"When it gets tired, put the phone down, and so will I."

"This is really silly, you know. We're reverting to adolescence."

"I don't care. Do you?"

"No. Who's going to know?"

"Exactly." He settled in a comfortable armchair and kicked off his shoes. A breeze blew in through the open door, remarkably cool after the very hot day. It was the fifteenth of September, not long now until the cooler days of autumn. He looked forward to them. "So," he said, "tell me about the most exotic place you ever visited."

Sarah felt restored after the burrito, and went back to work, tucking the phone under her ear. It was odd to work with the material at hand with him on the phone. As she matted a newspaper article from the mid-1920s about the brutal beating death of a Santiago youth, or a photo she'd shot in town, she couldn't help wondering how he would react to all of it. She wondered how all of them would react—her mother and father, Eli's family. The town itself, which loved its dramatic old story.

In the end, she had to get off the phone because she needed both hands. "Eight o'clock, Eli. Don't forget."

"I won't."

In spite of the fact that she'd had practically no sleep for more than twenty-four hours, and in that time she'd worked almost nonstop, she felt a wild, exhilarated sense of accomplishment in her task, unlike anything she'd ever felt for work before. It wasn't simply the chance to right old wrongs, to set right a story that had ruined too many lives already. She loved the way it was coming together, loved the way the multimedia images would mesh to tell a story simply and clearly. It was emotional material, and after so many years of working with commercial images, there was a surprising amount of satisfaction in that.

Finally, well past midnight, she was finished. She propped up the images, the photos, old and new, the letter and newspaper accounts, against the wall of the long room, and rearranged them over and over. She shifted this one to offset that one, stepped back, narrowed her eyes, moved another.

It was nearly dawn before she was satisfied, and as if waiting for that exact moment, her exhaustion belted into her like a sledgehammer. She showered twenty-four hours of grime from her skin and fell into bed without bothering about clothes, and slept the dreamless, dark sleep of a conscience assuaged. She had done all that she could possibly do.

The rest was up to them.

* * *

Joanna helped her hang the show, and she was strangely silent as she began to understand what the material was meant to accomplish. Sarah didn't prod her, but she felt a wave of nervousness. Oddly, it wasn't over the reactions the material itself might rouse, but a more egotistical, artistic anxiety. Was it good work?

When it was hung, a simple series along one adobe wall, Sarah stood back to evaluate it, and once again she felt a swell of excitement. "It's good, isn't it?" she said, her voice barely a whisper.

Joanna turned. "It's better than good, Sarah. I had no idea you could do this kind of work."

"Thank you." She smoothed her dress over her thighs. "My parents should be here soon."

"Do you want me to go or stay?"

Sarah took a breath. "I think tonight has to be intimate. Unobserved."

"Okay." Joanna hugged her. "Call me and tell me how it goes, okay? I'm going to be thinking about you every second."

"I will."

Sarah walked with her to the door of the tiny gallery. She saw her parents pull up down the street. Her stomach turned over. "Please," she whispered.

All at once the full reality of what she was doing hit her: she was gambling everything on this show, in a single, dramatic gesture to force her father and Eli into some kind of confrontation that might shake them both. Seeing her father on the street, panic hit her.

If this did not work, she would not be able to stay in Taos, just as she'd grown to realize how much she loved her hometown. She would lose the tenuous, fragile relationship with her father, and her newborn love with Eli.

She closed her eyes and took a deep breath, remembering

Octavia's words—only Sarah herself had the tools to end this war. She might not succeed.

Even if she failed, she had at last uncovered the truth of the terrible injustice done to two young people long ago, and the world would know it. That was something to be proud of—whatever it cost her personally.

The knowledge gave her courage enough to open the door and smile at her parents. "Come in," she said, and gestured to chairs she'd arranged for this purpose. "Would you like some coffee? I have some made."

"Not right now," Garth said. "You've got us both nervous, wondering what you're up to tonight."

"Well," Sarah said, sitting across from them, "I'm a little nervous, too." She folded her hands to steady herself, and plunged in. "I have put together a completely new kind of show, something I haven't done before. There aren't going to be many guests here tonight, and I wanted you to come early."

She looked at her father and took his hands. "Dad, I want to put the past behind us. I'm hoping you can forgive me for my anger, for all the lies I told, for all the awful things I said to you."

"There's nothing to forgive, Sarah. I was in the wrong more than you were. If I hadn't been so bullheaded—"

She smiled. "I may be a little bullheaded myself." She swallowed, bracing herself. "I've been thinking a lot the past few days, and we can talk as long as we need to when this is over, but first I want to take you both over here, and show you something." She sobered and looked at each of them in turn. "If any of this upsets you, I apologize in advance. But I really, really need you to listen to me before you say a single word."

Mabel spoke for the first time. "Just show us, Sarah. All this talk is making me even more nervous."

"You're right." Sarah rose. "Come with me, and listen while I tell you a story."

They followed her around the partition. Mabel made a soft, startled sound, but said nothing more.

Sarah picked up a sheet of paper. Tomorrow, the text from Deborah Lucero's book would be divided into paragraphs and hung beneath the appropriate pieces, but Sarah had wanted to guide her guests herself tonight.

"This is the story of the Santiagos and the Greenwoods," she began in a voice as cool as a museum guide's. "In particular, the story of Manuel Santiago—" she pointed to the miniature "—and his tragic love affair with Emily Greenwood."

"Good heavens," Mabel said, leaning forward. "He looks exactly like Eli, doesn't he?"

"Love affair!" Garth protested.

"You have to listen, Dad."

He scowled, but allowed himself to be led. She revealed, with text and illustrations, the history all of them had thought to be true...the rape and hanging, the suicide, the long history of war between the families, a war that had eventually reduced two proud, wealthy families to nothing. The story was documented with newspaper articles and old photographs taken both from the library files and Mabel's cedar chest. The final article detailed Eli's arrest twelve years before.

"And all of this," she said, "was built on a lie. Manuel and Emily were in love. She hanged herself not out of a misguided sense of disgrace, but out of grief." She stepped aside to point to the copy of the letter Emily had written to her Philadelphia friend, a letter Sarah sensed Emily had written out of a need to share something with someone who would not judge her. In it, Emily had poured out her feelings of passion for Manuel Santiago, who had asked her father's permission to marry her and had been brutally refused. Emily was not giving up hope, however. She suspected she would be able to force his hand. "According to neighbors' reports, she was almost five months pregnant when she killed herself.''

Garth and Mable were both utterly silent, staring not at the letter, but at the picture of Emily. Her father's face flushed, and he reached out one hand, as if to put his hand on the picture.

"Don't say anything yet." She took a breath. This was the hard part. "You know, for years I blamed myself for not fighting for my daughter. I was furiously angry—not at you, but at myself, for giving in." She looked away, focusing on Emily's happy face. "I really didn't think I'd ever get over it. But when I understood what had happened to Emily, I realized I was better off than poor Emily. Eli is still alive, and so am I. And somewhere, out in the world, is our child." It was the first time she'd spoken the words aloud, and it made her throat tight. "If fate is kind, maybe she'll come looking for me someday. But even if she doesn't, I gave her life. It has to be enough."

Mabel looked utterly stricken. "But Sarah, it wasn't your fault. We forced you. I don't know if I forgive myself."

Sarah shook her head, and took one hand of each parent into her own. "I forgive you both. You did what you thought was right at the time."

There was a suspicious moistness in Garth's eyes. He squeezed her hand almost painfully, and she realized he didn't want to speak for fear of giving himself away. With a mute gesture, he pointed at the last three photos. The first was Eli in the courtyard of the cottage, from the ones she'd taken of him standing against the post. The other two were shots Teresa had taken—the one when Eli had wanted to kiss her, and another, of the two of them the same day, standing side by side. Around them, sunlight gilded the grasses and edged the leaves of the cottonwoods, and overhead stretched the blue, blue Taos sky. A wind blew their hair from their faces, and they looked at each other with sober hope.

Sarah let them both go and stepped back. "These," she said quietly, "are exactly what you think they are. I saw him by accident the first night I came back."

She heard the gallery door open, and her nerves roiled again. Urgently, she looked at her father. "I need one more thing from you. Twenty minutes without losing your temper."

He looked as if he would dig in his heels and say no, but Mabel nudged him and, chastened, he nodded.

"Thank you. I'll be right back." She rushed around the partition and ran—hard—into Eli. In her nervousness, she laughed, grabbing his arms to steady herself.

Without missing a beat, he hauled her into him and kissed her. Not lightly. Not sweetly, but with passion and depth. "You had to be wearing that dress," he said. "Whew."

From behind the partition came the sound of her parents' voices, and Eli straightened, instantly wary. "What's going on, Sarah?"

"Sit down for a minute," she said, discarding her original plan. "I want you to see this show before the rest of the world sees it, but I don't have time to take you through it the way I thought I would, so I'm just going to say it really fast. I found out the rape was a lie. Manuel Santiago did not rape Emily Greenwood. She loved him. She was pregnant. She killed herself when he was hanged."

He stared at her.

"Now, I want five minutes, Eli. Can you give me that? Five minutes to just listen to me?"

"Sarah, I don't understand—"

"Five minutes, Eli?"

He gave her a puzzled frown, then nodded. "Okay."

Bracing herself with a deep breath, she took his hand and led him around the partition. She felt him go rigid beside her as he caught sight of her father, but she tightened her hand around his. "Five minutes," she whispered fiercely.

"Dad," she said, ignoring the blustery expression on his face, "I want you to meet Elias Santiago. Eli, this is my father, Garth Greenwood."

"We already—"

"What is this?"

"You said you would listen," she said, raising her chin. "So for once in your lives, do it."

She let Eli's hand go and went to stand between them. "Dad, I have been in love with this man for most of my life. I'm in love with him now."

Garth flushed but remained silent.

"Eli," she said, "I also love my father. The war the two of you fought tore me to pieces—and neither of you had to pay the price I did.

"I want you to look around you and see what this war has cost our families over these years. Generation after generation after generation we've been fighting and killing each other." She paused. "It has to stop now. We three have the power to make that happen, to call a truce." She looked at them both. "I love both of you, and I'm not going to choose between you. Either you make peace with each other, or I will leave Taos again and I will never come back."

For a long, long moment after she finished speaking, a deafening silence roared through the room. Eli and her father stared at each other. Sarah held her breath, praying in a silent chant.

Abruptly, Eli said, "No." He turned on his heel and walked out.

Sarah stared at his retreating back, feeling a howl of sorrow well up in her. She wanted to call after him, to beg him not to let pride tear them apart.

But she let him go. She had tried. There was nothing else to do.

Chapter Sixteen

It began to rain as Eli jumped in his truck, and he scowled as the first big, sloppy drops splattered on his windshield. It reminded him of waiting for Sarah beneath "their" tree the first night she'd been back.

It seemed a long time ago, but it had been barely a month. A month. His whole life had been turned upside down.

The day before she arrived, he'd been Elias Santiago, CEO of Santiago Teas, a successful, wealthy man. He'd turned around the Santiago fortunes.

Given enough time, he might even have forgotten the early betrayals in his life and found another woman to love, to be his wife. If not for Sarah's return, he might even have fallen in love with Jennifer, the beautiful and intelligent graphic designer who had created the new look for Santiago Teas.

He stared at the heavy rain. Sarah's return had brought

back the boy he'd been, helpless and a victim, a boy Eli had buried in his hatred and his need for vengeance.

With a roar of rage, he slammed his hand on the steering wheel. "Why did you come back?"

He started the truck and roared out of the parking place, driving aimlessly around the narrow back roads. But he could not escape his demons, or his rage, or his sorrow, and in defeat, he drove to the farms. In his mother's house the light was on. For a moment he considered stopping, but he drove on. He needed to be alone, to sort this out, to think it through.

Instead of driving to his own house, however, he found himself pulling up in front of his grandmother's. As if she'd been waiting for him, she sat on a chair pulled up before the open door, back far enough from the opening to be protected from the rain. Eli ran to the house and slipped by her. "What are you doing?"

"Rain is precious," she said. "It feels good."

"You'll get sick."

"No." She pointed. "Get a chair and come watch it with me."

He did, and sat down next to her. For a long time he only stared at the rain, listening to the splattering, pattering sound of it against the roof and the ground. "Sarah came to see you," he said.

"She did."

"Are you the one who told her there was no rape?"

Octavia smiled without looking at him. "I gave her a picture that looks like you."

"I saw it." It was an heirloom, like a war standard. "I'm amazed you gave it to her."

"She said it looked like you. I think she loves you."

"But she loves her father more," he snarled, and was instantly ashamed at the petty sound of it. With a groan, he dropped his head into his hands. "Did you know, *Abuelita*, that they were in love?"

"So much pride," she said. "So much sorrow over pride."

He raised his head and looked at her.

Octavia took his hand. "Don't you let pride ruin your life, too, eh?"

Eli thought of Sarah, holding Joanna's baby as he slept. "I never loved anything or anyone more than I have loved Sarah Greenwood," he said, and his voice sounded raw.

His grandmother nodded.

He thought he would wait until morning, but the rain would not let him. It seemed to call out to him as he left his grandmother's house, offering him a chance, a dream. And it seemed odd to him suddenly that every time anything had happened between him and Sarah since she'd come home, it had rained. So much rain for so late in the year.

So he went to his house and combed his hair and changed his shirt. It was no surprise to find Sarah's father on the porch of his house, watching the rain. Unmindful of the feel of it on his scalp, Eli approached the gate.

"Sarah isn't here," Garth said.

"I did not come to speak to her." He swallowed. "I would like to speak with you."

For a long moment Garth eyed him, and Eli thought he would refuse. Instead, he nodded. "I'll listen."

As Eli came up the sidewalk, Garth stood. Eli walked up the steps and stopped and faced his old enemy. Suddenly he discovered a strange sympathy with the old man, the same reluctance to lay down his arms.

And in Garth's face he saw the same measuring look, the same respect, as if they were two generals who had fought a long and difficult campaign in opposite camps. Finally Garth nodded, as if in approval.

Eli spoke. "My hatred of you made me a man."

"Mine lost me my daughter." He paused. "And yours."

A hard white flame of fury stabbed through him. "Yes. And my pride will make us both lose her again." He lifted his chin. "I love her," he said simply.

"So do I."

Eli bowed his head. "I have come, Mr. Greenwood, to ask your permission to marry your daughter." Powerful emotion rose in his throat, threatening to choke him, but Eli could not tell what it was—love or sorrow or regret. Maybe only hope.

"I watched you, all these years, you know," Garth said slowly. "I watched you build that business from nothing, out of air. Every time I heard your name on television or saw it in the newspaper, I wanted to get out my gun and shoot you dead."

Eli lifted a brow. "The feeling was mutual."

"What I wanted, Eli, was for you to end up dead, drunk in a ditch somewhere, so Sarah would finally have to admit I'd done the right thing." He paused, cleared his throat. "I can't even tell you how much I hated you for being what she thought you were."

Eli met his gaze.

"I can't promise I'll ever even like you, Eli Santiago, and I don't reckon you'll ever love me, either." He paused. "But I can respect you as a man, and I can't imagine a truer test of a man's faithfulness than what you've shown all these years. If she'll have you, I will come to your wedding."

"Thank you," Eli said. He turned to go, then turned back and extended his hand.

Garth took it. "Tell your mother to go to see Sarah's show."

"I will," he promised, and meant it.

But as he left the Greenwood house, Eli felt oddly unsatisfied. It should have felt better, to finally lay down his arms. He should have been joyful that at last he and Sarah would be together.

Instead, there was an ache in his lungs that he couldn't seem to dislodge, a feeling of loss so deep he felt his heart was being sucked from his chest.

What had he lost?

He found Sarah sitting on her porch, watching the rain, as her father had been. The cat sat beside her feet, cheerfully switching his tail. Eli wondered if she knew yet that she'd adopted him. Or been adopted.

"I seem to always be coming here to tell you I'm sorry," he said, sitting down beside her on the bench. She'd changed to a pair of jeans and an oversize white sweater that made her look very young. "That's why I'm here again. I'm sorry."

She touched his hand. "What's wrong, Eli?"

The gentle words pushed some button inside him, and, alarmed at the sudden surge of emotion, he stared hard at the rain. "I went to talk to your father."

"Oh." Disappointment clouded her tone. "Wouldn't he talk to you?"

"We talked." He swallowed, feeling the emotions ease away from his throat, enough that he could speak. "He said if you will have me, he would come to the wedding."

Sarah put her hand on his shoulder. "Was it so hard for you, Eli?"

At last he looked at her. "It wasn't. Not when it came down to losing you again." He ducked his head, choked out, "I just feel this pain now, since I talked to him. I don't understand it."

"Oh, Eli," she whispered, and moved close, putting her arms around his shoulders, pressing her face to his neck. "It's grief."

There was no stopping the swell of emotion now. It pushed up from his chest, through his throat, low and deep and agonizing. Blindly he reached for Sarah, pulling her into his lap, feeling his breath grow ragged and the undeniable and unmanly heat of tears in his eyes. He gasped against it, holding Sarah fiercely, tight as he could. "What…am I…grieving?"

She touched his hair, pulled his face into her neck. "For our daughter."

"Yes." Denial was stripped away, and the sorrow roared through him. He let himself weep for her, for the child they had both wanted, the child who had been taken from them. Unashamed, he let the grief out, and found his sorrow dissolving.

"I guess I thought it would all go away," he confessed at last. "Maybe some part of me thought she'd just be magically restored to us if we all came to peaceful terms."

Sarah stroked his hair. "I know."

He raised his head, cupped her face in his hands and kissed her fiercely. "We have each other now, though. No one can take that away."

"Yes. And we'll have more children."

His throat tightened again. "I would like that. So much."

"Me, too." She grinned wickedly. "Want to start trying right now?"

"Soon. There is something I want you to do for me now, Sarita."

"Anything."

"Pack what you need for tonight, bring your cat and come to the home I built for us."

"Now?"

He nodded. "I never want to sleep apart from you again."

"But your family—"

"It won't be easy, Sarah. I don't see that we'll ever have both our families over for Christmas dinner."

She laughed.

"And maybe it's always going to be me ducking your parents and you avoiding my mother, but I can live with that."

"So can I." A sudden blaze of wonder came over her

features, lighting her eyes and skin, and she put her hands on her face. "Eli," she said with wonder. "We're going to be married!"

And she promptly burst into tears.

Eli laughed, holding her close. "Yes, my love."

At last.

Epilogue

October 14, 19—
Mr. Elias and Mrs. Sarah Santiago
Santiago Farms
Taos, New Mexico

Dear Mr. and Mrs. Santiago,

My name is Crystal Madrid, and I'm writing to you because I found your names at the adoption registry. The people there said that means you won't mind if I contact you. (Actually, she remembered you guys— said you really hoped I *would* someday, so I hope this is okay.)

I have to do a genealogy for my history project this year, and my mother encouraged me to go ahead and look for you two if I wanted to. (She's told me I could since I was twelve, but I didn't want to until now, no offense. I'm her only kid, and my dad died when I was two, so I'm really all she has, but she wanted me to feel free about it if I ever wanted to.) I guess I am pretty curious.

It's kind of weird to be doing this, and even weirder to find out after all these years I might have been drinking tea you actually touched with your own hands. Or maybe it doesn't work that way, I don't know. My mom acted kind of funny when I first told her. She said she read a story about the family—your families—that I'd like. She saved it for you to tell me, though, if you feel like it.

Anyway. I have to do this project, and I'd like to meet you if you think that would be okay. We only live in Pueblo and would drive down for a day and a night if you can recommend a place for me and my mom to stay. She's looking forward to it, she says, but I think she's also scared I'm not going to want her to be my mother anymore. AND THAT'S NOT TRUE, okay? We really have to be totally clear on this. I'm all she has. I don't want to hurt her feelings, ever. But there's something inside me that wants to know you guys, too.

So, here's about me: I'm sixteen and almost five foot ten. Too skinny and no chest. I used to have blue eyes, but now they're gray, and I have black hair, which everyone thinks is permed and is just naturally curly. I'm not the greatest student in the world—I like to read and stuff, but math is boring and science is worse, so I don't do as well there. My big thing is singing. As long as I can remember, I've been singing—first at fairs and things, but lately I've been in some plays, here and in Colorado Springs. I might get to go to Denver to the Performing Arts high school next year, but I haven't heard back yet. (Cross your fingers.)

That's really all for now. I put my address and phone number at the bottom of the page so you can get in touch with me and let me know when would be a good time. I have to finish my project by Christmas vacation, though, so I hope we can do it sometime soon.

Sincerely,

Your daughter,
Crystal Madrid

* * * * *

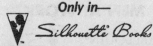

MEN at WORK

All work and no play?
Not these men!

July 1998
MACKENZIE'S LADY by Dallas Schulze

Undercover agent Mackenzie Donahue's
lazy smile and deep blue eyes were his best
weapons. But after rescuing—and kissing!—
damsel in distress Holly Reynolds, how could
he betray her by spying on her brother?

August 1998
MISS LIZ'S PASSION by Sherryl Woods

Todd Lewis could put up a building with ease,
but quailed at the sight of a classroom! Still,
Liz Gentry, his son's teacher, was no battle-ax,
and soon Todd started planning some
extracurricular activities of his own....

September 1998
A CLASSIC ENCOUNTER
by Emilie Richards

Doctor Chris Matthews was intelligent, sexy
and *very* good with his hands—which made
him all the more dangerous to single mom
Lizette St. Hilaire. So how long could she
resist Chris's special brand of TLC?

Available at your favorite retail outlet!

MEN AT WORK™

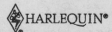 

Look us up on-line at: http://www.romance.net   PMAW2

Available September 1998
from Silhouette Books...

World's Most
Eligible Bachelors

THE CATCH
OF CONARD COUNTY
by Rachel Lee

Rancher Jeff Cumberland: long, lean, sexy as sin. He's eluded every marriage-minded female in the county. Until a mysterious woman breezes into town and brings her fierce passion to his bed. Will this steamy Conard County courtship take September's hottest bachelor off of the singles market?

Each month, Silhouette Books brings you an irresistible bachelor in these all-new, original stories. Find out how the sexiest, most sought-after men are finally caught...

Available at your favorite retail outlet.

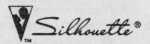

Silhouette ®

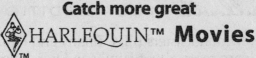

Silhouette ® SPECIAL EDITION ®

Newfound sisters Bliss, Tiffany and Katie
learn more about family and true love
than they *ever* expected.

A new miniseries by
LISA JACKSON

A FAMILY KIND OF GUY (SE#1191) August 1998
Bliss Cawthorne wanted nothing to do with ex-flame
Mason Lafferty, the cowboy who had destroyed her
dreams of being his bride. Could Bliss withstand his irresistible charm—the second time around?

A FAMILY KIND OF GAL (SE#1207) November 1998
How could widowed single mother Tiffany Santini be
attracted to her sexy brother-in-law, J.D.? Especially
since J.D. was hiding something that could destroy the
love she had just found in his arms....

And watch for the conclusion of this series in
early 1999 with Katie Kinkaid's story in
A FAMILY KIND OF WEDDING.

Available at your favorite retail outlet. Only from

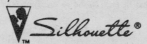

Silhouette ®

We, the undersigned, having barely survived four years of nursing school, do hereby vow to meet at Granetti's at least once a week, not to do anything drastic to our hair without consulting each other first and never, _ever_—no matter how rich, how cute, how funny, how smart, or how good in bed—marry a doctor.

Dana Rowan, R.N.
Lee Murphy, R.N.
Katie Sheppard, R.N.

Christine Flynn
Susan Mallery
Christine Rimmer

prescribe a massive dose of heart-stopping romance in their scintillating new series, **PRESCRIPTION: MARRIAGE**. Three nurses are determined _not_ to wed doctors— only to discover the men of their dreams come with a medical degree!

Look for this unforgettable series in fall 1998:

October 1998: **FROM HOUSE CALLS TO HUSBAND** by Christine Flynn

November 1998: **PRINCE CHARMING, M.D.** by Susan Mallery

December 1998: **DR. DEVASTATING** by Christine Rimmer

Only from

Silhouette®SPECIAL EDITION®

Available at your favorite retail outlet.

Silhouette®

SPECIAL EDITION™®

COMING NEXT MONTH

#1195 EVERY COWGIRL'S DREAM—Arlene James
That Special Woman!
Feisty cowgirl Kara Detmeyer could handle just about anything—except the hard-edged stockman escorting her through a dangerous cattle drive. Rye Wagner had stubbornly insisted he'd never settle down again, but a daring Kara had *every* intention of roping in the man of her dreams!

#1196 A HERO FOR SOPHIE JONES—Christine Rimmer
The Jones Gang
Vowing to reclaim his father's lost land, ruthless Sinclair Riker embarked on the heartless seduction of beguiling Sophie B. Jones. But Sophie's sweet, intoxicating kisses had cast a magical spell over him—and he ached to do right by her. Could love transform Sin into Sophie's saint?

#1197 THE MAIL-ORDER MIX-UP—Pamela Toth
Winchester Brides
Travis Winchester fought an irresistible attraction to his missing brother's mail-order bride. Even though he didn't trust Rory Mancini one bit, he married the jilted city gal after taking her under his wing—and into his bed. But he couldn't stop wonderin' if Rory truly loved her *unintended* groom....

#1198 THE COWBOY TAKES A WIFE—Lois Faye Dyer
Sassy CeCe Hawkins was forever bound to her late husband's half brother, Zach Colby. Not only was her unborn baby heir to the Montana ranch Zach desperately coveted—and half-owned—but a forbidden passion for this lonesome, tight-lipped cowboy left her longing for a lifetime of lovin' in his arms.

#1199 STRANDED ON THE RANCH—Pat Warren
When sheltered Kari Sinclair fled her overprotective father, she found herself snowbound with oh-so-sexy rancher Dillon Tracy. Playing house together would be a cinch, right? Wrong! For Kari's fantasies of happily-ever-after could go up in flames if Dillon learned her true identity!

#1200 OLDER, WISER...PREGNANT—Marilyn Pappano
Once upon a time, tempting teenager Laurel Cameron had brought Beau Walker to his knees. Then, she'd lit out of town and left Beau one angry—and bitter—man. Now she was back—pregnant, alone, yearning for a second chance together. Could Beau forgive the past...and learn to love another man's child?